D0724971

THE

SHAKESPEARE
KILLER

Books by Douglas J. Wood

FICTION

Presidential Intentions

Presidential Declarations

Presidential Conclusions

Dark Data

Dragon on the Far Side of the Moon

Blood on the Bayou

NON-FICTION

Please Be Advised

101 Things I Want to Say

Asshole Attorney

THE
SHAKESPEARE KILLER

DOUGLAS J. WOOD

PLUM BAY PUBLISHING, LLC
New York, New York
Morristown, New Jersey

Copyright © 2023 by Douglas J. Wood

All rights reserved. no part of this publication may be reproduced, distributed, or transmitted in any form or by any means, including photocopying, recording, or other electronic or mechanical methods, without the prior written permission of the publisher except in the case of brief quotations embodied in critical reviews and certain other noncommercial uses permitted by copyright law.

For permission requests, contact the publisher at the website below
Plum Bay Publishing, LLC
www.plumbaypublishing.com

Library of Congress Control Number: 2023904942
Hardcover ISBN: 979-8-9858564-2-2
Paperback ISBN: 979-8-9858564-1-5
eBook ISBN: 979-8-9858564-3-9

Cover Design: Dee Dee Book Covers
Interior Design: Barbara Aronica-Buck
Editors: Jeremy Townsend, Stephan Orovich and Kate Petrella

Printed in the United States of America

"One of the most fundamental questions people have about defense attorneys is, 'How can you do that? How can you go to bat every day for a person that you may not know is guilty but you have a pretty good idea that he's not so innocent?' It's a question that defense attorneys answer for themselves by not addressing."

—David E. Kelley, American television writer, producer, and former attorney

CHAPTER ONE

A Client to Die For

On the Gulf of Mexico off Key West, Florida

"Just sign the note," demanded the man sitting across from him.

Many considered Jacob Schneider among the finest criminal defense lawyers in the United States. He defended the most infamous of those accused of crimes. He had no interest in the innocence or guilt of his clients. That was not his job. His job—and at the core of his beliefs as a lawyer— was to ensure that every client was afforded his or her Constitutional rights and that the burden of proof to convict beyond a reasonable doubt remained with the prosecution. He used any maneuver that thwarted a district attorney or federal prosecutor from convicting his clients, no matter how guilty they may have been. Indeed, the more guilty the accused and the more heinous their crime, the more Schneider loved the challenge of winning. Even though that sometimes meant crossing ethical lines, he saw doing so as no different from the tricks and lies used by inept prosecutors or corrupt judges.

Now he was facing the most challenging defense in his

career. He needed to defend himself, something he'd never had to do.

"I said, sign the note. Do you not hear me?"

"I won't do that," Schneider responded, filled with the typical lawyer bravado that helped him win cases in court. He assumed the man was intent on completing the task before him—administering vigilante justice—but Schneider was confident he'd talk his way out of it.

He was being held in a chair by two men, and saw no point in putting up a struggle. It wouldn't help. He was only forty-two years old and in good shape, but there was no place to escape to. He was on a yacht far from land on the Gulf of Mexico for what he had thought was a meeting with a new client. The only defense he had left was his tongue.

When the man first contacted Schneider, he had told him that he stood accused of crimes with overwhelming evidence against him. He never said he was innocent, and Schneider didn't ask. He never did and didn't care. As a precondition to the meeting, the man wired $200,000 into Schneider's escrow account as a retainer.

When the new client greeted Schneider upon his arrival in Key West, he gave the right impression of having plenty of money to pay his attorney. His yacht was over one hundred feet with a crew of five, and had a main stateroom furnished in mahogany and leather with windows that allowed a panoramic view of the Caribbean. The two men sat down on the back deck, the sun shining. As the boat got underway, gently rocking in the calm seas, the salty air made conversation easy. As the sight of land slowly faded away, they talked about the beautiful coastline and the wonderful people of Florida. The crew set up a couple fishing lines in the back of the boat; the client told Schneider that perhaps they could catch their lunch. A butler who looked more like a bodyguard than a domestic servant served them drinks, and the two were getting along fine. Schneider found the man's accent mysterious and couldn't quite place it. Regardless, he was the type of client Schneider loved: guilty as hell and rich as shit.

The prospective client said he was facing charges in New York for murder, human trafficking, and pedophilia. Schneider didn't bother to question how this person was on a boat at sea well beyond the reach of authorities, but the accused appeared wealthy. Money for his defense was no object.

When they were just over four miles out, beyond the sight of land on Florida's flat landscape, the situation suddenly changed. The butler and a deckhand walked behind Schneider, firmly gripped his shoulders, and pinned him in his chair. Any friendly expression on the face of his client was gone. Schneider was shocked that the man intended to hurt him. He couldn't admit to himself that he was so foolish not to have investigated him before their meeting. But $200,000 in the bank made due diligence irrelevant to Schneider. Greed won out over caution.

The client turned abductor slid the note to Schneider and explained the situation. "You should sign the note," the man insisted. "If you don't, innocent people you love will be harmed or, perhaps, die."

"Look, I don't know who you are or what you want, but I will not sign this. I can't do that. I'm not sorry for anything I've done. So the note makes no sense to me."

Sighing, the man sat back in his chair, his eyes revealing a darkness in his soul. He was small, only five foot six, and heavy set with knuckles calloused from administering too many beatings. Looking at him now, Schneider realized that he looked more like a common thug than a wealthy defendant. Another mistake he had made.

"All those criminals you defended, and you believe you've done nothing wrong?"

"Criminals I've defended?" asked Schneider. "I don't understand what you mean. I'm a criminal defense attorney. It's my job to defend people charged with crimes. That's what I do for a living."

"Yes, it is what you do for a living, Mr. Schneider. And I understand you do it well. But you must now atone for letting the guilty go free. That is your sin."

"I can pay you," Schneider pleaded.

The man smiled. "This isn't a movie, Mr. Schneider. Not even money can get you out of this. But very well, have it your way. Don't sign the note. It's just too bad that your last memories will be how refusing to cooperate hurt so many others you care about. But that's a choice you can live with." He paused. "I'm sorry, I meant die with."

A third man, equally muscled as the other two men, approached, a thick rope in hand—rope like the one you tie to the anchor on an old sailing vessel. With a nod from the boss, he began wrapping the rope around Schneider, pushing him forward to get the rope around his back and pressing his arms to his sides to immobilize him.

Schneider was not a physical person. He relied on talking his way out of tough situations. It was an art he honed in summing up before countless juries. He knew no other way. But now, fear made him think his words would not be enough.

"Please . . . please don't do this! People know where I am. They won't let you get away with this." He felt urine soaking his pants as the fear set in.

"People know where you are, Mr. Schneider? Really. Like I said, this is not a movie and I don't give a damn if someone knows where you are or why you're here."

"Wait! I'll sign." Schneider cried.

"Good." The abductor nodded to the man to loosen the rope and free Schneider's right arm. "It's not as if we need you to sign, Mr. Schneider. But it only seems fair."

Schneider took the pen, his hand trembling.

"Sign the note, Mr. Schneider, and confess. Do one thing in your life that protects the innocent—your wife and your daughter."

With tears in his eyes, he signed the note. A neatly typed message that read:

> *I'm sorry for all the evil I've allowed to exist, all the lies I've let others make, and for all the harm I've done to good people. May God save my soul and forgive me for what I've done.*

Schneider dropped the pen, bowed his head, and prayed. He wasn't sure why, since he was not religious, but he needed to beg someone who might listen.

The third man finished wrapping the rope, immobilizing both his arms. The other two forced Schneider to his feet, holding him erect, his legs useless in fear. They dragged him to the deck.

As the sun set in the West, the day's beauty no longer had any meaning for him. The seas now had a growling swell. The air no longer smelled sweet. No other boat was in sight.

One man attached a small anchor to the thick rope, about ten feet from Schneider's body, heavy enough to make sure Schneider would sink. The second man held the other end of the rope so he could control the descent of the anchor. Without another word from their leader, the third man threw Schneider and the anchor overboard.

He quickly sank under the waves, stopping ten feet beneath them. The second man held the rope that kept his body from sinking to the bottom. Schneider tried to wriggle out of the restraints, but it was useless. After a little over a minute, his energy exhausted and reality clear, he surrendered to the inevitable, thinking of his wife and daughter, praying they'd be safe and that the man would keep his word.

After ten minutes, the three men pulled Schneider's lifeless body back on board, removing the ropes. The client sealed the note in a Ziploc bag and secured it in the zippered pocket of Schneider's jacket. They headed the boat back until they were about a half mile from shore, yet still out of the sight of any other boaters. Two of the men gently lowered Schneider's unbound body into the water.

The crew turned the boat away and returned to port.

Schneider's bloated body washed up on the beach three days later, just as planned. Fish and ocean bacteria ate most of his eyes and fingers. His face was unrecognizable. The killer wanted the body discovered before putrefaction and scavenging creatures dismembered the corpse as it sank to the seabed to be engulfed by silt. Were that to happen, the body would completely vanish within two months.

The local papers reported that authorities found a prominent American lawyer dead in an apparent suicide. The note found in his jacket confirmed it. A charter company also confirmed that a man with his name had hired a boat five days before authorities retrieved the body. Despite a search, they never found the boat. They assumed it sank at sea. Just as planned.

At his funeral in Manhattan, his daughter tried to

console his sedated wife, but to no avail. The cold weather and rain made the day all the more depressing. A local district attorney who often prosecuted Schneider's clients gave a lovely eulogy praising what a brilliant lawyer and father he was and how important Schneider had been to the legal community.

CHAPTER TWO

Meritorious Achievement

Headquarters, Federal Bureau of Investigation,
Washington D.C.

"We're here today to honor one of our finest," began FBI Director George Kinston. The Director stood at a podium in front of rows of chairs where about thirty FBI agents and staff sat in the main conference room of the Bureau. "Christopher DiMeglio has repeatedly shown himself to be a stellar agent of the Bureau who consistently solves complex cases, bringing the guilty to justice and the innocent to closure."

DiMeglio nervously sat in a chair to the right of the Director. Wearing a dark blue suit for the occasion, he felt out of place. DiMeglio didn't like public praise for doing what he considered was simply his job, although those present, Bureau agents and staff, were hardly the public. These ceremonies were private affairs.

Kinston, forty-one years old, was appointed a year earlier upon the resignation of the former director over a scandal involving the wife of a member of Congress. He was the U.S. Attorney for the Eastern District of New York with a tough reputation on crime and was responsible for successful prosecutions of some of organized crime's main capos. At six foot three, he was intimidating. He had played point guard on Princeton's basketball team and kept in shape through pickup games two times a week. But the Bureau needed heroes. DiMeglio fit the bill.

"In what proved to be a conspiracy well beyond what others thought, Agent DiMeglio saw past the obvious and identified a group of killers bent on murdering innocent men and women. The only sin of the victims was to be the offspring of members of the Ku Klux Klan. And while none of us harbors any sympathy for the principles and actions of the KKK, we cannot condone the murders in New Orleans, Atlanta, Idaho, and elsewhere. Were it not for Agent DiMeglio's refusal to give up, many more would have fallen victim to the psychotic killers."

Those assembled burst into applause. DiMeglio was popular in the Bureau, always ready to help others. Now chief of the FBI's Behavioral Analysis Unit or BAU, as it was known, DiMeglio ran the unit's five divisions of profilers, special agents, and staff responsible for assisting field agents and local police in tracking down and arresting criminals through profiling, predicting their actions, past and future. Most cases focused on violent offenders, serial killers, terrorists, pedophiles, cyber criminals, mass murderers, and kidnappers. At thirty-eight, he was one of the youngest Unit Chiefs in the FBI.

"Two years ago," continued Kinston, "Agent DiMeglio

arrived in New Orleans to help apprehend a serial killer. After an arrest and confession, the killer—the Bayou Slasher—was shot while being accompanied by Agent DiMeglio from the initial custody location to another. At first, everyone assumed the shooter was a disgruntled family member of someone the Bayou Slasher murdered, presumably a KKK member. Agent DiMeglio discovered, however, that was a mistaken conclusion. The Bayou Slasher was part of a much larger enterprise intent on killing the offspring of the KKK nationwide. A former Marine sniper with multiple tours in the Middle East and credit for hundreds of kills led the conspiracy. He turned his sense of patriotism into a recruitment campaign of like-minded psychopaths willing to follow him on a murderous spree for reasons only a sick mind like his could conjure. That he could convince others to join him on his quest speaks volumes about the persuasive powers of serial killers and the naiveté of so many others. Agent DiMeglio put an end to their killing spree."

More applause.

"Agent DiMeglio, please join me at the podium."

The Director continued, "Agent DiMeglio, it is my honor to award you the FBI's Medal for Meritorious Achievement. It's one of the most prestigious awards the FBI bestows on its agents; it acknowledges extraordinary and exceptionally meritorious service against extreme challenges through decisive and exemplary acts that result in the protection and the direct saving of life." Kinston placed the ribbon holding the medal over DiMeglio's head and led the room in another round of applause.

DiMeglio shook the Director's hand and turned to the audience for his obligatory acceptance speech, something no one would ever remember, including himself.

"Director Kinston, thank you for this award. I accept this with humility. The FBI's success is not founded on the actions of any single agent or staff member, but on the teamwork of many." If he were telling the truth, he'd say he alone solved the case of the Bayou Slasher but knew better than to let his ego go that far.

DiMeglio paused, took the medal in his hand, and looked at its face depicting an American eagle, olive branches and arrows in its talons. He was genuinely moved and grateful.

"In every case I handle," he continued, "I learn something new that reinforces basic principles of a criminal investigation. In the case of the Bayou Slasher, I learned to assume nothing and to suspect everyone. We never close a case until we have considered every alternative and eliminated every suspect. There are a lot of very sick people out there intent on killing. Our job at the Bureau and the BAU is to help find them. To help stop them. While I accept this honor, our entire team deserves it. Without them, I would not have succeeded. Thank you."

After a final round of applause, the crowd moved to the Webster Room, where congratulations continued and those gathered shared Champagne. These ceremonies were the rare occasion allowing on-the-job drinking. The cafeteria also served some poor excuses for hors d'oeuvres. The food at the Bureau was one reason most agents found excuses to eat at nearby neighborhood restaurants.

After an hour of celebration and congratulations, DiMeglio happily returned home to the quiet of his townhouse on Dunnington Place in Dumfries, Virginia, a development less than thirty miles south of Washington and only minutes from his office at Quantico. He bought it when construction of the community first began and prices were affordable for someone on an FBI agent's salary. The noise from the nearby train line also kept it affordable, but DiMeglio didn't mind the occasional rumbling from the tracks. It reminded him of the trains he heard growing up in suburban New Jersey. Maple, elm, and oak trees were scattered around the town, with a mixture of high-priced and affordable houses and well-kept parks. With a diverse population of under 6,000, it remained proud of its tobacco farming heritage, now long gone. DiMeglio particularly liked the Saturday farmers' market, where locals sold their goods and produce. It was a great place to relax with friends and meet locals.

That night, he decided to take a walk in the warm weather. He liked to observe people he passed and speculate whether or not they might be a suspect he was pursuing.

Knowing that so many serial killers were freely walking the streets and waiting to prey on their next victim, he couldn't help but be suspicious of people around him. Back home, he ended the night sipping a Jameson and enjoying his ego trip at receiving an award.

CHAPTER THREE

A Public Face

BAU Headquarters, Quantico, Virginia

It was 9:00 a.m., the day after the ceremony, when DiMeglio arrived at his office after a short ten-minute commute. He usually got in by 8:00 a.m. but was late that morning after nursing a bit of a hangover from the Champagne at the office and the Jameson he enjoyed back home. His decision to celebrate the medal proved costly when he awoke with a splitting headache that slowed him down.

DiMeglio liked how close the office was to his home. While the official rule was agents should be in their offices five days a week unless they were in the field, he and his team didn't follow those rules. DiMeglio was okay if he or a team member wanted to work from home. He turned his head away from official rules if they could get to the office quickly in case he needed them. Given the FBI rule that special agents must live within fifty miles of their home office, getting there in a reasonable time was rarely a problem. Since he didn't follow the rules of being in the office every day, he did not intend to enforce them on others.

Lenoir Peters, his executive assistant, greeted him, a Styrofoam cup of coffee in hand. Unlike DiMeglio, she was there every day and regarded the office as her personal domain.

"You're late," she scolded. "I made your coffee to go. The Director called and asked to see you. I have no idea why, particularly since you saw him yesterday. Is there something going on, or will this just become routine? Does he have a crush on you? Are you his new BFF?" Peters, a long-time veteran at the Bureau, had a dry sense of humor and enjoyed poking the bear. And at sixty-eight, white-haired and matronly looking, she had over forty years of government service, so no one was going to do a thing about whatever she said.

DiMeglio, not in the mood for banter and still nursing his headache, ignored her bait. "Nothing to worry about, Lenoir. If there was, I'm sure he would have told me yesterday. Call Kinston's EA and tell him I'll be there by 10:30. Thanks."

As he headed back to his car, he stopped. "Oh, and thanks for the coffee."

Lenoir smiled as if to say, "Good boy, now you can go."

The drive from Quantico to the FBI headquarters in Washington usually took DiMeglio an hour or more on the forty-three-mile trip. On days he wasn't in a rush, it afforded him plenty of time to think. On the other hand, going to headquarters was something he loathed doing. Not only was Washington a traffic nightmare and frenetic, but the commute also wasted precious time when he could be working on a case. As far as he was concerned, it was the unfriendliest place on earth. But being late to a meeting with the Director was not acceptable. At times like these, he appreciated his Dodge Charger RT, a government-issued car—his G-Ride, as government employees call it. It was fast and maneuverable, with over 350 horsepower. As he wove in and out of traffic, his speedometer hit 85 miles per hour on some of the route. He got lucky. For a change, the express lanes were open and he was able to cut his time avoiding the traffic-filled regular lanes. He could have used the siren on his car but the Bureau frowned on agents using that for regular business. If he was pulled over by the police, his FBI badge was a pass they respected. So a ticket was out of the question. Instead, it gave him an excuse to drive fast and hard.

In spite of his assurances to Lenoir, he feared seeing the Director could not be good. No agent looked forward to such meetings.

What could be wrong? I'm sure everything is fine. After all, I got the Medal for Meritorious Achievement yesterday!

But the FBI worked in strange ways, often creating more confusion than clarification. It was a daily battle for DiMeglio to convince his superiors, let alone the Director, that a particular case merited the BAU's involvement or intervention. In addition, the Bureau was short on field agents. So allocating resources was an ongoing problem Director Kinston had to solve.

In the back of his mind, DiMeglio always worried that

his indiscretion with Rebecca Simone would come back to haunt him. He'd broken a cardinal rule. He fell in love with a police officer he was assisting in an active investigation in New Orleans. His reputation suffered a serious blemish. Although the incident was in his file, he received only a mild reprimand, and no one held him responsible. The Bureau did not cite him for violating any rules. After all, he captured a serial killer in New Orleans and broke open one of the most notorious conspiracies in FBI history. Mission accomplished. The Bureau even promoted him! Certainly he wouldn't be facing the consequences of a lousy affair after all of his accomplishments. Or would he? Perhaps Director Kinston said nothing yesterday because he didn't want to spoil DiMeglio's moment in the spotlight.

But then, why even give me an award?

DiMeglio pulled into the FBI garage forty-five minutes after he left his office. The FBI's office is a massive granite edifice on Pennsylvania Avenue with eleven floors covering over 2.8 million square feet. An array of United States flags, dating from 1775 to the present, are displayed outside of the building. DiMeglio always felt a sense of pride when he saw the row of flags, knowing that his mission had a heritage worth the sacrifices and risks agents took, particularly in the field.

"Agent DiMeglio," greeted the desk clerk. "Congratulations on yesterday's award. And thanks for the Champagne!"

Despite the rules, the desk clerk didn't ask for an ID.

DiMeglio simply needed to sign the ledger. Everyone at the Bureau recognized him.

The clerk called the Director's assistant to tell him that DiMeglio had arrived. When the elevator doors opened onto the executive floor, Kinston's EA, Carter Gibson, greeted DiMeglio. Like DiMeglio's EA, Gibson was a long-time Bureau employee and took grief from no one. He immediately escorted him to the Director's office and followed him in.

"Mr. Director, you asked to see me?"

"Yes, Chris, please sit." The Director motioned to the chairs in front of his large oak desk.

The use of his first name settled DiMeglio's nerves somewhat.

He took a deep breath and briefly perused the office, strewn with memorabilia of Kinston's long career, including photographs of politicians he'd met or worked with over the years, his bar admission certificates, and other honors he'd received.

Noticing DiMeglio's curiosity, Kinston commented, "I'm like every politician on the Hill, Chris. I love to live with memories on my walls." He smiled and pointed. "I'm particularly proud of these front pages from the *New York Post* praising my success when we convicted Mafia Dons in New York."

Two chairs were in front of his desk, and a small conference table with four chairs and a couch were off to the side.

"Very impressive, Director," DiMeglio responded as he sat in one of the chairs. Out the window in the distance, he could see the Capitol dome.

Still standing in the office, the EA asked, "Would you like coffee or water, Agent DiMeglio?"

"No thanks, Carter, I'm fine."

"I know you don't want any tea," he responded with a smile. It was no secret that DiMeglio hated tea.

"Thank you, Carter," Kinston said to him. "Please ask Julie to join us."

Kinston stood and walked to the window of his office.

"Chris, the FBI's image is awful. Polls say our public trust is lower than it's ever been. We're fighting an endless battle with both sides of the aisle, arguing past mistakes and botched investigations. All they seem to want to do is question investigations they say we should have never undertaken, or investigations we *should* have undertaken but chose not to for political reasons. While some of the criticism is legitimate, most comes from blowhards in both parties."

Kinston walked back to his desk and sat down. He picked up a thick three-inch binder on the side of the desk and, with a thud, dropped it in front of DiMeglio.

"This is the latest file I have to review before testifying this afternoon at a Congressional committee hearing. Or maybe it's a sub-committee. I've lost track. All I can be sure of is I spend most of my time testifying before one fucking

Congressional committee after another, answering inane questions from political hacks. I can't take this shit much longer. The president appointed me to clean up the Bureau, not to be a professional witness. I intend to do my job and get the FBI back to the principles of its motto—*Fidelity, Bravery, Integrity*—and restore public trust. I need to put an end to the crap on the Hill."

With a tap on the door, Julie Frattarola, the FBI's assistant director of public relations, entered. She was the perfect picture of someone in public relations. Petite and a few inches over five feet, her brunette hair hung loose on her shoulders. It accentuated her figure, ample in many ways. She wore red-rimmed glasses that matched her dress and carried the obligatory notebook people in PR always had.

"Julie, thanks for coming." She took the seat next to DiMeglio.

"Good to see you again, Chris," Frattarola offered. DiMeglio nodded but chose not to respond verbally. He didn't know Frattarola well, but he believed public relations was something the FBI spent too much time and money on that often mischaracterized what agents did, usually through exaggeration and hyperbole.

"Julie, I was going to brief Chris about our new project. I'll let you tell him."

What the fuck is going on? DiMeglio wondered.

"Yes, sir," she responded. Then, turning to DiMeglio, she began, "We've been bouncing around ideas to improve the

FBI's image with the public. We've had the Director on the circuit talking about the Bureau, but we need the media to focus on a career agent who solves actual crimes. Someone who not only can talk the talk but someone who has walked the walk. Someone who represents the Bureau's mission and integrity. Of course, the Director is an obvious spokesperson, but he is a political appointee with no field experience. Worse, the negative press on the Bureau falls on him. That makes him a target, not a spokesperson. So for him, it's an uphill fight to gain public trust. Regardless, he has no time to be on the road with all his demands and the constant pressure from Congress and the administration."

DiMeglio was surprised at how calmly Kinston took the criticism, however veiled it was. True, Kinston was never a field agent with the FBI, but he was a celebrated U.S. Attorney who worked closely with the FBI throughout his career. Before becoming a prosecutor, Kinston was a naval pilot, enlisting right after he graduated from law school. Highly decorated, he served in two Middle East campaigns. He was tough and took grief from no one. At his confirmation hearings before the Senate, a member of the Judiciary Committee asked if his lack of field experience would be a detriment. He responded he had faith in the FBI agents who worked the cases and would be ready to lead them as director. While his answer was evasive, a slim majority confirmed him.

"Let's be honest, Chris," interjected Kinston, "the FBI is

still hurting from suspicion and scandals since Clinton. Since his administration and every administration since then, the Bureau has lost focus and chased more corrupt politicians than the criminals we're supposed to hunt down and stop. Despite my vocal assurances that my job is to restore the FBI to its core principles and avoid trying to clean up the swamp, I'm as much a politician as anyone on the Hill. I lack credibility, just like every bastard there. When I say let the politicians on the Hill clean their own houses, it falls on deaf ears. The role of the director has changed over the years, often in ways that don't help the Bureau. We need to let a real professional take the microphone, tell our story, and be the face of the FBI. Not a political appointee. Julie and I think that person is you. Your record for success is stellar. You've risen in the ranks through hard work. You'll be perfect for this."

Kinston and Frattarola could see the doubt, or perhaps shock, in DiMeglio's face.

"Chris," Frattarola reassured, "I understand you're surprised by this. We understand. It's often uncomfortable for an agent to face the press and public about his role and the cases he's handled. Even more daunting if it's not a pre-scripted press conference. But we can get you to a place where you'll become as expert in public relations as you are in criminal investigations. You'll find that press training is easier than you think."

"Yeah," interjected Kinston. "I've learned that the trick

is never answering a question and sticking to your story. It never ceases to amaze me how the press falls for that shit every day. You'll do fine, Chris."

"But Director Kinston, I'm not trained for what you're asking me to do. I don't have the experience that's probably necessary to deal with the press, even with training by Julie."

"Bullshit, Chris. You'll be fine. But there is one piece of bad news," continued Kinston. "I'm not reassigning you. You still need to oversee the unit and monitor its cases. To be credible, we need you to keep hunting down criminals. Besides, I don't have the personnel to replace you with an experienced agent. Hell, there isn't anyone qualified, anyway. But I can give you an additional assistant to help keep things organized and coordinate with Julie."

DiMeglio's mind was spinning, wondering how he could do both his day job and be a talking head for the FBI.

"I assume this is not something I have a choice about," observed DiMeglio.

"It is not," replied Kinston.

He knew an order when he heard one and resigned himself to reality, responding, "Okay, then. What's the plan? And Julie, I assure you I'll need a lot of help, but I won't need another assistant. Lenoir will coordinate with you."

"Great," interjected Kinston as he rose from his chair, indicating the time had come to end the meeting. "Then I'll leave you in Julie's capable hands."

As Frattarola and DiMeglio walked down the hall, they

remained silent. DiMeglio wasn't sure what to say, speechless at his new assignment. He had no experience and preferred being in the background.

As they waited for the elevator, Frattarola sensed his discomfort and broke the silence. "We'll start media training first thing tomorrow, Chris. My team and I will come to your offices. We'll be there at 10:00 a.m."

CHAPTER FOUR

Twisted Truth

BAU Headquarters, Quantico, Virginia

As promised, Frattarola and her team arrived at DiMeglio's office exactly at 10:00 the following morning.

Lenoir Peters showed them to DiMeglio's office. She made no secret of her displeasure at scheduling the meeting without first consulting her. She did not appreciate canceling other appointments and told Frattarola to coordinate only through her in the future. Frattarola took the order to heart, remembering that the Bureau only ran efficiently if the EAs wanted it to. So you always listened to them.

On arrival, Peters accompanied Frattarola's team into the adjoining conference room. Usually a mess of papers and evidence, Peters had cleaned it up and covered the charts on the wall that included notes and pictures relating to active investigations. She knew DiMeglio did not want anyone outside the BAU to see the Unit's work product.

Frattarola opened the discussion. "Chris, you're a natural. Not only are you a decorated agent, you're handsome and in great shape. And you look terrific in a suit. Before long, we'll make you the darling of Instagram and Facebook. You'll become the most sought-after bachelor in the FBI!"

Frattarola was astute in her assessment. At just under six feet, with brown hair and dark piercing eyes, even through wire-rimmed glasses, DiMeglio could mesmerize—an attribute he often used when interrogating suspects. For Frattarola's needs, he'd look perfect on camera, particularly if she could convince him to wear contacts.

Frattarola's demeanor immediately offended DiMeglio. "I haven't worn a suit in years, Julie, so I'm not sure any of them will even fit. And I have no interest in being a darling on social media or anywhere else. So if you try to package me, this will never work."

Frattarola raised her hands in defense and responded, "Not to worry, Chris. We don't intend to have you wear anything that's in your closet. I'll coordinate with Lenoir to have someone from Tom James come over and fit you for a new suit. They'll have some nice ties, too. And don't worry, we'll bury the cost in our PR budget."

"No, Julie, we won't bury the cost anywhere. I'll try on what I have at home, and if they fit, they'll work. If not, I'll get them altered. And I have enough ties."

"Okay, okay. I just want you to look your best." She made a mental note to make sure Peters made the appointment and got DiMeglio there. She knew he wasn't about to say no to Peters.

The others smiled, apparently endorsing Frattarola's thoughts on how DiMeglio needed to look. That sat poorly with DiMeglio. They might think him worthy of a cover on

Gentleman's Quarterly, but he did not intend to become the centerpiece of available bachelors. DiMeglio wasn't about to let anyone turn him into some stud to prance around on television and the internet. He wanted to establish some rules at the outset.

"Julie, I'm not at all comfortable with this. Don't package me. It's not who I am. I'm just an agent with a decent record and doing his job well. That's all I want to talk about."

"Of course, Chris. You make the rules. But it won't always go where or how you want it to. You need to be prepared. I'm sorry, but how you look makes a difference. Like it or not, the press and the public will judge you on your words and appearance and dissect you in every way possible. The press will probe you for weaknesses. That's what they do. The higher you rise in the public eye, the more they want to tear you down."

The others were feverishly taking notes; on what, DiMeglio had no idea, he was unsure what they were even doing there.

"And what kind of access will they want into my personal life? I will not allow them to make me a public punching bag by invading my privacy."

"I don't see that happening. You're not commenting on pending cases. Only past successes. If you stay on script and ignore questions you're not comfortable being asked, they'll move on. None of your reported cases have been failures. If they ask about one that went wrong or try to link you to one, tell them you weren't involved. If they push harder, keep giving them the same reply until they realize they're getting nowhere repeating the questions. Then they will stop and move on."

He wanted to believe her.

"Look, Chris, if there is something you need to tell me, tell me now. Whatever it is, we can handle it. If not, then we'll have to go with a different plan. But we were thorough in vetting you, and from what I've seen, there's nothing to worry about."

DiMeglio saw no point in being circumspect.

"I had an affair with Rebecca Simone, a New Orleans detective."

"I'm aware of what happened in New Orleans, Chris," she calmly responded. DiMeglio straightened a bit.

"Chris, we looked at you under a microscope for this assignment. Your affair with Detective Simone, while a technical transgression, was human. You saved many lives. And from what I read, you were quite the hero in how you did it. But it didn't end there. You followed up and found her killer and the leader of a murderous conspiracy. That story's not a problem, Chris. It's a golden opportunity to show you as human and vulnerable yet a hard-nosed FBI agent who knows how to get a job done no matter where the bodies lead."

That made sense to him, however twisted the logic may have been.

"And if Simone comes up in interviews? What do I say?"

"Say it's something you prefer not to speak about. Then, I'll take it from there and talk to them."

"No, Julie, no one is to discuss her with anyone. It is nobody's business but mine."

"Okay, Chris. Relax. I'll tell them neither you nor the Bureau will talk about it." Frattarola was lying. She knew that when it came up, and it would, DiMeglio would need to respond.

CHAPTER FIVE

A Killer View

Fairmont Century Plaza, Century City, California

"The view from here is amazing," she said as he joined her on the room's balcony in the Fairmont Century Plaza, a luxury Los Angeles hotel on the Avenue of the Stars in Century City. Overlooking the bright lights of the twin towers and the busy promenade below them, they could see LA's downtown skyline off in the distance.

They had met earlier that night in the lobby bar. She called and asked to see him about a sensitive matter. After a few drinks and some food, she invited him upstairs. Why not, he thought? It wasn't as if this would be the first time he'd been unfaithful to his wife in their twenty-seven years of marriage. He texted home that he'd be late. It was a text his wife often received.

"We'll have the view all night," he responded. "Why don't we both have another drink and have some fun?" leaving no doubt about what he wanted. After all, he'd spent over two hundred dollars entertaining her at the bar. It was now her turn to provide him with some entertainment. Judging from the way she was dressed, he suspected there was a lot more than the sensitive business matter she supposedly had wanted to talk about.

"Don't be in such a rush," she laughed. "Let's enjoy the view, and rather than a drink, let's try something else. Then I'll tell you a story you'll want to hear."

She lifted a small envelope from her cleavage, filled with white powder.

"I don't do drugs," he responded. That was not true. It had only been a month since he last had a few lines of cocaine. He was trying to kick the habit. At one point, it was costing him thousands a month. But he could afford it on the fees he charged criminals to represent them in court.

"Why don't you just tell me your story?"

"Come on, it's not going to hurt you, and it puts me in the mood." He certainly wanted her in the mood.

"If that is what it takes, sweetheart, then you have some. I'll watch."

"I won't do it alone. Please?" she implored while using her long red-polished fingernails to split the powder into four lines neatly arranged on the glass top of the balcony table.

"All right," he responded. "One line is all I want." He wanted to keep his wits and be sure he enjoyed what would come later.

"Perfect! You go first." She handed him a straw. He bent over, deeply sucking the line into his nose as he'd done so many times before.

An hour later, authorities found his body on the pavement, fifteen stories below the balcony. The note in the room read:

I can no longer forgive myself for the sins I've committed. I'm sorry for all I've done.

The routine autopsy found traces of cocaine laced with other barbiturates and hallucinogens that the coroner said he probably used to give himself the courage to jump. The coroner's report found that Stafford was still alive when he hit the pavement and had a lot of drugs in his system. Enough that would have incapacitated anyone other than someone experienced with drugs. Since the victim was a known user, the coroner concluded it was not enough to knock him out and disrupt his plans to jump. The final police report, following a routine investigation, noted that the deceased had a known cocaine habit that his associates said he was trying to kick. The reporting officer presumed that defense attorney Paul Stafford had a relapse. He later opined to his fellow officers that Stafford might have finally found a conscience after getting so many murderers, rapists, and molesters off because of legal technicalities, incompetent prosecutors, bought juries, or lenient judges.

Some witnesses in the bar that night recalled seeing Stafford with a woman, but not much more. No one there was acquainted with him, and the bartender said he hadn't seen Stafford in the hotel in the past. There was no evidence of any woman visitor in the room. It was booked in his name, paid for with one of his credit cards, something easily forged. Why he spent a night in a local hotel when his home was less than an hour away was of no concern to the police. Men often find comfort with women in hotels. Even hotels close to home. And the room was clean. No finger-prints other than his own and some from the cleaning staff, all of whom were off duty when Stafford died. The report noted some residue of the white powder on the balcony table and the one straw recovered at the scene. The police found nothing else and comfortably concluded Stafford was alone when he jumped. As far as they were concerned, whoever the woman was, she was never in the room with him. There was no evidence to conclude otherwise. And the police always—and only—follow the evidence. A few witnesses could describe the woman, but it made no differ-ence. The woman they described and the real woman who accompanied Stafford upstairs had no resemblance. That's how good disguises work.

CHAPTER SIX

Sully

Dunnington Place, Dumfries, Virginia

"Sully, I'm not a public speaker. And I sure as hell don't want to be an FBI poster boy." DiMeglio was relaxing on his couch at home after a long day of media training, Jameson in hand. The TV was on, but he wasn't paying attention to it.

Sully, the love of his life, remained silent, head on DiMeglio's lap, where it lay virtually every night.

"They think they can train me to trade sound bites with talk show hosts. Can you imagine me going toe to toe with Sean Hannity? With a reporter on *60 Minutes*? That's where they want to book me. I'm going to look like a fool and ruin my career."

With a low groan, Sully's head moved slightly.

"And this woman, Julie Frattarola. What a piece of work! Half the time, I'm not sure if she's training me or coming on to me."

Sully shifted, not happy with that prospect.

"All I hear is, 'Just stick to the story, Chris.' 'Don't worry if they bring up anything personal, Chris.' 'Everyone will be briefed on what is and is not fair game, Chris.' The bullshit never ends. I don't understand how people put up with the public spotlight. I just want to do my work and catch bad guys."

DiMeglio took a sip of Jameson, being careful not to disturb Sully.

"What will I say, Sully, if they bring up Becca?"

That made Sully stir, sit up on the couch, and glare at DiMeglio. The sixty-five-pound Catahoula Leopard, the official dog of Louisiana, always reacted badly at the mention of Becca—Rebecca Simone. Sully was her dog. He and DiMeglio bonded during the ill-fated affair DiMeglio had with Simone. Her death gave him custody of Sully. It was either take the dog or send him to a kill shelter. The two were now inseparable.

"Sully, you know they're going to ask me about her. What should I say?"

Sully let out a gentle growl. DiMeglio got the point.

"Alright, alright," he responded, rubbing Sully on his head. "I'll stop talking about Becca. Let's go for a walk and get some fresh air. I don't want to talk work any more tonight, anyway."

Sully sauntered to the door and waited for DiMeglio to fetch the leash.

CHAPTER SEVEN

Tonight's Hot Seat

Rockefeller Center, New York City

"From Studio 16, Rockefeller Center in the heart of New York City, it's the *Tonight Show* starring Jimmy Fallon. Tonight, join Jimmy and his guests . . ."

DiMeglio and Frattarola were sitting in the Green Room, which was barely green, along with another guest on the show. The room was a living room with a large sofa and comfortable chairs. Food and beverages of every kind were on tables lining the walls. Pictures of Fallon and the past hosts—Steve Allen, Jack Paar, Johnny Carson, Jay Leno, and Conan O'Brien—hung on the walls. DiMeglio thought of having some Jameson for his jitters, a bottle and a bucket of ice sitting on the side table, but Frattarola vetoed that idea. "You need to be sharp, Chris." A big-screen TV on the wall aired the show live, taped for actual airing later that night. With them was Martina Carpenter, the latest darling of the Hollywood press. She was there to promote her debut role in a movie where she played a bumbling police officer in pursuit of a cat burglar. DiMeglio had seen promos for it on TV but had no interest in seeing it. He found comedies about police work insulting. Regardless, she appeared completely disinterested in DiMeglio and Frattarola as she enjoyed a vodka on the rocks and watched the monitor. DiMeglio thought it ironic that he was following an actor promoting a just-released a comedic movie about police. He wondered if that was intentional and meant to set him up. He'd find out soon enough.

DiMeglio felt an appearance on the *Tonight Show* was beneath the dignity of the FBI. Although its guests were occasionally politicians or serious commentators, it was a comedy show. DiMeglio saw nothing humorous about what he and his team did. Kinston and Frattarola, however, felt its dominance in the demographics they wanted—adults ages 18 to 49 and 25 to 54 and critical adult-female demos—made it a perfect show to get the word out. Frattarola reminded DiMeglio that what matters is the audience, not the show.

"Don't be nervous, Chris. You'll do a great job," suggested Carpenter, obviously eavesdropping on the discussion between DiMeglio and Frattarola. "I hear you're an FBI profiler. That makes you smarter than anyone here, including Fallon. So just be yourself and have a good time."

DiMeglio responded, "If I were being myself, Ms. Carpenter, I'd be in the field working my cases, not wasting time on talk shows."

Before Carpenter could respond, a production assistant entered and took her to the stage.

Frattarola didn't want DiMeglio to be preoccupied. She whispered to him, "C'mon, Chris, try to get into this role.

It's an important one. And you've been doing a great job so far. Your interview in the *New York Times* was exactly what we needed. Just do the same when you take the chair next to Fallon."

A stagehand entered. "You're on next, Agent DiMeglio. Please follow me."

Frattarola straightened DiMeglio's tie and said, "You look great, Chris." He thought he should, with his $700 Tom James charcoal gray suit and official red and blue FBI tie. His EA insisted he buy the suit, even if he had to pay for it himself. Frattarola supplied the tie and was very pleased he agreed to use contacts after she suggested to him that glasses could create glare in front of cameras. That wasn't true, but it was all she needed to complete the changes she wanted.

Waiting behind the curtain, DiMeglio heard Fallon say, "Ladies and gentlemen, my next guest is a man who knows real crime and serial killers. He hunts them down and is here to tell us how the FBI always gets their man—or woman. Please welcome profiler and FBI Special Agent Christopher DiMeglio." The Roots, the *Tonight Show* band, started playing the theme of *Law & Order*. Hearing the song, DiMeglio concluded this show was more about entertainment than a serious discussion, furthering his disappointment that Frattarola booked him on it.

The stagehand gently nudged DiMeglio onto the stage as Fallon rose from his chair to greet him. The sign told the audience to applaud as the two shook hands and Fallon motioned DiMeglio to sit. Just what the production staff told DiMeglio would happen in his briefing before the show.

With his interview cards in hand, Fallon began, "I've got so much to ask you, Agent DiMeglio."

"Please call me Chris." Frattarola's training was to get the relationship with the interviewer on a personal level as soon as possible. First names help do that.

"OK, Chris. I'm Jimmy."

DiMeglio tried to see the audience, but the stage lights and cameras made that difficult. The brightness made him feel it was more an interrogation than an interview. The TV monitor off to his right showing him and Fallon on camera was also distracting, despite the instructions to look at the cameras and not the monitor.

Fallon sensed DiMeglio's nervousness and began, "Let me first ask, do I need a lawyer?" The audience's laughter in response eased the tension and DiMeglio relaxed.

"Only if you've done something wrong. Have you, Jimmy?" More laughter.

"Not that I'd ever admit." Fallon let the laughter subside, and the discussion took a more serious direction. "Tell me, Chris, what does an FBI profiler do?"

"It's not that complicated, Jimmy," began DiMeglio, now relaxed. Remembering Frattarola's instruction to keep it simple, he began, "Profilers look at unsolved crimes, usually violent ones, piece together leads and clues, and paint a picture of the type of person who would commit the crime. We create a profile that can identify possible suspects."

"How do you do that?"

"It's a process of elimination. We start with the facts and with assumptions we feel we can make. Things like location, evidence at the crime scene, and sometimes notes or other clues left by the criminal. Video of the area at the time of the crimes also helps. Today, there are cameras almost everywhere. Once we've done all that, we look for similarities and patterns. It's basic hard-nosed police work with a concentrated effort to paint a picture of the killer."

"Is that how you figured out who the Bayou Slasher was? The serial killer from New Orleans."

DiMeglio felt the knot in his stomach. He remembered what he'd rehearsed with Frattarola.

"More or less. In that case, the Bayou Slasher was one among a group of killers. We gathered clues. Eventually, the killer was exposed and apprehended. It led us to uncover a larger conspiracy to murder the offspring of members of the KKK. It turned out to be pretty ironic, with one set of psychopaths hunting down the innocent children of an equally repugnant set of psychopaths. But murder is murder regardless of the target. It was our job to apprehend them."

"Sounds a bit like a chess game, Chris." Frattarola smiled offstage. Fallon clearly read her briefing for the show's producers.

"For some, that's just what it is. Virtually all serial killers are psychopaths who see themselves as better than the rest of us and in total control of their lives and the lives of others. What they say, patterns in their movements and more reveals their psychosis. Wallis Manning, the man behind the Bayou Slasher, was an example."

"He was the real puppet master, right?"

"He sure was. Somehow, he recruited killers willing to take his orders. He's a stereotype of the manipulative nature of serial killers. They're often geniuses. Geniuses gone wrong."

"Did he say anything to you when you caught him?"

"That's the thing, Jimmy. He opened up like a mynah bird. He told us everything."

"Why would he do that?"

"Because, like so many serial killers, he wanted to brag about what he had done, and wanted to show me how smart he was. He wanted us to judge him as the best serial killer ever. They're pretty sick people."

"No kidding! Are you working on any cases right now?"

"Our workload is always filled with cases. Unfortunately, there is a lot of crime. The United States has over thirty-two hundred documented serial killers since we started keeping records. That number is almost twenty times more than in any other country. The next closest is England, with a hundred and sixty or so. But sorry, I cannot comment on active cases."

Fallon genuinely looked shocked. "Why does the U.S. have so many?"

"I wish we knew. Some say we keep better records, but that's a red herring. Even if other countries are off by 300 percent, we're still way ahead. And that doesn't count the over hundred and eighty thousand unsolved murders still on the books. We can't rule out serial killers behind some of those murders."

"And who are these killers? What is common among them?"

"The vast majority are white males in their thirties. A quarter or so is Black. While some are Hispanic, that number is small. And very few are women."

"Why not more women?"

"No one knows, although some research suggests it may be differences in the basic genetic makeup of men and women. Some studies speculate that, genetically, men are hunters. When they're serial killers, they become psychopathic with internal demons, pushing them to kill strangers with common characteristics, like prostitutes. Women are gatherers. As serial killers, they tend to know the victims they kill, often motivated by revenge for people who have hurt them. That kind of revenge has no bounds. And, interestingly, women serial killers are more likely to be motivated to kill for financial gain than men."

"Sort of like divorce lawyers!" Laughter from the audience.

DiMeglio stuck to the script.

"The bottom line, Jimmy, is there is a lot of crime in the

world, and the United States has the unfortunate privilege of being at the top of the list, far above any other country. And local police are often overwhelmed, understaffed, and ill-equipped to deal with it. So we're here to help."

DiMeglio could see Frattarola's broad smile from off-stage. She gave him a thumbs-up. DiMeglio tried not to let it affect his concentration.

Fallon continued, "You help local police? But is it like we see in the movies where the police and the FBI don't get along?"

"That's an unfortunate myth invented by scriptwriters in Hollywood. The FBI's mission is simple: to protect the American people and uphold the Constitution. Our mission is not to seek credit for what we do or to win popularity contests. We're here to solve crimes. Sometimes we lead those investigations. Other times, we assist local investigators."

"Suppose you needed to profile me. Or better yet, the Roots. How would you start?" Some light laughter from the audience.

Now it's getting silly, thought DiMeglio. But Frattarola warned him to remember it was a comedy show. DiMeglio didn't see the humor.

"Jimmy, what we do is not a parlor game."

Fallon's expression showed his disappointment. DiMeglio wanted to keep him on his side. Keep him away from tough questions and stay with softballs. He shifted his approach.

"But I suppose this one time, I can speculate. But I don't know enough about you or the Roots. So if there is something you or the Roots would like to confess, I'd be happy to listen."

"Like what?"

"Well, some folks have said you sometimes kill the monologue."

The laughter was barely audible and included some groans. DiMeglio knew his joke was lame. He remembered Frattarola telling him, "Chris, leave the jokes to Fallon." He should have listened.

"I'll quit while I'm ahead," responded Fallon, seeing the director make a gesture indicating a commercial break was imminent. He turned to DiMeglio, rose from his chair, and extended his hand. "Thank you for coming tonight." Then, turning to the audience, he added, "Ladies and gentlemen, FBI Special Agent Chris DiMeglio."

As the applause began, Fallon turned to the camera and continued, "Stay with us. After the break, we'll hear some great music from . . ."

The Roots played into the break. Fallon thanked DiMeglio off-camera and asked him to return when he solved the next case. DiMeglio was relieved that his first television appearance was over.

Frattarola was euphoric. "You were great, Chris. I was a little worried when you got so technical and stiff in the middle, but you hit the bullseye with the humor in the end.

And you got in the important talking points on the Bureau. Fallon loved it. Just keep it up."

Once in the black stretch limo supplied by the *Tonight Show* producer, on their way to the hotel, DiMeglio loosened his tie and leaned forward, looking at Frattarola as she sat across from him. "Julie, as much as I'll admit I enjoyed being on the show and meeting Jimmy Fallon, I still don't see how this is helping the FBI. And it's keeping me from my cases. So let's try to wind down this program. Okay?"

Frattarola shifted in her seat, keeping her eyes on DiMeglio. Her blue skirt moved up her thigh, exposing most of her legs. Her white blouse, enticingly opened at the neck, the cleavage inviting his stare. DiMeglio realized she'd unbuttoned the top an extra button more than she had at the show. As she moved forward to respond, DiMeglio leaned back into his seat to avoid an awkward moment.

"That's not my call, Chris. I'd like to keep my job. The plan is working. Our poll numbers are up. You're having an impact."

DiMeglio kept his focus on her eyes. "Poll numbers, Julie? Really? Is that why I'm doing this? Winning in the polls?"

She moved again, and the skirt moved more up her thigh. DiMeglio was doing everything he could not to stare. "Are you that naïve, Chris? Of course, it is. You may work in Quantico, but the FBI is knee-deep in the Washington swamp. So popularity with the politicians makes a big difference. And the polls are how we know if we're gaining their trust. And from that, their donations."

DiMeglio let out a defeated sigh, and stared at the car's ceiling.

Wanting to lighten his mood, Frattarola offered, "How about we get a drink at the bar to celebrate your first television appearance?" She stretched out her leg and affectionately touched DiMeglio's leg with the side of her shoe. Her skirt could not have gotten much higher.

DiMeglio considered it. Since his training began, she gave him the impression that she liked him more than just professionally. However, as memories of Simone returned, he responded, "As much as I'd like to, Julie, I'll pass." Nevertheless, he was careful not to close the door shut to something more at a better time. "I'm tired and I'd like to go to bed."

She smiled. "Get some rest, Chris. There's plenty of time to celebrate."

CHAPTER EIGHT

Carla

BAU Headquarters, Quantico, Virginia

The caller ID read, "San Diego Tribune."

DiMeglio usually ignored calls from numbers or names he didn't recognize. Yet he had to admit he was enjoying the limelight despite concerns about the time lost doing his actual job. Sitting at his office desk, knowing he had files to review and assignments to make, he preferred to ignore the call. He didn't have time for idle conversation. But he knew Frattarola would be unhappy if he missed a chance to talk to the press.

"Chris DiMeglio," he answered.

"Agent DiMeglio, thanks for picking up. My name is Carla Lane. I'm a reporter with the *San Diego Tribune*."

"Nice to talk to you, Ms. Lane. What can I do for you?"

"Please call me Carla," she responded. "And may I call you Chris or Christopher? I hate using last names. They're too formal."

I guess she has had media training, too.

"Chris is fine."

"I gather you're not here, but did you see the news reports on the death of Paul Stafford? He was a well-known criminal defense attorney in Southern California." DiMeglio was half paying attention to the call while he worked on the pile of papers in front of him.

"Sorry, no," he responded somewhat absent-mindedly. "I'm not familiar with him or the reports."

"Well, it's something you should look into. The investigation into Stafford's death, allegedly a suicide, has many holes in it. The local police don't seem to care." The criticism of the police got his attention. He put down the papers.

"I'm sorry to hear that, Carla. However, the FBI does not interfere with local criminal investigations. That is not the role of the Bureau. Nor is it mine. My job is to track down violent criminals. And to assist local police, but only when they ask for our help. The suicide—or murder—of your friend is not in my jurisdiction."

"He wasn't a friend, Agent DiMeglio. I never met him. Are you even listening to me?"

Now embarrassed, he tried to get back on track. "You say you've spoken to the local police?"

"I have, and as far as they're concerned, the case is closed, and finding a police officer willing to look into a criminal defense attorney's death isn't easy. They're all happy they no longer have to deal with him."

Smiling, he responded, "I'll give you that, Carla. I've known a few lawyers I don't particularly like either."

"I wasn't making a joke, Agent DiMeglio. I've taken a keen interest in this and have good cause to suspect this is not suicide and not an isolated murder. I think it's a pattern and a possible serial killer. I saw you on the *Tonight Show*. The FBI is hyping you as its top agent who hunts down serial killers. I think you have a case here that you should not ignore." He could hear the icy tone in her voice.

If DiMeglio had a dollar for every call he got from someone who claimed they identified a serial killer or a victim of one, he'd be a millionaire. He usually dismissed such calls with a polite brush-off. But all he heard in the back of his mind was Julie Frattarola's warning never to get on the wrong side of a reporter. He needed to be careful with any dismissal.

"I appreciate your concerns, Carla, but there are a lot of excellent investigators far better than I in the Los Angeles police department. I would imagine if there were hard evidence of a serial killer at large, the local police would look into it. Serial killers don't kill randomly. There's always a pattern. Multiple murders. And because their usual goal is to let people know what they're doing, they usually leave some clues. I assume there were no such clues in Mr. Stafford's case. So without more, I'd be hard-pressed to see the need for a further investigation, much less the involvement of the FBI."

"I understand. But you should dig a little deeper. That's what I did when I read the story about Jacob Schneider, another criminal defense attorney, who allegedly drowned off Key West. He left a note similar to the one Stafford left, apologizing for the bad things he'd done. It's as though the same person wrote both."

DiMeglio had a lot of work to do and wanted to end the conversation.

Using her last name for emphasis, he firmly responded, "Ms. Lane, two murders in California and Florida is insufficient evidence of a serial killer. Nor has any police department asked me to assist them in an investigation. So I can do nothing. As much as I'm sure you believe you're right, I'm afraid I can't help you."

There was a long pause on the phone. "Carla, are you still there?"

"Yes. Just at a loss for words. I wish I could convince you otherwise. I know I'm correct, but I can't get anyone to listen to me."

She hung up the phone. Despite Frattarola's instructions otherwise, DiMeglio decided not to tell her about the call. All she'd do was scold him for not turning the conversation into a story about how wonderful the BAU is at catching killers. Unfortunately, the growing piles of paperwork on his desk did not allow such diversions.

CHAPTER NINE

Hot Air on the Hill

Capitol Hill, Washington, D.C.

"Congressman Wilson, I do not agree that the FBI has lost its direction," replied Kinston as he entered the fourth hour of a Congressional hearing on allegations that the FBI had become a political tool for whichever politician was in charge.

With a bald head and substantial girth, New Jersey congressman Philip Wilson was an outspoken member of the House Judiciary Committee and a critic of the Bureau, as he was with just about any federal agency, even those supported by his own party. He preferred the role of being a thorn in the side of every administration. Wilson's seniority made him a powerful politician and one who did not back down from a fight, particularly if it might garner him headlines back home. Nor did he let facts get in his way.

"What I don't understand, Director Kinston, is why every administration in the last twenty years uses the FBI to advance political interests. Can you enlighten me? And can you tell us what you're doing about it? As I recall, we confirmed you to fix this mess. I don't see a lot of fixin' so far."

While sitting at a desk before the committee in an array

of a semi-circle of seats elevated in front of him, Kinston recalled his trial days as a U.S. Attorney and why the bench for a judge in court sits so high. Its purpose is to allow a judge to look down from his or her perch and intimidate those who appear before the court. In Congress, those elected to office and their staff similarly look down on witnesses before them for the same effect. But it didn't work on Kinston with judges and would not work on him with partisans like Wilson.

"Sadly, Congressman, every congressional session and administration accuses their opposition of corruption and calls the FBI to rout it out. Such partisan posturing and political witch-hunting wastes our time and resources." Kinston might have regretted his answer if he cared about not angering Wilson, knowing it undoubtedly displeased Frattarola and played into Wilson's anger. But he'd had enough. His comment, however, did get a rise out of the other committee members sitting in their hearing seats. Staffers started rustling papers behind them, hoping to be ready to arm their bosses with the information they'd need to ask tough questions and earn constituents' votes with a few good sound bites for the evening news. That was the downside of Kinston's honesty.

"Excuse me?" responded Wilson. He paused, making the mistake of giving Kinston an opening. Kinston's many years as a prosecutor honed his skills to strike when his opposition opened the opportunity. It had been a long day, and he was tired, done with taking any more grief from Wilson. But, since he now had the attention of the entire committee, he wasn't about to back down.

"Congressman Wilson, with all due respect, you understand exactly what I mean. As we have briefed you, your staff, and this entire committee, the Bureau investigates thousands of cases every year. When the Bureau begins prosecutions it originates, the Department of Justice conviction rate exceeds 95 percent. That happens because the agents of the FBI are doing their job at the highest level of competence. We take our responsibility seriously, and being pressured through political partisanship takes our eyes off the ball and does a great disservice to dedicated FBI employees and the public." Kinston paused, purposefully giving Wilson an opening in their thrust and parry game, a game Kinston loved. Wilson took the bait and kept attacking.

"I have nothing but respect for the employees of the FBI who are working every day to keep us safe. My question, Director Kinston, is why the FBI has seen it appropriate to be a political arm of whatever administration is in power?"

Kinston sat silently, considering how he wanted to answer the question and put Wilson back on the defensive.

"Director Kinston, do I need to repeat my question?" asked Wilson.

"No, Congressman Wilson, I heard your question. But I want to be careful and respectful in my response. The FBI, sir, is not a political arm of any administration. Perhaps you

have that misguided perception because you cannot accept
that proof of the political corruption that warrants an FBI
investigation comes not from elected officials or congressional and administration staffers carrying their bags. It comes
from our independent investigations and whistleblowers.
We follow up on those and decide if they have merit. But
when accusations come to us from partisan politicians who
have a grudge against another elected or appointed official
with opposing views, the process is compromised, and it
causes us to waste a lot of our time."

He was on a roll and not about to give anyone a chance
to interrupt.

"Nor does it help when politicians publicly make
demands of us. And it's even worse when Congress conducts its own investigations and parades witnesses in front
of cameras like you're doing today. Not only does Congress undermine justice when it conducts its investigations
publicly, but it also creates a circus. Even when a hearing
is behind closed doors, you tell the world what it is about
and leak information like drunk sailors. When the Bureau
takes on a matter, we quietly investigate and make no public
statement until we have a case that merits an indictment.
While you may perceive the Bureau as a political arm, we
are not, I can assure you, Congressman Wilson."

Wilson could see he wasn't getting what he wanted. "So
what, Mr. Director, is the solution? I'm sure you have an
opinion on that, too." You could have heard a pin drop.

Now is not the time to stand down. Not from this asshole.

"Unfortunately, Congressman, political corruption today is more rampant than ever. That's a consequence of the clash between partisan politics and reelection. My suggestion, Congressman Wilson, is that you and your colleagues clean up your own house. That will go a long way in assisting the FBI so it can do its work and keep Americans safe and their Constitutional rights assured."

Wilson's eyes focused on Kinston like a lion wanting to pounce. For him, it was getting personal. He wanted the last word and a good sound bite. As he leaned toward the microphone to take the interrogation further, Horace Suggs, a Congressman from Wyoming and a major supporter of the Bureau, cut him short.

"Mr. Chairman," Suggs interrupted, "my honorable colleague from New Jersey has gone past his allotted time, and I ask him to yield." That is Washington's polite way of saying, "Shut up, your time is up, and you're done." Wilson had no choice, leaned back, and dismissively said, "As my honorable colleague so kindly reminds us of the rules, Mr. Chairman, I yield and reserve my remaining questions for another time." On the Hill, there was no love lost between Wilson and Suggs.

Sensing the growing tension, the Chairman called for a break to calm tempers.

DiMeglio watched the testimony from his Quantico office with his team, Georgia Evans and Bradley Stokes.

Evans and Stokes had been DiMeglio's key team leaders for years.

Evans was all business with a dry sense of humor. In a profession dominated by men, she could hold her own with any of them. She could also put on the feminine charm and often had witnesses and suspects eating out of her hand. Perhaps her height of just over six feet and athletic physique helped her dominate a conversation or interrogation. Or it might have been her blond hair and deep blue eyes. Either way, she was a showstopper. She even had a way with women suspects where she could be empathetic with the worst of them. But what DiMeglio liked most was her intuition. She sensed things others failed to see. A minor detail she pointed out could often open a case and lead the team closer to a solution. So he always listened to her.

Stokes was the antithesis of Evans. He was a hard-nosed cop. Stokes looked the role at a stocky five feet eight inches, with his military haircut and tattooed arms. He took grief from no one. A graduate of Howard University's top criminal justice program, Stokes was proud of his Black heritage. He focused intently on overcoming prejudice in the Bureau, a goal he didn't hide from others. That sometimes unjustly got in his way and he was skipped over for some promotions. But he was okay with that. He enjoyed being on the street, squeezing informants, and finding the underlying cause of things. He wanted to solve crimes, not push papers. He worked well with the Bureau's techies, putting up with the arrogance that frustrated DiMeglio. Stokes had no problem being just as arrogant as the techies. Most of all, DiMeglio liked his unfiltered honesty.

"Jeez, Chris, the Director was pretty rough on Wilson," commented Evans. "Mind you, it's deserved, but I'm not sure that makes our job any easier."

"And it makes your new role as poster boy even more difficult, Chief," added Stokes, smiling.

Stokes always addressed DiMeglio with his official title, despite DiMeglio insisting he didn't need to. Evans told DiMeglio that Stokes liked to keep a distance from the brass at the Bureau. While it bothered him to think Stokes might see him as just another prejudiced or racist boss in the Bureau, he let it go. Evans assured him that was not the case and that Stokes thought DiMeglio was fair and even-handed. Regardless, Stokes was loyal to DiMeglio, and that made him part of the family DiMeglio protected.

Evans and Stokes looked at DiMeglio, waiting for his thoughts on the testimony.

He had nothing to add.

CHAPTER TEN

Prelude to an Ambush

CBS Studios, New York City

"I'm Lesley Stahl."

"I'm Scott Pelley."

"I'm John Dickerson."

". . . and I'm special correspondent Carla Lane. The FBI has a storied history of tracking down serial killers." DiMeglio's picture appeared on a photograph behind her with the title "The Profiler." His image was superimposed over puzzle pieces, some connected, others not. She continued, "Tonight we'll meet this man, Christopher DiMeglio, the chief of the FBI's Behavioral Analysis Unit—the profilers. He most recently hunted down the Bayou Slasher and a conspiracy to kill the children of members of the KKK. So who and where is the next serial killer? That story and others tonight on *60 Minutes*."

Unlike the *Tonight Show*, Lane taped DiMeglio's interview in a studio four days before airing. None of her questions and no briefing was given to him beforehand. Nor did he see the edited show before its airing. So, like everyone else, he had to wait.

When he heard Lane had become a *60 Minutes* correspondent and slated to interview him, he wished he hadn't blown her off when she called him about the suicide of a lawyer in Los Angeles. But he had no reason to think it was a murder much less connected to a serial killer. Nothing since had changed his mind.

DiMeglio expressed his concerns to Frattarola, but she reassured him.

"Don't worry, Chris. I'll handle it." But it was too late to change anything since the show was booked before the producers had told Frattarola it was Lane's episode. Frattarola was also troubled by the reputation of *60 Minutes* for uncovering matters best left confidential. Although DiMeglio had media training sufficient for the lighter shows, *60 Minutes* was another matter. Frattarola's fear was that Lane would be provocative in the interview in order to advance her career.

She told Kinston they should cancel the appearance, but the Director insisted they go forward and prepare DiMeglio for the worst. He had faith in DiMeglio. The demo for *60 Minutes* was exactly who they needed to target. It was worth the risk. She never shared her and Kinston's concerns with DiMeglio.

DiMeglio and Frattarola sat in makeup, getting ready for the taping. But, unlike the Green Room at the *Tonight Show*, nothing was welcoming in the room. No food or drink. Just a bottle of water. Other than a makeup chair in front of a mirror, the seating was limited to a couple of office chairs. When the makeup artist was done, Frattarola asked her to leave so she could have some private words with DiMeglio.

"Chris, look at this one as if you were a politician. You don't care what questions she asks. Just keep with the script and get out what we need in the interview. Stick to the talking points. Make sure you hit every one of them. If she strays into an area you don't like, use the excuse that you can't comment on active cases. We can stop the cameras whenever you'd like. Or end the interview entirely if you'd like us to."

"We can't quit, Julie. We're in it, for good or for bad. But what if she asks me about an inactive case, like the Bayou Slasher? What if she asks me about Rebecca Simone and whether I had an affair with her? I have to assume she knows."

"You're probably right that she knows about it, Chris. But if she brings it up, tell her the FBI does not comment on the private lives of its agents."

"Really? I'm sure that won't work. That answer is as much a confession as a ploy to avoid the truth."

"Don't worry, Chris. It's not a story. It's bullshit. Why don't you just say no? Deny it happened. Or say, 'Yeah, I had an affair. It had no impact on my investigation,' and leave it at that."

"I'm not going to lie, Julie. That never works."

"There you go again, Chris. Such a Boy Scout! Lying

does work. Every politician lies every day to get elected or reelected. And that includes the Director."

"I'm not a politician."

"You sure about that, Chris? As I see it, you're as much a politician as anyone elected. You persuade serial killers to talk to you and persuade them to give you clues about their whereabouts, why they kill, and more. It all leads to their eventual arrest. That's an amazing talent. The ability to manipulate someone who thinks they're smarter than you are, my friend, is the very definition of a politician."

A stagehand knocked on the door. They were ready to tape.

CHAPTER ELEVEN

Hanging by a Thread

CBS Studios, New York City

DiMeglio immediately felt pressured by the bright lights and the lack of an audience. Even in a comfortable chair across from Lane, he felt the room had the air of an inquisition. She sat in a similar chair, notepad in hand. A coffee table lay between them with a glass of water for each of them. She looked very professional dressed in a dark blue pant-suit with a high-collared white blouse, her light brown hair tied in a band hanging down behind her neck. Her makeup was subtle, without noticeable highlights. She looked professional and serious. Just what DiMeglio expected from a *60 Minutes* correspondent.

As he waited for the first question, he regretted that Frat-tarola agreed to the producer's request that no questions be pre-cleared. She told DiMeglio he was well prepared and had done well in other interviews. The preparatory sessions covered the possible questions. It was all he needed. He shouldn't worry. Besides, she told him, *60 Minutes* never gives its questions before an interview.

Lane was cordial as the interview began. "Welcome, Agent DiMeglio. I've wanted to meet you for a long time."

I bet.

"My pleasure, Ms. Lane. And congratulations on becoming a *60 Minutes* correspondent." Frattarola told him to use her last name to keep it professional and to be sure to start with a compliment. Unfortunately, it came across as canned.

Lane continued without acknowledging the compliment. She intended to cut it in the final edit, anyway.

"You're an expert in tracking down serial killers. Your record of accomplishment is outstanding. But the FBI has rarely let one of its profilers, let alone the top dog of the Behavioral Analysis Unit, do public interviews. Why now?"

DiMeglio went through his mental notes, just as Frattarola trained him to do. He could take as long as he liked to frame an answer. They'd cut any silent time in the editing room. So it was spin time.

"As long as it's not about a pending case or something confidential, I'm not aware of any restrictions on speaking, Ms. Lane. But, until the recent publicity on the Bayou Slasher case, I didn't have opportunities."

"And now you're the FBI's Mr. Popularity?" He didn't like her tone. She was challenging him.

"No. It just seemed that no one was interested. To be honest, what we do is quite boring. It's just basic police work. We follow every piece of evidence, track down witnesses who usually turn out to be dead ends, and keep grinding along. While the crimes are often sensational, what we do is not."

"The crimes are indeed sensational. And I'll get back to Rebecca Simone later. But first, how do you get into the mind of a serial killer? You're famous for the ability to do so. Is it intuition? Some secret talent? It can't just be basic police work. There's got to be more to it than that."

All DiMeglio heard was that she'd get to Simone later. His mind was spinning, and his heart was pounding. He was feeling very uncomfortable.

Lane broke the silence, sensing his discomfort and seeing a few beads of sweat on his forehead. "Chris, you okay? We can take a break if you like."

As his focus returned, DiMeglio replied, "No. I'm fine."

"I asked you how you find serial killers."

The director interrupted. "Cut. Let's get makeup in here to get the shine off his forehead." Once done, he signaled for the taping to begin again. DiMeglio was ready.

"When looking for a serial killer, we think of it as a jigsaw puzzle but one without a geometric shape. It's not a square or a circle. It's a free-form puzzle. We try to find pieces that fit where they often seem random." With the short break, DiMeglio calmed down and told himself that Lane was not on the attack. Yet. When he watched the actual show, he understood why Lane used puzzle pieces behind his photograph as the show opened.

"Serial killers," DiMeglio continued, "are predictable, depending upon the underlying emotions that motivate them and the common traits of their victims. Each act, and each piece of evidence, are parts of the puzzle we put together. When we have enough of the puzzle completed, we can predict their next move and hopefully apprehend them."

"But doesn't that mean to find a serial killer, they need to keep killing before you can get enough pieces of your puzzle together to catch them?"

The knot in his stomach returned, knowing his response—the truth—would be picked up by the papers as an admission that the FBI can't stop serial killers soon enough. But there was no stopping now.

"That is sometimes the case. Unfortunately, investigations take time, and the killings rarely stop while we're investigating."

"What's past is prologue?"

"Unfortunately, yes."

Lane looked at her notes, and DiMeglio took a sip of water. He was comfortable.

"And you've said that the connection between victims is always critical," Lane continued. "Isn't that what broke your last case of the Bayou Slasher—when you realized that all the targets were children of KKK members? Was that the breakthrough you needed to hunt down the killer and the puppet master, Wallis Manning?"

The knot in his stomach returned as he feared Lane would now bring up his affair with Simone.

"I wish I could give you some dramatic sound bite, but I'm afraid we found that connection through basic police work. I assigned an agent to look at the backgrounds of all the victims. It took him some time, but he found it. That was our first clue into the mind of the killer. We took it from there."

"But more people died before you caught her."

"They did, including a police officer. That was unfortunate."

"And you worked closely with her. Is that correct?"

He kept his stare directly at her eyes, wanting her to get the message that he did not appreciate where she was going. He responded, "Yes, I worked closely with her. Just as I did with the other officers of the New Orleans Police Department."

As she paused and stared at DiMeglio, he hoped she would not pursue the Rebecca Simone connection. If she did, DiMeglio would close down. But he knew her agenda was to pique his curiosity to pursue a serial killer, not to embarrass him. He knew that to get what she wanted, she had to make him feel comfortable with her. He was right.

"Let's move on to the kinds of serial killers you hunt down."

DiMeglio felt the weight on his shoulders relax. Finally, he was off the hook. At least for the time being.

"What makes them different, and what's common among them?"

Back to the script.

"The vast majority kill for sexual gratification, most

often because they had a perverse childhood of abuse. So they might target prostitutes, like Gary Ridgway, the Green River Killer. It's usually for the pleasure they get from the act of killing and the gratification they receive from their power over life and death. Others, like the Bayou Slasher and Wallis Manning, think they're on a mission. She and Manning thought their mission was to eradicate bigotry by killing the offspring of racists. They believed their mission justified the killings. Other killers, motivated by religious perversion, think God or evil demons are ordering them to kill. David Berkowitz, the Son of Sam, is an example of such a killer. If a serial killer targets children, he's likely a pedophile and probably has a history of child abuse. If he targets young women, as Ted Bundy did, he's trying to prove his masculinity, which, deep down, he lacks."

"Ted Bundy is particularly interesting. How did Bundy lure in so many women—intelligent women? Despite not knowing him, they willingly left with him. It doesn't make sense."

"Carla, even the Devil can assume a pleasing shape. However Bundy appeared, it was enough to get women to let their guard down. It's all part of the mystery that surrounds serial killers."

DiMeglio felt the interview was going well. So far, she was throwing softballs and avoiding his personal relationship with Simone. Frattarola cautioned him, however, not to let her kindness rope him in. The 60 Minutes model, since its inception in cutting-edge interviews from the likes of Mike Wallace, was to lure you in with kindness before they sprang tough questions and clips from hidden cameras. Since there would be no hidden camera segments, DiMeglio relaxed but kept his guard up for a potential attack.

"Agent DiMeglio, what makes someone a serial killer? How do you differentiate between someone who is just a murderer and someone who is a serial killer?"

Watching from offstage, Frattarola stiffened. Something in her gut told her that Lane was about to go on the attack. Lane's body language when she sat back, ignored her notes, and asked the question, spoke volumes. She was close to where she wanted the interview to go. Frattarola knew the question was a setup.

Stay on the script, Chris, stay on the script. Frattarola clenched her fists and stared at Chris. *Don't get too technical. Stay vague.* She considered interrupting the interview and warning DiMeglio, but it was too late. He started his answer.

"The classic definition of a serial killer is someone who has killed at least three people over an extended period, usually within a couple of months. The victims usually have a common connection, sometimes obvious, other times not. Then there might be a break as they plan their next move. Each murder makes them more confident. Bolder. And the bolder they become, the more likely they'll make a mistake."

"Three or more murders over an extended period? Each

with some common connection between the victims? Is that a fair definition of a serial killer?"

Here it comes, thought Frattarola. DiMeglio was oblivious to where she was going. She'd lured him into her web.

"In part, yes," he answered. "It's multiple killings of similarly situated victims."

She pulled out a newspaper clipping from the back of her notepad and handed it to DiMeglio. He could see in her eyes the satisfaction she felt at maneuvering him to where she wanted him to be.

The clipping was from the *Chicago Tribune*. A question, written at the top of the article in red ink that only DiMeglio could see, read, "Do you believe me now?"

"Agent DiMeglio, please take your time and read the article. It's short."

The director yelled, "Cut," and the filming stopped while DiMeglio and Frattarola read the article.

PROMINENT LAWYER COMMITS SUICIDE

The body of Joseph Bartlett, a leading Chicago defense lawyer, was found dead in his office, apparently having hanged himself. His secretary discovered him when she arrived at the office on Monday morning. His wife said he was off on a business trip, so she was not concerned when he didn't come home the night before his body was discovered. Bartlett was well known throughout the state for representing defendants charged with murder, rape, and other violent crimes. Flamboyant, he was never camera shy. At times, judges criticized him for using the press to sway juries with evidence that could not be admitted or misinformation he wanted to plant in the public mind. Some judges he appeared before even sequestered juries to thwart Bartlett's efforts to improperly influence juries when in normal circumstances, the jurors would be free to go home after each day of a trial. Police found a note at the scene, but did not disclose its content. It may shed some light on why he took his own life when he was one of the most successful attorneys in the city. Whenever he was defense counsel, very few of his clients were found guilty, at least for the crimes they were charged with. He leaves his wife and three children.

DiMeglio put the paper down on the table. The director waved to the camera operator to begin taping and pointed to Lane. Before the cameras started rolling, DiMeglio asked Lane, "It says they found a note. What did it say?" She didn't answer. The taping began.

"Now three dead lawyers," she continued. "Each a specialist in criminal defense. All of whom allegedly committed suicide. Is that enough of a connection, Agent DiMeglio, to suspect they all died at the hands of a serial killer?"

DiMeglio's mind was racing over the possibility. He remained silent.

"Any comment?" she inquired again.

Stalling as he mentally processed the facts, he responded, "I'm not sure what you're asking me, Carla."

"Okay. Let's get to the point. I already told you about two previous suicides by lawyers. We spoke about them months ago. And now I've told you that there is a third. That alone might not be surprising. It's no secret that attorneys are among the professionals with the highest suicide rates. But each of these lawyers were a prominent defense attorneys. Each secured mistrials or acquittals for violent crimes. Many of their clients were murderers. None of the now-dead lawyers had financial problems or professional pressures. They were all at the top of their game. Each left notes asking to be forgiven for what they'd done, presumably for securing freedom for murderers."

She paused, giving DiMeglio a chance to think before she asked her next question.

"So, Agent DiMeglio, is it possible these three killings are related and may be the work of a serial killer?"

Son of a bitch. I should have seen that coming. Keep your cool.

"Carla, I will not react to a newspaper article or speculate on the common traits between murders. This is all new to me."

She attacked. "That's not accurate, Agent DiMeglio. I previously told you about the first two and urged you to investigate whether there was a serial killer. At least two of these murders are not new to you."

On the defensive, he responded, his voice firm, "At this point, Ms. Lane, I have no basis for concluding that these dead lawyers are connected to a serial killer. It would require much more investigation to come to that conclusion."

"But will you look into it? Do you know enough to do that, at least?"

"Even if I did, I would not tell you. We don't discuss active investigations, even those we think will lead to dead ends."

"And that's where you think this one will lead?"

"Yes, Carla. Most likely like this one, too."

"Cut," the director ordered. The interview was over.

Frattarola was in Lane's face within seconds of the director's words.

"Carla, you had no call to blindside Chris with your personal speculation. We would have reconsidered the interview if you had told us you intended to do so."

"You agreed to no pre-clearance of questions, Julie. Frankly, he should have known I'd bring up our prior conversation. He's lucky I didn't bring up his affair with

Simone. And his answers were fine. Just what I expected. What's more important to me, Julie, is for him to take a hard look and confirm if my suspicions are correct. I want his help. That's why I didn't hit him with his problems in New Orleans."

DiMeglio took Frattarola's arm and led her away. He wanted nothing more than to get out of the studio. Looking back at Lane as they went for the door, he said, "Carla, let's talk soon."

CHAPTER TWELVE

It's Only Lunch

Commissary, Washington, D.C.

Lane chose the Commissary, a popular D.C. lunch spot on P Street about a half mile from DuPont Circle. She first suggested dinner, but DiMeglio turned that down. Lane suspected he wanted their meeting to be purely professional. That was fine with her, but she thought it was presumptuous for him to assume a dinner invitation would not also be professional. She had a story she wanted to break, not a relationship she wanted to pursue.

Lane's career was on the rise. She'd left the *San Diego Tribune* to become a special correspondent for *60 Minutes* and pursue her new job at the *Washington Gazette* as an investigative reporter, a position that allowed her to pursue just about anything she considered newsworthy or of interest to her editors and the paper's readers. Investigative reporters get a wide berth in what they cover.

She was waiting for him when he arrived, intentionally getting there early, as she did for all her interviews. Lane felt it gave her time to get comfortable and watch her guest's body language as they arrived. The Commissary could be noisy with its young diners, primarily locals, so she chose a table in a corner for privacy, making sure DiMeglio would face the wall to avoid distraction from the crowd.

As DiMeglio approached the table, she rose and greeted him. "Thanks, Chris, for accepting my invitation," she said, extending her hand. After shaking it, he sat down across from her.

Unlike what she wore in the *60 Minutes* interview, Lane purposely dressed to reveal a lot more. She wore a short pleated blue off-the-shoulder dress that showed just enough cleavage to interest any man, including DiMeglio. Her light brown hair hung down to her shoulders, and the light red lipstick accentuated her lips. She looked sexy and inviting.

DiMeglio had trouble taking his eyes off her, but he reminded himself to be professional. This was an interview, not a date. He began, "Before we get started, thank you for not bringing up my relationship with Rebecca Simone in our interview. Julie told me what you said to her. So you knew about it."

"I did, but that's not what I was interested in. My story isn't about mistakes you may have made in New Orleans. Instead, I'm interested in what you think about my belief that a serial killer is murdering criminal defense lawyers."

The server came, and the two agreed to split the Rustic Italian pizza. A pie with hot Italian sausage, roasted red peppers, caramelized onion, fennel, mozzarella, parmesan, and charred rosemary. For all intents and purposes, a fancy name for a sausage and pepper pie. She ordered a Diet Coke. He asked for a regular one.

"I'd like to hear more about your theory," said DiMeglio. "I admit the idea is intriguing. It's certainly possible for someone to target that group. It could fit into the psychopathic model of a serial killer. However, with only three victims in distant locations, it's hard to see a connection or pattern that raises concerns. But I'm willing to listen."

"It just strikes me as too coincidental."

He smiled. "You need to meet my team. They think there is nothing coincidental. That's a trait good profilers need."

"So what makes you decide to pursue a case?"

"Most start with nothing more than an observation. Then the coincidental becomes consequential, and we see a pattern sufficient to warrant a closer look. I'm not sure we're there yet." He remembered what Frattarola had told him to say before he answered questions. "But anything I say to you today is off the record. Can you agree with that?"

The pizza arrived, and the server gave them plates, serving one slice to each of them.

Off the record or background only were common requests, but the last thing Lane wanted to agree to. If she said she had an unnamed source in the article, it would be a tough sell to her editor. She needed to name names.

"Not completely," she responded. "But how about this? Everything is off the record unless I ask you for a comment

I can attribute to you or, as we often say, someone high in the Bureau?"

"Given our history and the *60 Minutes* interview, that would be tantamount to using my name. But I'll agree to your ground rules if you let me review any article before you publish it." That was not the script Frattarola gave him.

Lane shook her head. "Tell you what, Chris. I'll let you preview the article for comment, assuming I ever write one. You can then tell me what you think, but I cannot agree to make changes unless I believe they're appropriate. Otherwise, my editors will never agree to publish. We don't give approvals to people outside the paper."

"Okay, that will work," replied DiMeglio. While he didn't think it was what Frattarola wanted, it was okay with him. He resolved to be careful about what he told Lane and control the narrative until it made sense to be more public.

They took a few minutes to enjoy the pizza. Then, DiMeglio returned to the subject, concerned about any initiative by a reporter.

"Carla, the timing when the public is informed of the possibility of a serial killer being at large is important. It's a tactic we use to flush them out. But if we make the announcement too soon, the killer might change his targets or methods. If announced too late, the killer may have already gone into hiding or vanished. While we can never be certain of the right timing, it's too early now. This is not the time for you to write an article. We're not even sure we're dealing with a serial killer."

"I'll keep that in mind."

The server refilled the drinks.

"Tell me why, beyond the similarities you've already told me, you're so convinced the lawyers are victims of a serial killer."

"I'm not sure there's much else to tell, Chris. The killing of three famous criminal defense attorneys who routinely take on the worst of the worst has the markings of some sort of vendetta. Whether or not you call the killer a serial killer, the fact remains that it's tough to explain the similarities as mere coincidence. You must at least agree with me on that point."

He did.

CHAPTER THIRTEEN

A Bark as Bad as its Bite

Dunnington Place, Dumfries, Virginia

DiMeglio poured himself a glass of Jameson on ice and sat on the couch, thinking about the day and his lunch with Lane. It only took a few seconds before Sully joined him, head on his lap.

As he rubbed the back of Sully's neck, DiMeglio said, "Well, Sully, it seems there might be a serial killer out there who has a real hard-on for lawyers."

Sully stirred a bit as DiMeglio took a sip, pondering the case. Did he have a serial killer on his hands?

"But I'm not sure if it's the case or the reporter I want to pursue."

Sully got up and walked away. The dog had a way of letting DiMeglio know that his relationships with women were never promising. Worse, while Sully put up with DiMeglio's long absences and dog walkers when DiMeglio was chasing down murderers, he took it out on DiMeglio by shunning him when he returned, particularly if it was with a woman in tow.

"C'mon, Sully, give me a break!"

Sully let out a low growl, loud enough so DiMeglio could

hear it, and sauntered into the other room. DiMeglio took another sip and turned on the TV.

"Stupid dog," he muttered.

CHAPTER FOURTEEN

An Open Mind

BAU Headquarters, Quantico, Virginia

DiMeglio gathered his team in his conference room at the Quantico headquarters the following day. As he usually did before early morning meetings, he stopped and picked up some bagels, cream cheese, and lox. Stokes brought coffee from Starbucks. A Grande four shot cappuccino for DiMeglio, a tall latte with skim milk for Evans, and a black Venti Americano for himself. Evans brought her appetite. It was their routine.

"A reporter is pressuring me to open a case and see if we have a serial killer targeting criminal defense lawyers."

"Wow," replied Evans. "I can identify with that! I can give the killer suggestions on a few lawyers I'd love to see on his list. Like the names of both of my divorce lawyers."

She'd been married twice. No children. In each instance, she couldn't balance her life as an FBI agent with any semblance of a stay-at-home spouse. It just wasn't in her. As a result, both husbands eventually left her. That's when she gave up looking for long-term relationships and turned to Tinder.

"Ditto," added Stokes. "Maybe we just let this guy keep up the good work!"

"You've been married for over twenty years, Brad, and you've never hired a lawyer. So what's your beef?" asked DiMeglio.

"I just like to agree with Georgia. She treats me better when I do." That elicited a laugh among them. The banter continued.

"Hey, we could call him the Counselor Killer," suggested Evans with a grin.

"Or the Lawyernator," added Stokes.

"Okay, guys, now that the humor's out of the way, let's toss it around. Personally, I'm not sure there is enough here. The reports say each of them committed suicide. That's sadly common for their profession, and I'm sure there are plenty of criminal defense lawyers haunted by some scumbags they freed and put back on the streets. They may have all simply died by their own hands."

"What else do we know, Chris?" asked Evans, now serious.

DiMeglio went through all the facts Lane gave him.

"We need a lot more to open a file, Chief," concluded Stokes. "These three guys died all over the place. At least one of them was killed outside their hometown. That's a lot of distance for a serial killer to travel and a big disconnect. We're busy enough and don't have time to chase down what's only a hunch or a reporter's obsession with a story."

"That's what I've been thinking," observed DiMeglio.

"Wait for a second," interjected Evans. "No doubt your first reactions are right. But it is plausible that some psychopath has it out for criminal defense lawyers. Perhaps someone who thinks the justice system is letting too many people off. Or someone who has had enough with prisons and parole boards releasing allegedly reformed murderers only to see them kill again. There are plenty of people who think the judicial system is in ruins. So maybe a vigilante wants to fix it himself."

"And travel all over the United States to do it?" asked Stokes. "If he has a vendetta, there are plenty of targets in any large city. Doesn't seem to have the efficiency we usually see."

"There are plenty of serial killers whose areas of operations spanned states," countered Evans. "Like Samuel Little. He confessed to a thirty-five-year spree that killed ninety-three women in nineteen states. So I'm not willing to write it off. It deserves a deeper look."

"Okay," DiMeglio agreed. If Evans saw something he and Stokes missed, it was meaningful. It was her superpower, as DiMeglio would tell her. "Let's pursue Georgia's gut feeling and set up a board."

CHAPTER FIFTEEN

Breaking the Mold

Headquarters, Federal Bureau of Investigation,
Washington, D.C.

"He can't be serious."

"He is, Chris," responded Frattarola as they walked toward Kinston's office.

"The idea is ludicrous. Embed a reporter into our investigative team? This is not a war zone. It's never been done."

"Well, it might be unique, but working closely with the press is not. Hoover did it constantly, and Eliot Ness never met a camera he didn't like. Comey did it behind the scenes, leaking information when it served his purpose. So working closely with the press is not something new for the Bureau."

"It is for me. And look what it got Comey."

Kinston's EA immediately took them into Kinston's office. They sat in their usual seats in front of his desk, waiting for him to arrive from another meeting.

"Chris, remember our conversation about politicians?"

"Yeah, so what?"

"Look at all the pictures the Director hangs in his office. Pictures of him with one politician after another. And you don't think he's as much a politician as anyone else on the

Hill? This entire exercise is about politics, Chris. That's why he wants to embed a reporter with you. To get the most political spin he can."

Before DiMeglio could reply, Kinston arrived.

"Good to see you both. It looks like your PR tour is doing well, Chris. I saw you on *60 Minutes*. You had Lane eating out of your hand." He sat in his chair behind his desk.

"Thank you, Director, but I was lucky. She laid off the controversial stuff. She never mentioned the issues with Becca Simone," replied DiMeglio.

"Lucky or not, Chris, you're doing a great job. I hear you're going on *Hannity* next. That's likely to be a real trip. He hates the Bureau and me. Says he respects the agents, though. So he may be nice to you."

"We'll have Chris prepared, Director," interjected Frattarola.

"Good. So what do you think of my idea, Chris? I'm sure Julie told you all about it."

"She did. But with all due respect, Director, embedding a reporter with my team is a bad idea. It will be very disruptive and risk the release of confidential information; it could undermine our active investigations. We can't trust the press."

"I expected that response from you, Chris. And I respect it. But we have a serious image problem. And it doesn't get better no matter how many times I testify or how often Julie puts out success stories. You are the only thing we have out there right now that's working. So we need to take advantage of that success."

DiMeglio did not want to give up. "Director, our investigations involve very sensitive issues. We work on vague assumptions and sometimes what seem to be preposterous ideas. Profiling is often about throwing everything against the wall and letting one thing lead to another. And most unsettling is the reality that to succeed, we usually need a killer to keep killing. That's a spin we don't need in the press. Our success is often at the price of innocent victims. I'm not sure any reporter can appreciate that, much less report it fairly."

"I can think of one reporter who will be fair," responded Kinston.

DiMeglio saw it coming.

"Carla Lane. She's shown a keen interest in this investigation and seems comfortable with you. She has a vested interest in the story. We can ensure she keeps it all confidential, and we'll get confirmation from the *Gazette* that they will also respect our rules. When you solve the case, assuming it is a case, it will be a major victory for the Bureau. Even if there is no case, I'm sure you can manipulate her to write a favorable article. I want to make the complexities and process part of any story. It will show how hard we work to get results unfiltered by politics."

DiMeglio was resigned that the decision was final. "How much access do you expect me to give Lane, sir?"

"That's your call, Chris. But I'd err to the side of caution and make her a real part of your team. Win her over. Shit, she might even give you some useful clues. After all, she is an investigative reporter. And a good one, from what I hear."

Frattarola added, "But what we really want, Chris, is for you to get her to tell the true story about the FBI and get congressional heat off the Director."

Typical PR bullshit, thought DiMeglio. *She was going wherever the wind took a story.*

"Yeah, that too, Chris," offered Kinston.

"Why can't we just leave that to a TV series?"

"Because the FBI is out of favor everywhere. Depending on Hollywood scriptwriters is not the answer. We need to create the change from within," responded Frattarola.

"But you do need to watch more television, Chris," observed Kinston as he pressed the intercom button on his phone to talk to his EA.

"Yes, sir," Gibson immediately responded.

"Has Ms. Lane arrived?"

"Yes, sir, she's right here."

"Please bring her in."

CHAPTER SIXTEEN

Ground Rules

BAU Headquarters, Quantico, Virginia

Stokes and Evans were waiting in the conference room, arriving immediately after they got the text from DiMeglio. He, Frattarola, and Lane were on their way from seeing the Director. DiMeglio drove in his car, and Lane was with Frattarola. From his car, he briefed Stokes and Evans on the phone, telling them that at the meeting, he wanted to address the elephant in the room before it got any bigger. Driving well above the speed limit, he was far ahead of Frattarola and Lane.

"This is bullshit," said Stokes, arms crossed as he and Evans waited for DiMeglio to arrive. "The last thing we need is some fuckin' reporter watching over our shoulders."

"I agree, Brad, but that's what the Director wants, so we'll have to make the best of it," replied Evans.

"Why can't Chris just say no? The Director can't force him to do this."

"Really, Brad? That attitude is exactly why the Bureau has passed you over for promotion so many times. Do you honestly think Chris, much less you or I, can make whatever decision we want? Unless you want reassignment to a field office in Alaska chasing polar bear poachers, I suggest we make this work for Chris. I'm sure he's no happier than we are."

DiMeglio entered the room, motioning them to stay seated. He took a seat at the table with them.

"OK, I agree, this is bullshit," he began. "But that's what we've been dealt. So we'll have to deal with it."

"Whatever you say, Chief, but I don't see how we can trust her," Stokes said. "She's the press. All she wants is a sensational story."

"And we can't give her confidential information, Chris," added Evans.

"I know that, Georgia. And I'm not suggesting we trust her, Brad. We'll keep everything close to the vest. We can meet without her as well. We'll investigate just like we always do. For all I know, this is a wild goose chase, anyway. If that turns out to be the case, we'll get rid of her quickly. So we'll play this one day at a time."

Frattarola and Lane arrived, and Lenoir Peters brought them in. DiMeglio stood and motioned toward his conference table, and stood at one end.

"Carla Lane, this is Georgia Evans and Brad Stokes, key players on our team." Georgia and Brad stood and shook hands with Lane. "And, of course, everyone already knows Julie." DiMeglio motioned for Lane and Frattarola to take a seat at the table.

"Let's address the issue and get it out of the way,"

DiMeglio began. "We don't like the idea of having Ms. Lane on the team. To my knowledge, the Bureau has never done this before. We don't know what rules apply. We'll have to make them up as we go along."

Lane shifted in her chair. She didn't expect DiMeglio to be so blunt despite Frattarola's warning in the drive that he was likely to be so.

"How about starting with confidentiality, Chief?"

DiMeglio almost grinned as Stokes played the bad cop. He always did. DiMeglio depended upon it. He wanted to be sure Lane got the message that she was not welcome on the team, hoping she'd quit.

"Ms. Lane and the *Gazette* are both under a very strict written NDA," responded Frattarola. "They know we're allowing Ms. Lane to be part of ongoing investigations and understand that any information leak would constitute an obstruction of justice. In writing, we have made it crystal clear that we will take a breach of our agreement very seriously. Is that all correct, Ms. Lane?"

"Yes, Julie. I understand."

Lane was not a reporter to cower or not rise to a challenge. She'd done enough crime reporting to stand up to any cop. Now was not the time for timidity.

"But let me be clear as well," she began. "I get it. You don't want me here. But I'm here to stay. I promise I'll try my best not to get in the way. But I will ask questions. That's my job. And I expect honest answers. I'll keep it all confidential. I simply want to pursue a story about your work, particularly serial killers. Maybe a serial killer is targeting defense attorneys. There will be no leaks."

That wasn't good enough for Stokes. "With all due respect, Ms. Lane, that's rich. A newspaper reporter saying there will be no leaks? And in Washington, D.C., no less? Your kind lives and dies by leaks. And once something is out there, it can never be recalled. So I hope you understand that what we do can often be the difference between life and death. So don't screw up."

"My *kind*, Agent Stokes, knows what's at stake."

CHAPTER SEVENTEEN

Une mort choquante

Avenue Montaigne, Paris, France

Marie Létisse was among a few women who excelled as criminal defense attorneys, particularly in defending murderers. Based in Paris, she defended some of the most demonic killers in France, including terrorists who murdered and maimed dozens of innocent people in newspaper offices, shopping malls, and on public transportation. She'd been a prosecutor for ten years and an expert at using the ropes—and the tricks—of criminal law in a country steeped in a history not known for due process or fair trials. Her mission as a prosecutor was to do the right thing and keep dangerous criminals behind bars. But when repeatedly overlooked for a deserved promotion, she concluded it was because she was a woman in a male-dominated world. She was right. So she quit and vowed to show the system— indeed the world—that no one, no man, no woman, no one could beat her at the game. She turned from doing what was right to whatever she needed to do to win an acquittal for her clients, regardless of how guilty they might be.

And she proved to be very good, with a winning record that was the envy of every criminal lawyer in France. She rose to lead the criminal bar and became an international spokesperson at key conferences on the art of criminal defense. With it came considerable wealth that afforded her pleasures no prosecutor could dream of, including a multi-million-dollar apartment on Avenue Montaigne, the most expensive street in the posh 8th arrondissement of Paris. In the late 17th century, women in mourning for their lost husbands gathered on Avenue Montaigne, then known as widows' alley. But that changed as the 18th century unfolded. Today, it is home to opulent wealth and high-fashion retailers, including Louis Vuitton, Chanel, Yves Saint Laurent, Gucci, Prada, and Versace.

Her apartment was old and always needed repair, but its fine art and history as the residence of some of France's royalty in centuries past gave it a regal feeling. Létisse, unmarried and unattached, enjoyed being alone in her apartment, away from the pressures of her work and the many clients she considered reprehensible. Her only companion was her cat, Gaston, a pet she rescued from a kill shelter, naming him after a client acquitted on multiple murder charges.

They found her dead in her bathtub, electrocuted by a hairdryer dropped in the water. In modern homes, circuit breakers would have prevented the dryer from killing her. Indeed, the local police saw it as odd that the safety measures in the appliance itself didn't work. Upon examination, the investigators speculated that someone might have tampered with the dryer, turning it into a deadly weapon. Or it was just bad wiring.

There was also a note, just like the others. Létisse lamented all the wrong she had done in defending murderers and terrorists and hoped for forgiveness. There were no signs of a struggle. No fingerprints other than her own. They also found Gaston in the kitchen, lying dead beside a bowl of poisoned food. The investigators, confused, wondered if this was a tragic accident, a bizarre suicide, or murder. But why would a murderer kill an innocent cat? They concluded the cause of her death by electrocution needed further investigation.

The local press ran with the story. Some international media outlets also picked it up, but not many. It was just another dead lawyer.

Lane emailed DiMeglio a copy of an article in *Le Monde*, the Paris newspaper. She included a Google translation to be sure he could read it.

CHAPTER EIGHTEEN

Fox in the Henhouse

News Corp, Studio J
1211 Avenue of the Americas, New York City

"Hello. Welcome to *Hannity*. On this busy night of political disasters and mistakes…"

DiMeglio sat in the Green Room waiting to go on stage, knowing that this interview would be more difficult given Hannity's criticism of the FBI and allegations by just about every host on Fox that Washington politicians have weaponized the Bureau. Unlike his prior television appearances, the telecast was also live. That raised his concerns. He reminded himself of Frattarola's admonition not to let Hannity pull him into a political debate. That was Hannity's turf, not his.

The Green Room was like the others he'd seen. Comfortable with food and alcohol if you wanted it. Only he and Frattarola were in the room, waiting for a call to Hannity's desk. Before arrival, Frattarola told him not to talk aloud about anything while in the Green Room. "It's bugged," she warned. DiMeglio found such a fear absurd, but was okay with not talking about his job. The interview circuit was exhausting, and he was growing tired of hearing himself pontificate on the BAU and success stories of the FBI.

"Julie, just in case they are listening," he said, "and since I'm not allowed to say anything, I guess I'll have a drink and relax." He got up and poured himself a Jameson, appreciating that what he drank was stocked in the Green Room. Frattarola said nothing, but her expression made it clear she approved of neither the comment nor the drink. At this point, he didn't care.

With a knock on the door, the stagehand said, "Mr. DiMeglio, you're on next." DiMeglio took one more drag on the Jameson, followed the staff producer, and sat at a desk across from Hannity. The show was on a commercial break.

"Thanks for coming, Agent DiMeglio," began Hannity as the director counted down with his fingers, indicating the commercial break was approaching its end. "Sorry we didn't have time to talk before you came on. I'm a great fan of the FBI's agents. The people who do the actual job of the Bureau."

"Thanks, Mr. Hannity. Please call me Chris."

"Good. Call me Sean."

The show's director completed the countdown. They were live.

"Welcome back. The FBI is under attack. It's been weaponized by politicians looking for scapegoats. It's lost its direction. My sources say that's all going to change. I hope that's true. Welcome Chris DiMeglio, chief profiler at the FBI, who assists local police in tracking down violent criminals. He is one of the most successful agents in the Bureau and is now speaking for the FBI and its renewed focus. Welcome to *Hannity*, Chris."

DiMeglio's stomach turned, not responding. Instead, he nodded and reminded himself, "*What would Julie tell me to say?*" He now regretted having the Jameson.

"So, Agent DiMeglio, let's get right to it. The headlines are clear. What's gone wrong with the FBI? Why did it become a political tool for progressives, and what is going to change?"

Are those questions or accusations?! DiMeglio could see Hannity was wasting no time getting to his political agenda. *Stay calm. Stay on the script.*

"Sean, the FBI hasn't gone wrong. Unfortunately, the media has focused on a few investigations involving allegedly corrupt politicians. In reality, we do far more than that. Our mission is to protect the American people and uphold the Constitution of the United States. We do that by tracking down, arresting, and assisting in the prosecution of terrorists, cybercriminals, serial killers, and more. Paramount in what we do is protecting the civil rights of all Americans."

Just what Julie told me to say.

"I apologize, Agent DiMeglio, but that sounds like a canned response." Hannity would not make it easy for DiMeglio. "You have to admit that the FBI has become a tool for political agendas."

DiMeglio wished Julie could help him respond. "Sean, it's not my place to comment on political debates. I'll leave that to you. But the FBI has been unfairly maligned by both sides of the aisle, depending upon whose ox they choose to gore."

Take that, asshole.

"But why then, Agent DiMeglio, does it at least look like the FBI spends most of its time on investigations spurred on by Congress aimed at past and present politicians, including their families? Most of the investigations seem overwhelmingly targeted at conservatives."

Change the agenda, Chris. Change the agenda.

"Because that's the spin media reports, Sean. That's not why I'm here. I want the public to learn about our great work and not feed the media pipeline with innuendo and fake news." He could see Frattarola wince standing offstage.

Hannity paused, realizing he would not drag DiMeglio into a political debate. DiMeglio hoped he'd go to a commercial break and end the ordeal.

"Okay, then. Let's talk about your work. Tell us more about your job when you're not appearing on talk shows."

He could hear Frattarola's voice in his head, "*Don't take the bait, Chris. Stick to the facts.*"

"When I'm not appearing on talk shows, Sean, I'm Chief of the Behavioral Analysis Unit. What most folks refer to as the profilers."

"And you mainly chase down serial killers, right?"

"That's been my focus, but the unit does much more. I prefer to think of the unit as profilers of serial criminals.

That can include financial crimes, pedophiles, and more. It's not just killers."

"And I understand you're very good at that."

Finally, a softball.

"We're all very good at it, Sean. The Bureau has been the world's most successful law enforcement agency in solving complex criminal schemes. We've saved countless lives and livelihoods."

"Let's hope the new leadership of the Bureau shares your views, Chris." Seeing no reaction from DiMeglio that might lead to a discussion on the FBI leadership, Hannity continued, "But I have to admit, I love stories about serial killers. They make for some of my favorite television series and motion pictures."

Really?

"It's always interested me that so many people are fascinated by serial killers, Sean. Since I spend all my time hunting them down, they hold little fascination for me. They're just murderers. What makes them so interesting to you, Sean?"

Hannity seemed taken aback by the question. He was supposed to be asking them, not DiMeglio.

"I hadn't thought about it," he said. "But I guess it's because they're so mysterious. And to be honest, that mystery makes me want to know more. But how serious is the threat of serial killers, Chris? Or is it more of a Hollywood plot than a neighborhood reality?"

He's throwing more softballs! Perfect. Hit the agenda.

"Since 1980, Sean, there have been over 185,000 unsolved murders in the United States alone. Every year, we add another 6,000. Those cases have all gone cold. We estimate that as many as 2,000 serial killers are responsible for those cold cases. The United States alone has more serial killers than every other country in the world combined."

"That's more than I expected. How many are out there who haven't been caught?"

"Over time, hundreds if not thousands. Serial killers have been around for millennia. But if you're asking me how many are out there as we sit here, my guess is there could be as many as fifty active serial killers prowling for victims every day."

"Fifty?!" replied Hannity with surprise.

"Unfortunately, many of them will never be caught despite our efforts. But that does not stop us. We deploy dozens of agents every day to hunt them down."

"Hold on, Chris." Hannity seemed to be still reeling from the numbers DiMeglio recited. "You're telling me there are as many as fifty serial killers out there right now, and most of them will not be caught? That you, the FBI, and local police, can't find them? That's a scary statistic, Chris."

DiMeglio silently kicked himself. That wasn't the spin Julie wanted in the press, even though it's the truth.

"It is scary, Sean. Worse, we continue to make it easier for killers to find victims. People openly post on social media, chat rooms, dating services, and websites, where they disclose far more personal information than they should. As a result, they put themselves in harm's way. I caution everyone to think twice before they share their innermost thoughts online. You may feel liberated telling the world what you think. But you may be signing your own death warrant."

Still dumbfounded, Hannity responded, "Serial killers use social media to find victims?"

"Every day, Sean. Every day."

"Wow. But I want to get back to the fifty who you say are out there. That amazes me. What can the FBI do to stop them? Isn't it fair to say that despite all the cases you've solved, it's just a drop in the bucket?"

Don't take the bait.

"We work at it every day, Sean. It may be a drop in the bucket to you, but we approach it, using your analogy, one drop at a time. One life at a time."

"How?"

"Every serial killer has a motive. They have a pattern. Sometimes it's obvious. Often it isn't easy to see. We look at every connection. We put together a profile. That profile eventually leads us to the killer."

"One killer at a time?"

"One killer at a time," replied DiMeglio.

The director cued Hannity that he was approaching a commercial break.

"Thanks again for coming on the show, Chris. Perhaps

we can dig deeper into the FBI's problems with politicians next time." DiMeglio chose not to respond as the music introducing the break rose, and the cameras stopped taping.

"Sorry if I was rough on you about politicians using the FBI as a tool. But you cannot deny it's happening, and if you and Director Kinston are telling the truth, that's where the Bureau needs to change."

"That's above my pay grade, Sean. My job is to stop murderers."

DiMeglio could not have gotten off that stage fast enough.

CHAPTER NINETEEN

Bait

BAU Headquarters, Quantico, Virginia

"Okay, Carla, if you're so convinced we have a serial killer on the prowl, we need to flush him out."

The team gathered in the Quantico offices for an early morning meeting. Carla added to the routine menu by bringing some pastries to accompany the bagels.

"And what do you propose, Chris?" asked Lane.

"If nothing else, serial killers have inflated egos. Most think they are God-like and should be revered like one. They at least want acknowledgment. They crave publicity. So we eventually want to let him know we're on to his game. Make him a little nervous."

"Won't that make him go into hiding and stop or take a break?" asked Lane.

"It might. But it's a risk worth taking. It's time to have you write an editorial. I'd like you to give him a reason to reach out to me."

The Op-Ed in the *Washington Gazette* was short and simple:

WHO IS KILLING THE LAWYERS?

Among professionals, lawyers are near the top of the chart on suicide. So a dead lawyer here or a dead lawyer there who killed themselves isn't that surprising. Particularly when they've left a note saying they took their own lives. Such was the case with Marie Létisse in Paris just a few weeks ago. And with Jacob Schneider from New York, Paul Stafford from Los Angeles, and Joseph Bartlett, who died in Miami.

Far-flung locations. Different ways they died. They found Létisse dead in her bathtub in Paris, the victim of electrocution. Schneider drowned in the Florida Keys, Stafford jumped from a Los Angeles high-rise hotel, and Bartlett hanged himself.

What connects all these dead lawyers?

Each was a celebrated defense attorney who successfully got some of the most horrific criminals acquitted on what many people considered rock-solid cases that even the most inexperienced prosecutor should have won. Unfortunately, many of those they defended and helped stay free, killed again before they were eventually stopped by going to prison for life, being shot by police, or executed in the gas chamber, by lethal injection, the electric chair, hanging, or a firing squad.

Each of the lawyers was at the top of their game. None of them had any financial problems. None of them showed any reason to want to take their own lives. Those who had families were living happy lives. None of them faced any personal challenges. Suicide made no sense. Yet all but the Létisse case are closed. All certified as suicides.

The findings also noted the lack of evidence at the scenes, causing police to believe no foul play was involved. There were no fingerprints. No signs of struggle. No witnesses. Nothing on surveillance cameras. So suicide was a convenient conclusion and an easy reason to close a case. But was it too convenient?

Are these cases too similar to write them off as routine suicides? Is there more to it? Does an investigation need to be undertaken?

Readers may recall when this reporter confronted Christopher DiMeglio, the Chief of the FBI's profiling unit, on *60 Minutes*. I gave him a clipping from a local paper reporting on the death of Joseph Bartlett, the third victim, in a suspicious line of dead lawyers. He avoided making any conclusion or speculating about any connection. Then I sent him the clipping on the death of Létisse.

Are these deaths coincidental, or is a serial killer targeting famous defense attorneys who have set criminals free? And how does this killer operate internationally, let alone across the United States? These are good questions for Agent DiMeglio to ask. The only person who can answer them is a serial killer who might be responsible for the deaths.

CHAPTER TWENTY

Perhaps We Should Talk

Marine Corps Dog Park, Quantico, Virginia

The first contact came in while DiMeglio exercised Sully at the Marine Corps Base Dog Park in Quantico. It was his and Sully's routine on most weekends when he was not on the road. While not the most beautiful park in the area, it allowed Sully to run free and play with other dogs while DiMeglio could sit on a bench and relax, occasionally engaging in small talk with other dog owners.

"Perhaps we should talk," read the simple text on his phone from an unidentified caller. The texter used the Signal app.

DiMeglio avoided texting. The lines are too insecure. Signal, however, is an independent, double-encrypted service that assures anonymity unless you can access the phones on both sides of a conversation. Each user is anonymous to others unless they choose to identify themselves. They can also use an alias that has no connection to a real person. If you know a user's name or number on Signal, you can send confidential and secure messages that do not reveal your identity or location. Because of its security, Signal is among the favorite texting apps of the criminal world and the bane of police. Nonetheless, many law enforcement professionals use it for confidential communications with informants or undercover officers. That's why DiMeglio, like virtually every other FBI field agent, had it on his cell phone. So long as someone knows his cell phone number, they can send him a message that does not reveal who or where they are.

"Who is this?" DiMeglio typed in reply.

The bubbles that pop up when someone types in a text message exchange immediately appeared. The sender had something to say.

"Someone I think you want to talk to."

"Why?" typed DiMeglio.

More bubbles.

"Because you're looking for me."

DiMeglio usually told texters not to waste his time unless they identified themselves and got to their point quickly. When they didn't, he'd simply block their number and hope never to hear from them again. But Lane's editorial was too fresh in his mind to dismiss any lead.

"I'm looking for lots of people," he typed. "And I don't have time for games. Unless you tell me who you are and what you want, lose my number."

No bubbles. No response. The first session was over.

Sully was at his feet, holding a Frisbee in his mouth. Where Sully got the Frisbee was a mystery. DiMeglio didn't bring it. But if Sully saw something he wanted from another dog, he took it. And now, Sully wanted to play Frisbee. So

DiMeglio threw it as far as he could, Sully in pursuit. As he waited for Sully to return, he texted Evans and Stokes to get to his office.

When Sully returned, DiMeglio put the leash on his collar and dropped the Frisbee on the bench. Sully knew it was time to leave and didn't put up a fight. He never did. They drove directly to DiMeglio's office, a five-minute drive. Sully took his usual position on the couch, leaving no room for anyone else.

Evans arrived dressed in typical weekend clothes—jeans and a polo shirt. "Brad is right behind me. He looks like he just came from the gym. And I bet he smells that way, too!"

Within a minute, Stokes arrived. Evans was right. DiMeglio pointed to the conference table, and they all sat down.

"We may have our first communication with the killer. I received a text on Signal suggesting I should talk to the sender," DiMeglio began.

"Or to a prankster, Chief," responded Stokes. "As far as I'm concerned, Lane's editorial was an open invitation for every kook out there to call you. It's not as though your number is unlisted. It's on your LinkedIn profile. Anyone with a computer can find it."

"It's there, Brad, so that people can contact me," responded DiMeglio. "You might want to list your number, too."

"I'll think about it." Stokes guarded his privacy despite his role as an investigator. He knew, however, that just about everyone in the Bureau used Signal and that, eventually, he'd have to make himself available on the app and his social media profiles. Of course, like most agents, he could use a separate phone for personal calls. But that was all too complicated for him. And he liked things simple.

"Is there anything in the texts that gives us any clues, Chris?" asked Evans.

"No. Just an invitation to speak. So you're probably right, Brad. Wishful thinking on my part. I guess we just wait and see if I get another text or if we're contacted in some other way or by someone else."

"Hopefully, before the next murder," offered Evans.

"I doubt we'll be that lucky," concluded Stokes.

CHAPTER TWENTY-ONE

The Game Begins

Dunnington Place, Dumfries, Virginia

Four hours later, DiMeglio's phone beeped. He was home trying to decide what to have for dinner. It was usually some kind of frozen dinner or an Uber Eats delivery from a local restaurant. The phone's beep ended his search of the freezer.

"It's me again," read the text. DiMeglio went to his couch and sat down. Sully laid down next to him, head in his lap.

"And who is 'me again'?" typed DiMeglio. "Unless you give me a good reason to continue, this is over and I'll block your number."

"You can do that, but I'll just use a different phone to contact you. Sooner or later, you'll want to listen."

"Why?"

"Because I can give you the name of the next lawyer who is going to commit suicide."

With Lane's editorial, the story about a search for someone killing lawyers was out, so claiming to know who was next in line lacked credibility. DiMeglio's natural inclination was to agree with Stokes that the person on the other end of the line was just another kook looking for his day in the limelight. But something piqued DiMeglio's curiosity. This caller was toying with him. Most kooks wanted instant gratification. This caller was different. Patient. A trait of serial killers.

"Why should I believe you? Everyone in the world knows we're looking for someone who kills lawyers."

The bubbles repeatedly appeared and disappeared. The texter was thinking.

"Why don't you just call me? It's a lot easier," typed DiMeglio.

The response came quickly. "Come now, Agent DiMeglio. Please don't take me for such a fool. Let's just keep our conversation on Signal. No doubt you know why." DiMeglio did. All he could do was play along. It was the caller's game.

"Okay, so who is the next lawyer that's going to commit suicide?"

"Not so fast, Agent DiMeglio."

If this was the killer, DiMeglio needed to build a relationship with him. Unless DiMeglio built some trust, the killer would never open up, provide clues, make mistakes, or confess and ask for help. But something told DiMeglio that this killer didn't want help and had no remorse. At least not yet.

"Sorry. Tell me about yourself. And please call me Chris." Start simple.

No bubbles.

"And what should I call you?" DiMeglio typed, hoping the texter had not ended the conversation.

Bubbles.

"Please don't play me, Agent DiMeglio. I've read your FBI manual on profiling."

"I hope you found it interesting. I wrote much of it."

"Yes, I assumed that. To be honest, I found it simplistic. Too obvious." A superiority complex, noted DiMeglio. Another trait of serial killers.

DiMeglio texted Lenoir Peters, his EA, "Lenoir, please ask Georgia, Brad, and Carla to join me at the office in a half hour. I may have the killer on the phone."

Lenoir was unlike most EAs. She was not a nine-to-fiver and constantly monitored her phone and email seven days a week. DiMeglio could always depend on her.

He sent the next Signal text, wanting to keep the conversation going. "I'm not trying to play you," typed DiMeglio. "I just don't know what to call you."

Bubbles.

"If you need to call me anything, you can call me Dick."

"Okay, Dick. What do you want to talk about?"

"Are you a fan of Shakespeare, Agent DiMeglio?"

"I am familiar with Shakespeare, Dick. Why?"

"It was Shakespeare who wrote in *Henry VI*, 'The first thing we do, let's kill all the lawyers.'"

DiMeglio smiled and shook his head, responding,

"Okay, I'm familiar with that scene. Now I understand your name. You're quoting from the character, Dick the Butcher. Right?"

"Very good, Agent DiMeglio. You got one right."

"And that's what you want to be called?"

"It works for me."

Wanting to keep the conversation going, he typed, "Dick the Butcher wanted to get rid of the only people who could stop him from committing the crimes he planned. Shakespeare meant that if you kill all the lawyers, chaos will ensue. So only the lawyers kept criminals at bay."

Bubbles.

Dick wrote back, "Exactly. As I said, Dick got it right."

"So you want chaos?"

"No. I want dead lawyers."

"Why?"

"That's enough for today, Agent DiMeglio. We'll talk again soon."

DiMeglio typed quickly, not wanting the conversation to end. "But what is the name of the next lawyer who is going to die? Are you going to tell me?"

No bubbles. The second session was over.

It took him less than fifteen minutes to get to his office. Evans and Stokes were already there.

"Where's Carla?" asked DiMeglio.

"She told Lenoir she had another story she was pursuing.

And that's fine with me. The less we see of her, the better," responded Evans.

DiMeglio let them read the text stream.

"Shakespeare? What the fuck is that about? And Dick?" asked Stokes. "What kind of fucking name is that? That's not at all inventive. Serial killers want names that reflect fear and control. Not a wimpy name like Dick."

"It's Dick the Butcher, Brad," noted DiMeglio. "That's a pretty good name for a serial killer."

"Wow, Chris, I'm impressed," added Evans. "I didn't know you were so up on English lit."

"As if you are, Georgia?" offered Stokes.

"Either way, it looks like the three of us are going to have to learn a lot more about him, the Bard of Avon. In high school, Sister Agnes, a nun we liked to call Sister Agony, made us read Shakespeare, hammering one interpretation after another into our adolescent brains. We were convinced it was her way of punishing us. I think I've read nearly all of them. But I never thought Shakespeare would become involved in my work. So now we need to look at the darker side of his writing. If the killer is enamored with Shakespeare, then we'll find hints in his plays."

"I think Dick could be the real deal, Chris," offered Evans. "He's creative and smart. Not some head case who's looking for glory. He's patient and obviously loves to play the game. All signs we've seen before. He may well be the killer."

"Maybe," responded Stokes, "but he hasn't told us a single thing we don't already know. And he cut off the call before he told you who the next victim would be. So he's either an imposter or a killer out to play the game as long as he can."

"And if he's telling us the truth, there's some lawyer out there who is about to die," DiMeglio concluded.

CHAPTER TWENTY-TWO

Missing

Dunnington Place, Dumfries, Virginia

"Did I miss anything?" asked Lane on the phone. It was late, and DiMeglio was sitting at his kitchen table finishing a bucket of chicken and sides he picked up at a local Bojangles while reading articles online about Shakespeare's work, looking for hints and quotes he could use with Dick.

"Sure did. I think we may have connected with the killer." He threw a piece of chicken to Sully, who was patiently waiting for handouts. "Still too early, but it's promising. Your editorial flushed him out. I'll let you see the text trail tomorrow. But he calls himself 'Dick' and claims to know the next lawyer who will die."

"Intriguing. Is that kind of communication typical of serial killers?"

"It's not unusual for serial killers to bait the police. They often like to make it a game of cat-and-mouse. It gives them greater pleasure when they get away with something right under our noses. A real power trip."

"So now what do you do?"

"We wait. There's nothing else we can do. Our tech folks

will look at the texts, but Signal is impossible to hack. At least, that's what I understand. So our hands are tied."

"Signal?" she asked. DiMeglio explained to her how the app worked and why criminals liked it. He was surprised she didn't know about it.

"When do you think he'll call next?"

"Soon. As much as I hate to say it, it might not be until another lawyer is murdered."

"That's so sad."

"Yeah. So, what was the other story you were working on?" DiMeglio wanted to change the subject since there was nothing more to say about the investigation.

"Oh, nothing. Just some story my editor wanted me to run down. It was a dead end. Maybe I'll have better luck next time. Unfortunately, most of what we chase turns out to be nothing."

"I know the feeling. I'll see you in the office tomorrow."

"I'm looking forward to it."

CHAPTER TWENTY-THREE

It's Personal

Dunnington Place, Dumfries, Virginia

Five days had passed since DiMeglio had received the last text. A few phone calls came in from people who claimed they knew the killer or had seen something pertaining to the case. DiMeglio had some agents follow up, but the calls turned out to be useless. Typical for the BAU. The vast majority of "tips" they received from the public were dead ends.

"Hi, Agent DiMeglio. It's Dick."

DiMeglio was home sitting on the couch, done for the day, enjoying his evening with his usual Jameson on the rocks and Sully's head lying on his lap. As Kinston recommended, he was watching more crime shows. Tonight it was *FBI: Most Wanted*, and while he found himself enthralled by the show, each scene was a misrepresentation of the reality he faced every day. An FBI agent's life was nothing like the Hollywood portrayal. That's why he refused to watch *Criminal Minds*, a series about the BAU. He knew the inaccuracies would drive him up the wall.

He muted the TV and typed "Hi" and nothing more. DiMeglio wanted to let Dick lead the conversation and avoid angering him into hanging up before he could learn more.

"I see another poor soul's burdens forced him to take his own life."

"Who are you talking about?"

"You haven't heard? Your old friend, Percy Armand, is dead. I'll give you a minute to look for a press report. He committed suicide early this morning in New Orleans. I know you are quite familiar with that city. And if memory serves me correctly, you're very familiar with Armand's eccentric reputation."

DiMeglio's heart sank. He swiped the screen on his phone to access Google while Dick was still on.

NEW ORLEANS TIMES-PICAYUNE

Prominent Lawyer Found Dead

After a call from the housekeeper, Police found public defender Percy Armand. Armand was a well-known and highly respected criminal defense attorney in NOLA. He took on infamous cases involving murder, child abuse, and kidnapping, including the defense of Wallis Manning, the co-conspirator of the Bayou Slasher. Preliminary reports conclude Armand committed suicide in his French Quarter home by cutting his wrists. The razor police say he used was beside him on the blood-soaked bed. While an investigation is underway, the police said they saw no foul play at the scene and have no suspects.

DiMeglio composed himself. He would have leaped through the phone and strangled Dick if he could. Now a friend was dead, and it became personal. While he and Armand were on opposite sides of the Bayou Slasher investigation, DiMeglio respected him. He was truly dedicated to his clients.

Armand was wealthy through an inheritance from a very successful father. But he wanted nothing to do with the family business in shipping. Instead, he went to law school at Tulane and took a low-paying job as a public defender to pursue his passion for Constitutional law upon graduation. He never left. And he didn't deserve to die.

But DiMeglio, keeping his composure, knew he needed to understand more about Dick, so he suppressed his anger and typed, "Why should I believe you had anything to do with it?"

As he waited for Dick's response, he grabbed the pad on the coffee table to take notes of any observations during the call. They might help in building Dick's board and establishing a profile.

After a couple of minutes, with bubbles appearing on and off, Dick responded with a long text, "Do your own investigation. It will show that he cut his wrists along his arm, not across his wrists, as would be typical. That hasn't been reported. The longer cuts make it harder to stop the bleeding and best assure death. Look for the note. Hidden just for you. I assume the police found it. But just in case, it's in the lower left-hand drawer of the desk in his bedroom, along with the pen he used to write it."

DiMeglio noted Dick took his time typing the texts, obviously careful with his grammar and spelling. The writing was also somewhat formal, rather than the usual casual style of text messaging. DiMeglio wrote on his notepad: "Patient," "Grammar," and "Educated."

"Why did you kill him? Give me a reason, Dick."

"I didn't say I killed him, agent. I just said he was dead. In due time, I will explain it all to you, dear. In due time."

The third session ended.

DiMeglio wrote down, "Loves the game."

Sully nudged DiMeglio. It was time for a walk. *FBI: Most Wanted* would have to wait.

CHAPTER TWENTY-FOUR

It's Personal

BAU Headquarters, Quantico, Virginia

It had been over a year since DiMeglio was in New Orleans on the Bayou Slasher case. But he and Raleigh Broussard, now Superintendent of Police, kept in touch. DiMeglio occasionally asked Broussard for his insight, remembering that it was Broussard who set off the light in DiMeglio's mind with a suggestion that eventually led to the arrest of the Bayou Slasher. It was the first call he made the morning after Dick's third text conversation.

When he heard Raleigh's deep voice answering his phone, DiMeglio could picture him sitting at his paper-strewn desk, his office probably a typical mess. "Raleigh, sorry to call you unexpectedly, but I'm working on a case. I think Percy Armand may be the victim of a serial killer."

"What? I was told he committed suicide. Are you saying that's not the case?"

"I am. I've now had text conversations with someone who calls himself 'Dick the Butcher,' the name of a character from a Shakespeare play. He gave me details of Percy's death that I have not seen in the press."

"Like what?"

"Did your detectives find a note in the desk drawer?"

Broussard pulled up the police report on his computer screen. "They did."

"And were his arms cut along the length instead of across his wrists?"

"Shit," responded Broussard.

DiMeglio asked, "How secure is the crime scene?"

"Good question. Unfortunately, the local precinct did not see it as an active crime scene and thought the poor slob committed suicide. The note proved it for them. That was easy since there isn't a cop in NOLA shedding a tear for this guy."

"Were any forensics taken at the scene?"

Broussard scrolled through the police report. As Superintendent, he was often the last to get involved in a local matter, depending upon officers filing reports he could retrieve on his desktop computer. He read what little had been reported so far.

"The report says they followed normal procedures for a suicide investigation," he responded to DiMeglio. "There was no sign of a struggle or any other evidence to show anyone else assisted him in the suicide. They ran the usual sweep and found no prints. Nothing unusual." He sighed. "Until now."

"Raleigh, don't you think it's odd that Armand would hide a suicide note? That's not how people kill themselves. They want the world to read their last confession. They don't put them in desk drawers. And we both knew the guy. If he committed suicide, which I doubt, he would have gone out with fanfare, not a quiet death in his bed."

"I hear you, Chris."

"And what about the cuts? My guess is each arm had cuts that were six inches or longer. Am I right?"

"Yep. That's what the report says. And these fuckin' officers thought that was consistent with suicide. Unbelievable."

"Someone might cut one arm that way. But cutting two is another matter. Someone else obviously cut him. Percy didn't have the disposition to do that to himself. Not the Percy I knew."

"Nor the one I did," responded Broussard. "But Percy was an odd duck. If he committed suicide, it wouldn't surprise me if he put the note in the drawer to play games with us."

"But that doesn't explain why I got a text from someone telling me where it was or how he was cut."

"Yeah. You're right. Damn. Not another serial killer in New Orleans! That's all I need! When are you coming down to catch this one?"

"I'm not. I don't think the killer is in New Orleans, Raleigh. The other murders were all over the country. One was in France. This operation makes the last one we worked on together look like amateurs."

"I'll put some better detectives on it, Chris. And I'll call the coroner to make sure they do a full autopsy, assuming they haven't already screwed that up. For all I know, he's already cremated."

"I appreciate that. But would someone be cremated that quickly after a suicide?"

"Unfortunately, that's what we usually do here in New Orleans. He had no family still alive, so an immediate cremation is likely. New Orleans doesn't have enough cemeteries. I also doubt there's anything left at the scene, so my guess is they'll hit dead ends. The usual informants will probably be worthless as well. If this was a murder, the killer was a professional."

"Agreed. But Dick's not a lone wolf. The murders are too distant from one another. And too varied. Regardless, please secure whatever is left of the scene. I want our crime lab to take a look. There might be something the locals missed."

"I'll need to take that up with the mayor, Chris. But that won't be an issue. She still thinks you're a hero. But last I looked, I don't take orders from the FBI. So I'll clear it with her."

"Thanks, Raleigh. Call me when I can send in my team. I'll let you go now. But before I do, how are you doing? I should have asked you that first. I'm sure you're leaning back in your chair enjoying one of your stinky cigars."

Broussard was known for smoking cigars in his office. His daily fares were cheap ones he bought on the street from local rollers. They stunk up the entire office, but no one had the guts to tell him to stop. When he solved a case, he'd break out his Padrons. He often asked DiMeglio to join him. Cigar smoking was a habit the two had in common, although enjoying a Padron was a rare treat for DiMeglio. Worse, he'd been spoiled by having Broussard's expensive Padrons and didn't enjoy cheaper ones anymore. Premium cigars were well above his budget as an FBI agent. His maternally motivated EA approved since she abhorred smoking.

Laughing, Broussard responded, "I've seen better days, Chris. I wish I were smoking one now. But after my promotion and move to this office, someone complained to the mayor that I was smoking inside the building. I got a note from her ordering me to stop. Seems the enjoyment of a smoke in any public building is prohibited here. So now I have to go for walks every day to enjoy a cigar. When I find out who complained, it will be hell to pay for them!"

DiMeglio smiled. Broussard was all bark, no bite. He knew the former New Orleans Saints linebacker was really a gentle giant, in spite of his physical demeanor.

"It's because they love you, Raleigh. And you're now in that big, beautiful office. The walks will keep you in shape. Look at it as a perk that came with your promotion to superintendent."

"I'd rather be back on the street."

"Yeah, I like the ground game, too." There was nothing else to say. "See you soon, Raleigh."

"Wait, Chris," Broussard said. "Before you go, how are you enjoying being the new poster boy for the Bureau? You did well on *60 Minutes*. But I can't believe you really wanted to do that. Hannity must have been tougher. We never pictured you as a talking head."

"If you only knew, Raleigh. It's a shitshow at the Bureau. Using me as the shill for the Bureau's future is evidence of that. It's nuts here. But the good news is I'm still investigating cases, and this latest one fascinates me. How could it not? After all, the idea of killing successful defense lawyers has a bit of ironic justice," DiMeglio said.

Broussard didn't laugh, not appreciating DiMeglio's dark humor after a friend was murdered. "Well, if you'd like, I'd be happy to review what evidence you have so far. I might come up with something, and a new set of eyes wouldn't hurt."

"I may take you up on that, Raleigh, but not yet. It's too early in the investigation, and there's not enough for me to show you."

"OK. Just know the offer stands. Dick the Butcher, huh?" asked Broussard.

"Yeah. My staff thinks it's pretty lame for a serial killer."

"Then I'll leave you with this, Chris. Don't like the name he picked? Then change it before the press does."

DiMeglio hung up and buzzed his EA. "Lenoir, it looks like we may have a serial killer on our hands, just like Carla predicted. Ask her, Georgia, and Brad to meet me in the conference room at 11:00. We need to get started."

CHAPTER TWENTY-FIVE

Boards

BAU Headquarters, Quantico, Virginia

"OK, let's go over what we have so far," began DiMeglio.

In the two hours they'd been meeting, the three FBI agents posted sticky notes on two whiteboards at the front of the conference room. They divided the boards into four sections, and labeled them "What We Know," "What We Need to Know," "To Do," and "Dick." Under "Dick," they posted transcripts of his text conversations with DiMeglio. The individual notes were in no particular order since they had yet to find enough to begin a profile that might separate suspects from victims and witnesses. The right edge of one board included photos of each of the murdered attorneys and how they allegedly killed themselves written beneath their pictures.

> <u>What We Know</u>
> Kills criminal defense attorneys
> Staged to look like suicides
> Crime scenes scrubbed—professional
> If professional, very expensive enterprise

Not likely done by one individual acting alone

<u>What We Need to Know</u>

The gender, age, ethnicity, nationality, and location of the killer(s)

How victims are picked

Why each feigned suicide was staged as a different method

Things in common between the dead lawyers

Whether the killer(s) is seeking vigilante justice

Whether judges and prosecutors could become targets

<u>To Do</u>

Reexamine crime scene reports

Interview family members of victims who have died

Interview colleagues, partners, and staff of victims

Interview defendants represented by murdered lawyers and their families, both in and out of prison

Get the technology team on case to try to track texts and hack Signal

<u>Dick</u>:

Took the name of a Shakespeare villain, Dick the Butcher

Educated

Patient

Articulate

Likes the game

Won't speak, only texts

Knows technology—uses Signal

Photos:

Jacob Schneider—Drowned

Paul Stafford—Jumped

Joseph Bartlett—Hanged

Marie Létisse—Electrocuted

Percy Armand—Slit wrists

"Shit," Evans muttered. "We don't have squat. Just five dead lawyers."

"Yeah, but my guess is our killer is a woman. Why would he—or she—call Chris 'dear' in a text? That's how a woman would talk. Not a man."

"Brad," responded Evans, "you're such a Neanderthal. That may have once been the case, but in today's society, men actually do say 'dear' and 'honey' and are not afraid of showing their feminine side. You really need to get up with the times."

"Nah. I kind of like being a Neanderthal. Fits my personality."

"I won't argue with that," added DiMeglio. "And you're right, Brad, we can't leave out any possibility at this point. For all we know, using 'dear' may have been intentional to create a false impression. But what we have is at least a start."

"That reminds me of the old joke," replied Stokes.

"Please, Brad. I'm too tired for your sick humor," Evans warned. "Don't tell me it's the one that asks what ten dead lawyers are."

"You got it!" Stokes said. "It's a good start!"

DiMeglio and Evans shook their heads and groaned. Lane gave Stokes a piercing look. He apparently got the message and changed his tone. "I'll get the techies to look at what we can do with Signal. I doubt there's much, but they keep coming up with new tricks."

"Good," responded DiMeglio. Turning to Evans, he added, "Georgia, have someone get us a list of the dead lawyers' partners and staff, and add prosecutors and judges where they practiced who botched cases or gave out lenient sentences."

"That's going to be a lot of people," offered Stokes. "Like flies to shit, lawyers attract lawyers."

"Brad," added Evans, "cool it with the jokes. It's not working."

Stokes leaned into her, smiling. "Why? Do they offend you, Georgia? I sure don't want to offend your innocent ears." DiMeglio allowed the banter between them to a degree, but Evans's glare made it clear she wasn't playing the game. Stokes backed off and added, "We'll need more manpower, too, Chief."

"That will not happen, Brad. We're all we got. So let's keep focused. Georgia, get a list of the defendants, particularly repeat offenders." Turning to Stokes, DiMeglio added, "Brad, look at the families. I doubt we'll learn much from them, but we need to follow up on every possibility if we hope to stop the killer. Or killers. Remember, the more we eliminate, the more we learn."

"Is there anything I can do?" asked Lane.

The three agents looked at her as if they'd forgotten she was still there.

If either Evans or Stokes answered Lane's question, they'd tell her to go home. Or worse. But the team was stuck with her, and DiMeglio needed to make her part of the team or face the wrath of the Director.

"Sorry, Carla, I didn't mean to exclude you," he lied. "Is there anything, in particular, you'd like to work on?"

"I can see the families and colleagues of the dead lawyers and possibly the criminals they defended. I can also tap into reporters in the local papers for background."

Stokes, seeing it as an opportunity to drop what he considered a wild goose chase, replied, "That's a splendid idea, Carla. I'll get you the list right away."

DiMeglio saw through his ploy.

"Good, Brad. And I want you to accompany Carla on the interviews. We need an agent's eyes on these people, too." He was not about to let Stokes pass the buck. And he needed someone to keep an eye on Lane. She was not a trained agent, and she could not be allowed to run off on her own investigating an active case. He kept reminding himself that she was a reporter, not an official team member.

"And where are *you* going, Chris?" asked Evans.

"Idaho."

CHAPTER TWENTY-SIX

Past Transgressions

Idaho Maximum Security Institution, Kuna, Idaho

The Maximum Security Institution in Kuna, Idaho, houses the state's most dangerous male prisoners. It has a capacity of 549 inmates and is surrounded by a double perimeter fence, razor wire, and electronic detection systems. Snipers in the tower and dogs patrolling the space between fences, made escape a deadly option to consider. Coupled with its brick and gray outside walls, there is little that is welcoming about it despite its Pleasant Valley Road address. Inside, polished concrete floors and rows of cinder block 9'x10" cells make it abundantly clear to inmates that they are under the thumb of an authority that is not to be questioned. Inmates are allowed an hour of exercise in an outdoor enclosure but otherwise spend their time in solitary. So there is little interaction among prisoners except on rare occasions that they share prison duties in the kitchen, laundry, or elsewhere.

It is also where the state carries out the execution of prisoners by lethal injection. Wallis Manning was among a half dozen waiting on death row for their appeals to run out. He was found guilty of six counts of capital murder, although he committed or caused many more. One of America's most infamous serial killers, he was apprehended by DiMeglio and local authorities after a killing spree in Coeur d'Alene, Idaho, where he targeted the offspring of white suprema- cists, the so-called neo-Nazi Skinheads. Before the Idaho murders, Manning and others who helped him, including the Bayou Slasher, targeted the children of KKK members in New Orleans. DiMeglio suspected Manning was guilty of other atrocities, but with a death sentence already over his head, there was no point pursuing them. Instead, he left that to the locals.

DiMeglio requested an audience with Manning through the Management Assistant in the Warden's Office. He had found it sometimes helpful to have conversations with incarcerated serial killers about current cases. Their narcis- sistic personalities led them to speak openly and show off what they believed to be their superior intellect over their captors. Manning was just such a killer.

To accommodate visitations, the prison had two rooms where physical contact was possible. These are most often used by an attorney visiting a client or law enforcement personnel interviewing an inmate. Each room has a table where the visitor sits across from the inmate. A security officer sitting in an elevated observation booth monitors visits in both rooms. Conversations, however, can neither be heard nor recorded.

"Well, well, well, Christopher DiMeglio in the flesh.

You're my first visitor. I was wondering when you'd come by."

Maximum security prisons have color-coded clothing to signify a prisoner's status and any risks associated with the inmates. At the Idaho prison holding Manning, inmates who behaved wore green, and those who worked in the prison were issued blue denim pants and orange hooded sweatshirts. Inmates in isolation, solitary, or segregation might also wear yellow jumpsuits and coveralls. Yellow was also used when an inmate was being transferred to court. Inmates can also purchase various articles of clothing from the prison commissary, such as athletic shorts, sweatpants/shirts, T-shirts, and baseball caps, but only in the prison's official colors of gray, green, blue, and white. No clothing, however, may have any gang-affiliated logo. Personal clothing may only be worn while inmates are in their cells, during visitations, and when allowed outside for recreation.

DiMeglio was surprised to see Manning dressed in prison green. He could have worn personal clothing. A guard later told him that Manning spent as little money as possible at the prison to protest his incarceration. The only exception DiMeglio could see were his slip-on sneakers and a gray T-shirt underneath the smock. Because he was on death row, he would generally be shackled on the rare occasion he was outside his cell or the penned-in exercise yard. The rules, however, did allow him one "contact" visitation per month. He chose to use it for DiMeglio's appointment.

With the consent of the visitor, he could be unshackled.

Manning's head was shaved. He looked tired and as if he'd had a hard time in prison. The deep scar on his right cheek that he didn't have when first imprisoned was probably evidence of it. It didn't surprise DiMeglio. His weight looked down to only about 175 pounds, a good 50 pounds lighter than when apprehended. When caught, he was in prime physical condition from rigorous workouts that he'd stopped once in prison. And given Manning's psychotic mission was to murder children of white supremacists, it didn't surprise DiMeglio that the prison inmate population put a price on his head. Now he looked like a frail, broken man, not the Marine he once was.

"How have you been, Wallis? I brought you a Coke." Inmates were not allowed to bring food or beverage into the meeting room. Only visitors could do so, provided they purchased it from vending machines outside the room.

"Thanks. I've seen better days, Christopher. While I spent time in prison during my trial and before sentencing, I ran into some trouble. But now, they keep me away from the general population, so I'm safer now." Pointing to the scar, he added, "That wasn't the case when you caught me. It's ironic, isn't it? They saved me from being murdered when I was stuck with the general prisoner population so they could kill me themselves. Now I only get to interact with other prisoners on death row."

"I'm sorry to hear that." But, of course, DiMeglio wasn't

sorry but wanted Manning to be at ease and more likely to be open in the conversation.

"Yeah, I bet you are. But don't worry. The discussions I have with my buddies on the row can be entertaining. They love to claim they're innocent. Don't we all?"

"You're not innocent, Wallis."

"No. I guess I'm not. So what really brings you here, Christopher? I doubt it's listening to my complaints. What do you want?"

"Wallis, I'd like to talk to you about a hypothetical I've been thinking about." DiMeglio could not talk to Manning about the facts of the case for fear of leaks. As it was, if Dick the Butcher found out DiMeglio visited Manning, it might raise his flight impulse and shut him down. So he wanted to give Manning as little to work with as possible.

"Hypothetical, huh?" Manning understood exactly what was going on, but looked forward to the banter.

"Yes, strictly hypothetical."

"Sure, Christopher, I'd be happy to talk to you about your hypothetical. It's not like there's anyone here with half a brain who can carry on an intelligent conversation. They're all morons, particularly the guards and warden. So tell me your bedtime story."

"Good. Let me get right to it. You targeted children of the people you hated rather than those who were the actual sinners." DiMeglio intentionally used religious terms to appeal to Manning's God complex. "Why?"

Manning finished the Coke. "Can I get a coffee or something else to drink?" It did not surprise DiMeglio that Manning started with demands.

"No, Wallis, you can't. The rules don't allow food or beverage in the meeting rooms unless the visitor brings them. And all I got you is the Coke. As it is, I agreed you didn't have to be shackled. So there is nothing more I can do."

"Yeah, I noticed that. Thanks. But what if I leaped over the table and strangled you? I could easily kill you before any guard gets close enough to stop me. And what do I have to lose? I'm in line for the needle, anyway." Now Manning wanted to create fear. That didn't work with DiMeglio. He knew Manning too well after months of trailing and eventually capturing him. Manning wanted to have a conversation, not more time in solitary. But first, Manning wanted to establish his Alpha status with demands and threats. Typical. But not something DiMeglio intended to put up with.

"Wallis, can we dispense with the theatrics? You know you can't have anything else to drink, and you have no intention of trying to harm me. You're not that stupid. So unless you want to get to my question, we can call it a day, and you can rejoin the half-brains, as you like to describe them."

Manning smiled, "OK, OK. I'll play by your rules, Christopher." He paused, gathered his thoughts, and added, "We took out the children of racists and supremacists because that was the best way to ensure the evils propagated by their bloodline would end." An ex-Marine, Manning was prone to military jargon.

"But you had most of the murders committed by others. Why didn't you do them?"

"I didn't need to. I did my share. Others believed in my cause. They saw the light. It was a very simple plan. And brilliant."

"Brilliant, huh? Is that why you're sitting here on death row, Wallis? That doesn't sound very brilliant to me." DiMeglio had to be careful not to agitate Manning too much. He needed him to keep talking. But DiMeglio could push the limit because Manning had no place to go and was happy to have a visitor.

"Say whatever you'd like, Christopher. You're not going to get me mad. You never could. That's why it took you so long to find me. I kept calm and told you very little."

"But eventually, you made enough mistakes to get yourself caught. Then, with each new communication, you gave up a little more. You must have known I would eventually put it all together and find you."

"No, Christopher, I never thought you or anyone else would catch me. You sort of became a friend and an intellectual equal. Well, almost an intellectual equal. You wanted to learn from me. I appreciated that. And you certainly had a lot to learn. But I guess I have to give the devil his due. You won in the end."

So typical, thought DiMeglio. A superiority complex is central to the way serial killers think. DiMeglio knew it was their greatest weakness and opened them up to what psychologists call "talk therapy." The more he talked to them, the more comfortable they became with him. Over time, they open up. They begin to trust him. And that's when they make mistakes. Manning was no exception.

"And that's why I'm here, Wallis. I want to know why serial killers think differently. I want to understand why you killed innocent people. Then I might understand why others do as well."

"I've never killed an innocent person, Christopher. The sins of the fathers fall on the children. They're just as guilty because they continue the evil seed. History has shown us that countless times."

"Is it that simple, Wallis? If it is, why not kill both the parents and the children?"

"It's less efficient. The fathers will die soon enough. So what's your hypothetical, Christopher?"

"Say there's a killer murdering lawyers who represented criminals that committed homicides and worse. It could be for revenge. Or just a psychotic belief that they need to change society, sort of what you're thinking was."

"You mean like that reporter talked to you about on *60 Minutes*?" Manning saw DiMeglio's surprise at the question. He added, "Christopher, even those on death row get to watch TV. And hearing that you were appearing on the show, I had to watch. So your hypothetical isn't quite a fairy tale after all, huh?"

"OK, you have one up on me, Wallis. But what do you think is in the killer's mind?"

"I'm flattered that you'd ask me that."

"Takes one to know one, Wallis."

"Yeah. I suppose. What's inside your killer's mind, Christopher, is revenge. A vendetta. A belief society needs to change. Or all of that. Or none of it. But if he is a serial killer, Christopher, he's committed to his cause, whatever that is. You didn't stop me until you caught me. He'll be no different."

"So what is it you're telling me I should do, Wallis? Nothing you've said so far is very helpful."

Manning smiled, and responded, "Christopher, why would I want to make your job easier? It's too much fun watching you play the game. But I will tell you this, you won't catch your killer until you earn their respect and, even better, their friendship."

"Wallis, I'm not inclined to want to be friends with any serial killer."

"I know that, Christopher. But your killer doesn't. Yet."

That's all DiMeglio needed from Manning. Confirmation of some of his thoughts and the unsettling idea that he needed to make Dick think he was a friend when all he wanted to see is the killer burned at a stake. DiMeglio would later write *talk, efficiency, dedication to cause, trust, friendship*, and *superiority* in his notebook. They all applied to Dick as much as they did to Manning. They'd later add them to the board. But now it was time to leave.

"Thank you, Wallis. You've told me what I needed to hear. I'm done here." DiMeglio rose from this chair.

"Wait!" implored Manning. "Don't leave yet. Other than lawyers, I haven't had a visitor since I came here. And there's no one here who I can intelligently talk to. So let's talk for a while in the time we have left. I'll talk about whatever you'd like. On the row, I only get an hour a day outside, mostly in a cage, except when I get to spend a little time on the ballfield and feel some grass under my feet. And no one comes to visit." He was desperate.

DiMeglio signaled for the guard, sitting back down in his chair. He was finished and wanted to be sure he, not a psychotic killer, got in the last word.

"Wallis, there are families who can never again talk to the loved ones you killed. Whether the fathers were sinners isn't important. The victims had done nothing wrong. They were just trying to live their lives. Some were even running away from the racism and prejudice that poisoned their families. So I couldn't care less that there is no one with whom you can have an intelligent conversation. Live with it, at least until they put a needle in your arm. Then you can have a conversation with God."

Manning sighed in disappointment and stood as the

guard ordered him to. He was led out, his hands now cuffed behind his back.

Before the guard took him through the door, Manning added, "Christopher, continue playing his game like you did with me. He'll start to trust you and let you into some of his secrets. And come see me again when you catch him."

DiMeglio knew the game. He knew he had to gain Dick's trust. Make him think he wanted to learn from him. Show respect. Push for more in every conversation. When dealing with a god complex, look for forgiveness, not permission.

DiMeglio took the next flight home.

CHAPTER TWENTY-SEVEN

It's Just Dinner

Four Provinces, Falls Church, Virginia

"I'll have an Irish Manhattan."

"I'm sorry, sir, I'm not familiar with that," responded the server. He'd already taken Lane's order for a Chopin vodka martini. Straight up, three olives. She was very specific.

"It's a traditional Manhattan except with Irish whiskey. Jameson would be fine."

The server left to fetch the drinks.

DiMeglio made the reservation at Four Provinces in Falls Church, popularly known as the 4P's, because it was one of his favorite spots. He made sure to reserve a table on the patio. The weather that night was comfortably in the 70s, and their table was away from the crowd's noise in the pub itself. So the patio was very amenable to conversation.

"I hope you don't see me as a thorn in the side of your investigation, Chris. But what you do is a fascinating story, and watching the process you use to profile an unknown killer is something the *Gazette's* subscribers would love to read. It could even make a great TV show, too."

"I have no problem with subscribers or television viewers reading or watching what they enjoy," DiMeglio answered, smiling. He added, "I'm even getting into some of the FBI shows myself. The Director told me I needed to get a life. Same thing Evans and Stokes tell me. The Director told me to start watching TV shows about the FBI! As if I'd enjoy watching anything so distant from reality."

"I can ask our TV reviewer to give you a list of good shows, if you'd like," Lane said, smiling as well. She sat back, enjoying the more comfortable relationship as DiMeglio's professional façade faded.

"Please do, but let's get back to reporting on the case," replied DiMeglio. "Honestly, I don't like a public spotlight on the unit. What we do is very technical, and the more we're seen by the public, the more attention everyone will give to serial killers. They want that attention. But giving it to them can backfire. And I don't want serial killers to be aware of what we do. It makes them smarter. Also, because we don't know how many are out there, too much news reporting will increase paranoia, and people will start thinking there's a serial killer around every corner. We don't need that. It's not healthy."

The server brought DiMeglio his Irish Manhattan and Lane her martini.

"I understand," she replied. "But you don't give my readers enough credit. They understand the violence that's out there and can deal with it. Contrary to what you might think, a piece on the unit will make people feel safer. It will give them a sense that real pros are looking after them."

"Really? Even when you tell them that most serial killers are never caught?" He took a sip of his drink and added, "Just remember our deal. I get to see anything you're going to publish before you put it out there." Lane was already nearly done with her martini.

"Agreed. Again," responding with an emphasis on "again" to drive home to DiMeglio that she did not need to be reminded.

The server brought Lane another martini. "Are you ready to order?" he asked. They hadn't even looked at the menu. The server realized that and added, "Why don't I give you a few minutes? I'll be back."

"Do you like this restaurant, Chris? I've never been here."

"I do like it. It's an Irish pub off the beaten path, just outside the capital. So it's mostly just ordinary folk here. I suppose there might be some bureaucrats or politicians among them, but they're few and far between. So I feel comfortable here. And it's close to my home."

"Then you order for me."

"But I don't know what you like," protested DiMeglio.

"Then surprise me. I'm sure I'll love it. You can't go wrong if the food is as good as their martinis."

The server returned, notebook and pen in hand.

DiMeglio didn't wait for the server to ask. "We'll start by splitting the Irish Potato Croquettes."

"They're great," responded the server. "And for the main?"

"The lady will have the Chicken Tullamore, and I'll have the Bangers & Mash."

The server asked Lane, "And would you like another martini?" DiMeglio hadn't realized how quickly she polished off the first two.

"Sure," she responded. The server walked away. DiMeglio kept one copy of the menu in case they had dessert.

"So, what did you order? I know what Bangers & Mash is, but not Chicken Tullamore. It sounds very Irish."

"It's the Irish version of comfort food, grilled fresh breast of chicken, Tullamore Irish whiskey cream sauce, fresh market vegetables, and mashed potatoes. And the croquettes are corned beef, cabbage, and cheddar with an Irish mustard dip."

"So I'm starting with corned beef disguised in a taco and finishing with chicken cooked in whiskey. Am I close?" jokingly asked Lane.

Two hours and another martini later, Lane's curiosity was running high. DiMeglio was nursing his second Irish Manhattan. He hoped the bread pudding they had shared for dessert was soaking up some of the alcohol to keep Lane's wits in order, although there was no sign they were in any way impaired. *This girl can certainly hold her alcohol,* thought DiMeglio.

"Chris, you've been doing this a long time. You've undoubtedly seen a lot of gruesome stuff and unexplainable murders."

"There's not much I haven't seen, Carla."

"Right, and you can get into a criminal's mind. No. A murderer's mind. That's fascinating. But I'm wondering something."

"What's that?"

"What makes someone murder an innocent person they don't even know? The question may seem naïve, but a lot of us make false assumptions. I get why someone might murder someone they know, but a serial killer? That's where I don't get it. I need to understand."

"OK, well, let's start with the basics." He held up his drink.

She held up her glass and touched his. "To the basics!"

"To the basics!" he toasted back.

"First of all, the relative simplicity of murder investigations can be surprising. Why it's the subject of so many TV shows is beyond me. They never get it right. The more of them I watch, the angrier I get at how they mislead viewers." DiMeglio paused, took a drink, and looked around the now empty patio. While the weather had cooled, it was still comfortable. He could see the waiter hovering in the corner hoping the two of them would finally leave. DiMeglio chose to ignore him. He was enjoying his company with Lane.

With another sip of her martini, Lane said, "Please go on, professor." DiMeglio smiled at that.

"Okay, most victims know their murderer. Very often, they're a member of the same family. They might have a criminal history, drug addiction, or mental illness. Or a history on the streets. But that's not always the case. It might be a crime of passion, like when a husband kills his wife and her lover when he discovers them in bed. It can also be a murder prompted by putting an end to abuse. Or it might be nothing more than a random drive-by. Of all those murders, most are solved, often with a confession."

After another sip of his Manhattan, DiMeglio was getting comfortable in his professorial role.

"Then there's the group who kill for hire. That's a tiny group and usually kills someone who has wronged another crime family member. Mafia stuff. They're sometimes caught, but it's about a 50/50 shot. On the other hand, when someone is hired to kill outside a crime family, like when a husband hires someone to kill his wife, that's different. In most of those cases, the murderer is caught, and the husband is arrested and tried for the same crime. The killers screw up because they're not professionals, or the killer turns the husband in. Or the wife, if she's the one who hired the killer."

DiMeglio, pointing to his now empty Manhattan, waved to the server for a refill.

Lane pointed to her martini as well. The server understood.

"Then we move on to serial killers," DiMeglio continued. "They're an entirely different story and were the topic of my master's thesis at John Jay. That thesis got me into the FBI and assigned to the BAU."

The server delivered the drinks.

"Serial killers are all psychopaths at some level. Most of them had an awful childhood with parents who did drugs or were abusive, often sexually. Just a screwed-up life where filial love was nonexistent. They are paranoid, impulsive, and at odds with reality. Yet they can be very calculating and careful to cover their tracks while at the same time craving recognition. Many are on the genius scale and can act like your friendly neighbor. They often hide in plain sight. Others may leave hints or find pleasure in being named, like Son of Sam or the Bayou Slasher. Some also like to collect souvenirs from the victims and crime scenes. It might be a body part of a victim, a piece of clothing, or a picture. Killing for many of them gratifies them. All of this helps us profile a serial killer. We take the clues and hints we get and put them up against common stereotypes. Eventually, we get a pretty accurate picture."

"Then why are so many serial killers never found if you can profile them with such certainty?"

"For several reasons. First, many stop before they can be profiled. In fact, many are never even discovered and stop before we know they're serial killers at all. Second, most local police departments are not properly equipped to investigate. Third, serial killers commit their murders in multiple jurisdictions, so many local authorities are involved and can butt heads. Or worse, each thinks it's investigating a single murder and never connects the dots. Last, some serial killers take breaks and pop up months or years later. Like Dennis Rader, the BTK Killer, or Lonnie Franklin, the Grim Sleeper. They both took years off on their killing sprees. They were eventually caught, but other files go cold, and connections are lost forever."

"Such theatrical names! How do they get them?"

"Most of the names come from the press. Rader gave himself the name. It stood for bind, torture, kill. Franklin got the name because the time between killings was so long. Like the Grim Reaper, except he was the Grim Sleeper."

"Then we need to work on a better name. When I write the article, Dick the Butcher doesn't work. I'll think of something."

"Don't glorify him, Carla."

"I won't. So where does Dick fit in, Chris?"

"I don't know yet. It's too early. Clearly, Dick is on some sort of vendetta that justifies killing lawyers. But we have to be careful not to make too many assumptions. A mission is normal for serial killers and usually involves psychosis related to a perversion of religion or worship of the devil. Or revenge. That might be the case here. But, for some reason, this serial killer has a real hard-on for criminal defense lawyers who got guilty people off. I've investigated a lot of serial killers, but this one is different. His mission may be some twist on vigilantism. They're the toughest to find."

DiMeglio waved for the check.

"That's enough for tonight, Carla. I'm beginning to feel

these Manhattans. We can hold another class tomorrow. Would you like some coffee?"

She smiled back, "No. I can't stand coffee. Tea is more my preference. But I don't need anything else. And I look forward to our next session."

The Uber ride to drop off Lane was uneventful. They both said nothing to one another. Then, when DiMeglio walked Lane to her door, she turned, drew him near, and gave him a deep kiss. It caught him off guard, but that didn't diminish the enjoyment.

She drew back. "Chris, I had a great night tonight. Let's call it our first date." She was through the door and out of sight before DiMeglio could respond.

Oh my God, Sully, what have I gotten myself into?

CHAPTER TWENTY-EIGHT

Dead Ends

Holcomb, Kansas

Now two weeks on the road interviewing potential sources, Stokes and Lane were growing tired of both the tedious task and of one another. The many nights at a local Holiday Inn or other discount hotels were taking their toll. Stokes made it no secret that, for him, Lane was a nuisance. After a week of trying to get on his better side, Lane gave up. For her, it was now one day at a time.

On the road yet again, this time on Interstate 70 in Kansas, they were on their way to the next appointment. The endless landscape of cornfields and cattle ranches dotted with occasional windmills generating power added to the boredom of the ride. And the tension between them. They could drive for hours and barely see another car or truck. After the first few days, they'd run out of anything to say to one another. Now the drives mainly were mile after mile of silence, interrupted by occasional questions from Lane. Breaks for meals were the same.

Lane broke the silence as they passed yet another ranch with dozens of grazing cattle. "Brad, we've spoken to more than a dozen people connected to the dead lawyers and have nothing. We've driven thousands of miles. I hope I never see another cow in my lifetime. So what makes you think interviewing more will get us anything?"

"I doubt it will, Carla. But if we tell Chris we gave up asking questions after a dozen or so interviews, he'll have our heads."

"So we keep chasing dead ends?"

"This is the tough side of police work. We're not chasing dead ends. We're doing what you don't see on TV or in recruiting brochures. And it's also most of what we do. We gather evidence. Follow leads. Interview people. Not because we expect to find a magic bullet that solves a case but because, to use Chris's words, the more failures we have and the more false leads we uncover, the closer we get to the solution. In case you haven't noticed, Chris loves sayings like that. He has posters all over the office with that kind of bullshit motivation."

She had noticed posters containing pithy statements related to police work strewn all over DiMeglio's office and conference room. Posters with sayings like "Evil is powerless if the good are unafraid," by Ronald Reagan; "Blessed are the peacekeepers, for they shall be called the children of God," from Matthew 5:9; Henry Ford's "When everything seems to be going against you, remember that the airplane takes off against the wind, not with it," and the quote often attributed to George Orwell, "People sleep peacefully in their beds at night only because rough men stand ready to do violence on their behalf."

But DiMeglio's favorite from an unknown author was, "When you think about quitting, remember why you started."

"OK," said Lane, resigning herself to yet another day on the road. "Who is next on the list?"

"Amanda and Alicia Schneider, the wife and daughter of the first victim. They moved to Holcomb, Kansas, to escape the suburban city life they lived before Schneider's murder. The fuckin' town's in the middle of nowhere."

Waze offered them three routes to Holcomb from Kansas City. Stokes chose the longest route, which would take them just over six hours. The shortest route would have been five hours, virtually all on Interstates. But Stokes liked to see more of the rural areas, and an additional hour made no difference to him. It pleased him that Lane found the scenery so ordinary and boring. Without having someone like Evans around to annoy, Lane got the brunt of his perverse sense of humor.

They exited Interstate 70 just before Topeka and took 335 southwest to Emporia, where they picked up state highway 50 to Dodge City. They then took state highway 400 for the last hour of the ride to Holcomb. Once in Holcomb, they took a rural road. Eventually, they turned on a dirt road leading to the Schneider's house. If it weren't for Waze guiding them, they'd have never found the address. The wife and daughter wanted to be as far away from anyone as they could be. Schneider's wife reluctantly agreed to meet when Lane called her.

The two were welcoming, but it proved to be yet another interview that led nowhere. Neither the wife nor daughter offered anything new Stokes and Lane could use. Between tears and anger, they remembered Schneider as a good father and husband. Certainly not suicidal. They sorely missed him. They appreciated the efforts the FBI was making to find his killer. Lane took a few photos on her iPhone in case she might want to use them in an article.

After that interview, they spent the night at the Comfort Inn in nearby Garden City. Dinner was at Applebee's. It was their go-to place since it had beef for Stokes, salads for Lane, and a good bar. Early on their trip, Lane gave up on suggesting more places that are interesting. Stokes vetoed anything that wasn't down-home American food. At dinner, Lane was reading about the town on her phone. "Hey, listen to this. Holcomb is famous as being the home of the Clutter family, who were murdered in 1959, inspiring Truman Capote's best-selling novel, *In Cold Blood*." She looked up at Brad, who for the first time in days actually smiled.

"I wonder if they're living in the old Clutter house?" she speculated. "Or just how far away the house is from them. Certainly, they must know about it. Imagine trying to escape the pain of losing a father and husband, only to end up in a town known for one of the bloodiest murders in literature."

"Seriously, Carla, I'm beginning to worry about your obsession with murders. If my memory serves me right, the Clutters were murdered by a couple of misfits who thought they'd find a bunch of money in the house. The whole thing went south when they didn't, and four innocent people died."

"You're familiar with the case?"

"Carla, I'm a profiler. It's part of my business to study murderers. And besides, Capote was a brilliant writer. His book is terrific. I gather you also read it."

"No, I haven't. I only learned about it on the ride when I looked up the town on Google. But now I will read it. What happened to the killers?"

"Perry Smith and Richard Hitchcock were both hanged."

"Hanged!? They still do that?"

"They did back in the day, particularly in the West. Now, most states execute by lethal injection, although some let the condemned inmate choose other methods like electrocution, firing squad, or gas chamber. I like to call that their final menu. The last one that allowed hanging was New Hampshire. But they have since abolished the death penalty."

"And you follow all that, too?"

"Of course I do. I want to know all the ways they can execute the bastards we capture."

"I gather you believe in the death penalty."

"You bet I do, Carla. If you investigate enough murders

and see the evil I've seen, you can't think otherwise. Unfortunately, some people, particularly serial killers, can never be reformed and deserve to be executed. It's black and white to me."

"Have you ever been to an execution?"

"No. It's not something I want to witness. I've got enough images in my mind of dead people. I don't need more. No one does."

"I think I'd like to see one so I understand the psychology. I bet some of them say things at the end that might give clues."

"Not usually. I've seen the last words of most of them. If they say anything, and most don't, it's not a request to be forgiven."

"Has Chris ever been to an execution?"

"I don't think so. You'd have to ask Chris. My guess is he's seen enough demons, too. Watching them die won't provide any closure for him. Or for me."

The conversation ended, they finished dinner, and called it a night. Back in his hotel room, Stokes poured himself another drink, recalling all the evil he'd seen and the toll it had taken. Evans was right that he'd never called a lawyer about his marriage. But years of couples' therapy were the only reason his marriage stayed intact. He finally passed out.

In the morning, nursing a hangover, Stokes decided that despite what he said to Lane, he had enough and would tell DiMeglio that they'd exhausted the list of cooperative witnesses. While not exactly true, Stokes had no reason to believe they'd find out anything new by interviewing anyone else. Clearly, the victims did not know their killer, and questioning their families and colleagues was a waste of time.

He'd also had enough of chaperoning Lane and giving her lessons on police work and serial killers. She was filled with questions, and Stokes had no patience to endure them any longer. After weeks of dinners filled with one question after another at Applebee's or in diners and local gin mills, he was done.

DiMeglio reluctantly agreed but was OK with it. Unlike Stokes, he enjoyed answering her questions and was increasingly enjoying her company, ignoring the reminder in his head not to make the same mistake twice.

CHAPTER TWENTY-NINE

Déjà vu

Dumbarton Place, Dumfries, Virginia

The relationship between DiMeglio and Lane progressed beyond a professional level after what began as another business dinner and more questions from Lane on criminal investigations. When the two were in the Uber, he asked her if she'd like to meet Sully, since he had to take him for a walk.

"Really?" she asked. "Is this how you're going to seduce me? With a dog?"

He smiled and responded, "If that works for you, yep."

"Finally. I was wondering how many dates we needed to have that ended with only a kiss goodnight."

DiMeglio told the Uber driver to skip the first stop.

In the morning, the two agreed to keep the relationship to themselves, at least during the investigation. It troubled both of them that Lane's objectivity could be questioned if she published a positive story and the affair between them became public. DiMeglio wondered if he had some sort of need to get involved romantically with women who were connected to his work. He was drawn to the mystery and risk. As for Lane, she was working on a lead and saw no reason not to enjoy herself while she worked.

Sully disapproved. Whenever Lane stayed over in the apartment, Sully refused to be near her. He'd usually find his spot in the spare bedroom and ignore the two of them. At other times, Sully would lie outside the bedroom doorway, spying on them. Much like he did during the New Orleans liaisons between Rebecca Simone and DiMeglio, except that then it was to keep an eye on DiMeglio and protect Simone. By the time he got adopted by DiMeglio, his loyalty shifted. Now he was not about to let Lane into his life. And if he could help it, into DiMeglio's life as well.

Lane noticed it. "Sully doesn't seem to like me," she said as she lay in bed one evening, looking at the big dog parked in the doorway.

"Don't worry about it. Sully's just an old fool with memories of his last owner. Unless you're a serial killer too, he's not likely to take a liking to you."

"But he likes you, Chris. And you're not a serial killer."

"True, but I kept him from a shelter and a probable needle. My guess is he knows he owes me. I'm also the only one who feeds him or takes him for long walks."

"You talk as if the dog knows what you're saying."

"Trust me, Carla, that dog knows exactly what I'm saying. Sully also knows what I'm thinking. Call me crazy, but he's a lot smarter than either of us."

Sully stirred, seeming to know that they were talking about him, and made mildly angry eye contact with Lane, even showing some of his teeth. He had a subtle way of letting someone know how he felt.

"See, Carla, he's smiling at you!"

"That's not a smile, Chris. But let's see if we can make him a little jealous." She rolled on top of DiMeglio with obvious intentions, her hand finding its way to his thigh.

On hearing DiMeglio groan, Sully, head hanging, walked off to the living room and jumped up on the couch.

CHAPTER THIRTY

Fishing

BAU Headquarters, Quantico, Virginia

"Hi, Agent DiMeglio."

"Dick," DiMeglio typed, "why are you contacting me today?"

DiMeglio was in his office. The text came in at 10:00 a.m.

DiMeglio continued, "Are you ready to tell me how you're involved with Percy Armand's death? And the deaths of Jacob Schneider, Paul Stafford, and Marie Létisse?"

"It's so fitting they took their own lives. Don't you agree, Agent DiMeglio?"

"Come on, Dick. You and I both know they didn't commit suicide. At least not willingly."

As he waited for Dick's next text, DiMeglio yelled to his EA to get Evans and Stokes into his office.

"Did you ever wonder how many people they hurt by helping criminals keep out of prison? How many innocent people died because of their actions?" asked Dick.

"They didn't keep people out of prison, Dick. The prosecution failed to establish their case to put them in prison. You can't blame their lawyer for that."

Evans and Stokes arrived and took positions behind

DiMeglio, looking at the phone over his shoulder. DiMeglio wanted to gain more trust with Dick.

"Of course, I can, Agent DiMeglio. They knew their clients were guilty. And they used all their skills to set them free despite that guilt. So they did keep them from going to prison. Don't be naïve. You can blame incompetent prosecutors and judges, too. But it all starts with the lawyers who defend the killers."

"Keep him typing, Chris," urged Evans.

"OK, Dick, let's say I agree with you," typed DiMeglio. "How long do you intend to continue this? How many lawyers do you plan to kill? There are an awful lot of them out there, Dick."

"It is a burden, Agent DiMeglio," Dick responded. "I think I need to be more efficient."

A chill ran down the back of DiMeglio's neck.

"What do you mean by more efficient?"

"Do you ever go fishing, Agent DiMeglio?"

"Fishing?" DiMeglio asked aloud. Looking at his colleagues, he added, "Where is he going with this?" Both shrugged.

"Rarely."

"But you know a little about it, right?"

"OK, what's your point?"

"I'll ask the questions, Agent DiMeglio. OK?"

Keep playing along.

"Fine."

"So, Agent DiMeglio, when you go fishing, where is the best place for the fisherman to catch fish?"

DiMeglio hated playing games invented by suspects, particularly riddles. But it was their way of lauding themselves above someone. They always need to feed their ego. So it was the game he needed to play.

"Sorry, Dick, I'm not good at riddles. I guess it's wherever the fish are."

"You're close, Agent DiMeglio, but you can do better. Where is the best place for the fisherman to fish?"

"Where there are a lot of fish?" DiMeglio guessed.

"Exactly. Where there are schools of fish, often with one type feeding on the others. A target-rich environment for everyone hungry. You should ask yourself, where are the schools of fish? Where is the easy prey for predators? Fish are easier to catch when they're all together. It's a lot more efficient."

DiMeglio's spine tingled again. Dick intended to be efficient. DiMeglio was ready to type but knew it would be to no avail. The fourth session was over. There would be no more bubbles today. Dick was gone.

"He's going to hit somewhere with a concentration of lawyers," speculated Stokes.

"Then the most obvious fishing grounds are conventions," concluded Evans.

CHAPTER THIRTY-ONE

Efficiency

Zoom Conference, Washington, D.C.
and Philadelphia, Pennsylvania

Alan Kramer was the Chair of the Alliance of Criminal Defense Attorneys. With nearly 3,000 members, the elite among defense lawyers attended the annual meeting. It had a small section for public defenders but concentrated on supporting private practitioners. As a result, its annual get-together was always at a posh resort. Successful attorneys are not shy about flaunting their wealth, and Kramer was no exception. He drove expensive cars and wore Armani suits, Hermès ties, and Gucci shoes. The Franck Muller Cintrée Curvex watch on his wrist completed the image of success he cultivated during his forty-year career as one of Philadelphia's premier lawyers.

While some of those who attended the annual conference used the meeting sessions to satisfy their state bar's minimum requirements for continuing legal education (CLE), most attendees networked, swapping war stories and drinking. In fact, most of them lied on the CLE filing forms, attesting that they attended the educational sessions. So much for integrity.

"I'm not sure what you're telling me, Agent DiMeglio. Are you saying someone is going to attack our convention?" Kramer agreed to a Zoom call with DiMeglio. He had no interest in inviting the FBI to his offices, much less going to Washington.

"I can't be sure," responded DiMeglio. "But it's a possibility. We've been tracking a serial killer who targets defense attorneys. He has a real vendetta against them. But we're not sure where he plans to strike next. But he gave us a warning that is concerning."

"And what warning would that be, Agent DiMeglio?" It was clear on the video feed that Kramer was only half listening to DiMeglio, distracted by other papers he was reviewing. He was acting as if this was merely a courtesy call from the Bureau.

"Mr. Kramer, this is serious and deserves your undivided attention. So whatever else you're working on, please put it aside for a few minutes."

Kramer looked up at the screen. "Agent DiMeglio, I'm giving you the attention this call deserves." The sarcasm was apparent.

"Mr. Kramer, he's killed at least four lawyers so far. Maybe more. His targets have been successful defense attorneys. Much like yourself. Makes them look like suicides."

"And how do you know this?"

"He and I have been exchanging texts."

That got Kramer's attention. "You're actually talking to him!?"

"No. Just texts. It's not unusual for serial killers to reach out to those pursuing them. They often like to flaunt their killings and want to expose what they believe is police incompetence."

"That's probably not so hard," Kramer sarcastically replied. "What did he say?"

"He talked in riddles about fishing and where to go to catch fish. His answer was you go to where they concentrate in large numbers. That's about all he said. It's our guess that a convention of defense lawyers would be a perfect place to fish."

Now Kramer looked more serious and had put aside whatever else he was working on. "But he can't get dozens of lawyers to commit suicide, agent. You said that's his MO."

"It is so far, but serial killers can change when an opportunity presents itself."

"So, what are you asking me to do? Cancel the convention? That is not an option. It's only ten days away. Tell my members that if they come, some psychopath might kill them? That's also not acceptable."

"I can't stop you from having your convention. Nor am I suggesting you cancel it. But I can offer you additional security. We can keep an eye on attendees to see if any might look like or exhibit the behavior of someone who might be dangerous. And if he does anything, we'll be there to take him down quickly."

"So you're asking me to let law enforcement chaperone a group of defense attorneys. Better yet, the FBI. I can only imagine how that will go over with my members. It's like letting the fox into the henhouse. But I assume I don't have a choice. Am I right?"

"You can say no. Then if something happens, it's all on your shoulders. But if you can live with that, enjoy the Miami sun and surf."

"I assume you will be discreet."

"If we do our job right, Mr. Kramer, you won't even know we're there."

DiMeglio, together with ten agents he temporarily pulled off other cases, arrived the day before the convention began. Director Kinston thought DiMeglio was chasing a windmill and reluctantly agreed to let him have additional support. But only for the convention.

They set up their base at the Radisson Hotel, a block from the convention at the Fontainebleau. Even when hunting a serial killer, FBI budgets didn't pay for the Fontainebleau.

His first impression of the conference venue was the snobbery of its location and its attendees, the vast majority of whom were men. Defense lawyers did indeed do well. And the women at the lobby bar and pool! The local police warned him that many were "professionals." If they were,

DiMeglio decided they must be some of the most beautiful professionals he'd ever seen. But he guessed the defense attorneys only wanted the best money could buy. He wondered how the female members of the alliance felt about the misogyny and objectification so apparent at the convention. No doubt Evans and Lane would have a thing or two to say about that, and Stokes would have a few off-color jokes to add to the discussion.

DiMeglio and his expanded team, some dressed as bellhops and clerks, set up observation posts at the registration desk, in the meeting rooms, and at the planned events. DiMeglio secured press credentials for Lane so she could roam the conference floor and see if she could get a sense of folks who might not belong there. Possible suspects. People with things to hide were often uncomfortable with reporters. It was a long shot, but it might work.

Sensors were set up to detect explosives in a variety of locations. Most registered attendees were members whose photographs were in the alliance files. The speakers also supplied photos and biographies to help hype attendance at their sessions. Although it was impossible to clear all 700 of those attending, let alone other tourists and hotel guests, Kramer helped DiMeglio's team identify who among his members had won well-publicized cases where they freed violent defendants. He was on the list himself. Unfortunately, statistics on such wins are not in any database. So it was all from memory. While searches of the personal websites of the alliance members attending had information about wins, they were not helpful. Understanding the difference between facts and hyperbole on an attorney's website was impossible. So much for the truth, the whole truth, and nothing but the truth.

When done, they identified 23 lawyers as potential targets. Each had recently won a big case against what seemed to be overwhelming evidence that justified a conviction. Just the kind of lawyers Dick the Butcher liked to target.

Two days before the start of the convention, Kramer and DiMeglio met in Kramer's room at the Fontainebleau, the Le Ciel Suite, the most expensive accommodation in the hotel, with a king bedroom, adjoining living room, and a private office. The two were sitting on its wrap-around balcony, the largest in the hotel, overlooking the white sand of Miami Beach. DiMeglio guessed that Kramer negotiated the $1,360 per night room as a free perk for hosting the convention at the hotel.

It was only 11:00 a.m., but Kramer was already enjoying a cocktail as he lay on a chaise lounge in his shorts and a polo shirt. His baseball cap read "Not Guilty" on the front. DiMeglio wore cotton trousers and a lightweight open-collared short sleeve shirt. He turned down Kramer's offer of a drink.

"Are you going to notify the potential targets of the threat and give them a chance to cancel coming?"

"We don't intend to notify anyone. If you feel inclined

to do so, that's your choice. All we have now is a hunch. No proof. So while we're setting up surveillance, we're not revealing our plans or concerns to anyone other than you and, where necessary, local authorities."

"So they're guinea pigs? Bait for your killer?"

That's precisely what they are, you putz.

"Not at all," responded DiMeglio. "We're going to do all we can to protect them. To protect everyone at the convention, including you. The Miami Beach police are informed, and we'll also coordinate with them. We'll be discreet and interfere with your convention as little as possible."

"Then I guess I have nothing to say," responded Kramer. "And frankly Agent, if the local police know, in no time it will spread throughout the convention. Cops have relationships with the local defense bar that assures secrets are short-lived."

"That's probably true, Mr. Kramer, but I suggest you not be the one who tells them."

"Don't worry, Agent, I'm not about to put a damper on the convention with empty warnings based upon mere suspicions. If someone brings it up, I'll just say a crime-ridden city like Miami warrants protection. And if asked why the FBI is here, I'll say I know nothing about it."

DiMeglio didn't believe that Kramer, with his inflated ego, could keep anything confidential. But with the convention being Kramer's moment to shine, the additional warning might temper his enthusiasm to talk.

CHAPTER THIRTY-TWO

Arrogance

Lobby, Fontainebleau, Miami Beach, Florida

DiMeglio tried to reach out to Dick, hoping to learn more about his plans and whether his team's hunch that he'd strike at the convention was true, but he got no responses from any of the numbers used by Dick in the previous text conversations and suspected he was using burner phones. Previous efforts to trace them had failed, so he assumed he might be texting to phones long ago discarded. But he nonetheless texted on the chance they'd connect.

The conventioneers began assembling, arriving in limos, taxis, and private cars. A few drove Ferraris, Maseratis, and tricked-out Escalades. Others rode up in classic antiques. Rich and pretentious lawyers were invading Miami Beach. They fit right in with the tourists and revelers ordinarily in Miami and South Beach, except they wore more bling.

DiMeglio marveled at how friendly the registered attendees were with one another as he watched them arrive. Adversaries who eat and drink as friends. It was as if they were all part of a big family. Hugs were common, and bantering with playful insults was the norm. It reminded DiMeglio of scenes from movies depicting meetings of the Dons of the

Mafia. All friendly on the surface but always plotting to kill one another if the opportunity arose. The only difference was that the lawyers arriving at the convention were also there to have a good time and brag about their victories, some honestly believing they were protecting their client's Constitutional rights. All they really wanted was to feed their bank accounts.

The day passed without incident, and DiMeglio returned to the hotel.

The following day, he and Evans had breakfast at the Crema Gourmet Espresso Bar, a short walk south of the hotel. DiMeglio enjoyed the quiet of the local coffee shops. Stokes and Lane were roaming around the convention site, monitoring the meeting areas with other agents assigned to the surveillance.

"Georgia," DiMeglio began, "I sometimes wonder if lawyers actually are the problem."

"I get how you feel, Chris. I thought about being a lawyer once but realized I'd never make it representing scumbags. It's hard enough working for them."

DiMeglio smiled, and Evans quickly added, "But not you, Chris. You're not one of the scumbags. Working for you is a pleasure."

The server brought DiMeglio his salmon omelet and Evans her Greek yogurt and fruit. Evans had a skim latte and DiMeglio, his usual macchiato—a shot of espresso with a dab of steamed milk on top.

DiMeglio wanted to get back on track. "So, getting back to the problem of lawyers, I guess even they have their rights."

"And I suppose serial killers do, too," remarked Evans.

Nodding his head in agreement, DiMeglio said, "There are two kinds of serial killers. The rational ones and the irrational ones. The irrational ones are the toughest to catch. They kill randomly. No obvious connections between victims except for being in the wrong place at the wrong time. Almost impossible to predict their next move."

The server returned to ask if everything was OK. Servers with stupid questions was one of Evans' many pet peeves. If something was wrong, didn't they think a person would complain? Instead, she answered firmly, "Not yet. We just got our food." As the server walked away, he got the message to leave them alone.

Fearing she might have one of her meltdowns, DiMeglio interjected, "Georgia, relax."

"Sorry."

DiMeglio continued, "Then there are the rational ones. They need a reason to kill. It's always a psychopathic reason, but, nonetheless, a reason. They can be profiled and connections can be made between victims, revealing patterns that can eventually lead to an arrest. But the one thing common with virtually all serial killers is a misplaced sense of deity that eventually grows into a sense of immortality. They think they will never be stopped, much less caught. That's when they got sloppy. Make mistakes."

"And is Dick a rational killer?"

"I believe he is. And I think he's well on the way to making a mistake if we can string him along and gain his trust. But, unfortunately, that will mean more lawyers die before we can stop him."

He waved to the server for the check. In DiMeglio's mind, Dick the Butcher was as good as caught. It was just a matter of when and how many more lawyers had to die.

CHAPTER THIRTY-THREE

Where's there's smoke . . .

Outside the Ballroom, Fontainebleau,
Miami Beach, Florida

Day three, the last day of the convention. It was time for the black-tie dinner finale.

"Boom" was all the text read.

DiMeglio, phone in hand, briskly walked toward Evans across the ballroom, standing at an opposite door. "Georgia, I think he planted a bomb in the ballroom. The text simply reads Boom. There are over 700 lawyers in there!"

Stokes joined them. "I heard you say something about a bomb."

"Yeah. My guess is it's in the ballroom."

"What do you want to do, Chief?"

"We have no choice." He turned to Evans. "Georgia, find the hotel manager and tell him there is a credible bomb threat. Have him set off the alarm to empty the hotel."

Evans was on her way before DiMeglio finished the order. "Brad, get the Miami PD bomb squad here, stat. They need to start looking. Get others on the team to use our scanners and see what they can find. Try to do it discreetly until the alarm goes off. And where is Carla?"

"As far as I know, Chief, she's working the floor like you asked."

"Find her and get her out of here."

DiMeglio went into the crowd to find Kramer. With a group that big, he expected it to be a challenge. There were over sixty tables with hundreds of lawyers milling around, networking with one another. But as luck would have it, Kramer was on the side of the stage in front of the room, getting ready to make his big speech. His script was about to change.

As DiMeglio approached, Kramer could see the concern on his face.

"Mr. Kramer, we have a credible bomb threat, and the hotel is about to sound the alarm to empty the premises." He showed Kramer the text. "I suggest you get to the microphone and warn your members so they can start an orderly exit while my team comes in and locates any bomb."

"Jesus Christ, that assumes there is one, Agent DiMeglio. We've had an incident-free convention for three days. Nothing has happened. You're worse than Chicken Little. So now, at the last minute, you want me to panic the members that someone is about to blow them all up? I'm supposed to do that on yet another one of your hunches, Agent DiMeglio? Nothing has gotten in here without being inspected. The area has been scanned. Now you want me to turn everything on its head over a one-word text you received. No wonder your agency has such an awful reputation."

As much as he didn't want to, DiMeglio ignored the insult. He was there to save lives. Even the lives of idiots.

"We might be wrong, Mr. Kramer. But are you willing to risk the lives of your members? Besides, the hotel is going to sound the alarm, anyway. I'm just giving you the courtesy of a warning so you can tell them before they hear it. And I assure you, it's likely to be the last courtesy I give you!"

Kramer approached the microphone, shaking his head. Before he could say anything, the hotel alarm went off, and the pre-recorded announcement calmly asked everyone to leave the premises in an orderly fashion. Under the hotel's emergency protocol, no reason was given in the announcement. As far as the hotel was concerned, the guests didn't need to know why. They just needed to get out.

The lawyers sitting at their dinner tables and milling around looked confused. These were not people who took orders well. They seemed unconvinced with little intention to leave. The tone of the announcement was more of a request than an order. While a few got up and started walking out, most stood frozen in place, continuing their conversations.

Now at the podium and pointing at DiMeglio, at his side on the stage, Kramer began, "Everyone, may I please have your attention." He tapped his hand on the microphone to help. The crowd quieted. Again pointing to DiMeglio, he continued, "This gentleman is with the FBI. They are investigating a serial killer who wants to kill defense lawyers like you and me."

To DiMeglio's surprise, laughter rose in the room.

"I'm serious, folks. This is no joke. He told me there might be a bomb in the hotel, maybe even in this room. His suspicions are based upon what he calls 'credible' evidence."

More laughter.

"So we should be safe rather than sorry. Please calmly leave the hotel. I suggest we all meet at the pool, where I hope the bar remains open. Drinks are on me!" It was as if Kramer wanted to make this a circus show. Turning to DiMeglio, he quietly added a whisper the microphone could not pick up, "I know these idiots. I have to give them a reason they should get out."

As the two walked off the stage, a series of bangs reverberated in the room as smoke began rising from the centerpieces on a few tables. No explosions. Just a lot of smoke. But it was enough to panic the lawyers remaining in the room. They immediately went from calm complacency to chaotic compliance, rushing to the doors, almost trampling over one another.

A few more centerpieces made a popping sound and started spewing smoke. DiMeglio stood there, waiting for an explosion. Nothing. Just an occasional pop as more smoking centerpieces.

His phone buzzed.

The text read, "Imagine what could have happened, Agent DiMeglio. A bomb could have rid the world of a couple of hundred lawyers efficiently and effectively. Just imagine."

The fire department arrived, dousing the floral center-pieces as Evans and Stokes tried to prevent damage to the evidence.

"How did you get the flowers past security?" DiMeglio typed.

"I didn't get anything past anyone, Agent DiMeglio. But if I were to use my imagination, I'd suspect the florists are the last to arrive. After all, the flowers must be fresh. And all the stems sit in water jabbed into Styrofoam shielded in aluminum foil, a perfect place to hide something. That's fundamental, Agent DiMeglio. But you missed it. Make sure you note that for the future. You may be getting sloppy."

"So there never was a bomb?"

"My dear Agent DiMeglio, I never said there would be one. I never even told you where it would happen. You led me there. All I said was that killing all the lawyers might be done more efficiently. You decided a convention might be a good hunting ground."

Son of a bitch, we've been played. And how the fuck did he follow us to Miami?

"How did you know we'd be here? We haven't texted in weeks."

"When you told the cops what you're doing, you told the world. Miami cops are no different from any others. I'm surprised all those lawyers stayed once the police told them why you were there. Just shows how stupid they are."

Evans was at his side, looking over his shoulder at the

screen. "Son of a bitch," she said. "Does he have contacts in the Miami PD?"

The next text read, "But don't feel bad, Agent DiMeglio. You got my message out to a lot of the people who should start worrying about their lives. Perhaps some will change their ways, find another line of work, and stop freeing the guilty."

"We played right into his hands, Georgia. We were made fools."

DiMeglio waited a minute, thinking about how to respond and draw out more information from the killer. But before he could, bubbles appeared. Dick was typing.

"But I don't want to disappoint you. Room 5146. *Crack the lawyer's voice, that he may never more false title plead.* From *Timon of Athens*, Act IV, Agent DiMeglio."

The fifth session was over.

CHAPTER THIRTY-FOUR

Overdose

Room 5146, Fontainebleau, Miami Beach, Florida

They found Justin Haynes dead in his bed on the fifth floor of the Fontainebleau. The Miami medical examiner, already at the scene, said Haynes died of an overdose. An orange plastic bottle of Lexapro from CVS lay on the floor, open and empty. According to the label, Haynes' doctor prescribed it. The note on the bedside table was simple, just like all the others, apologizing for doing so much wrong to so many people. While DiMeglio assumed the scene was wiped clean like all the others, he told the Miami PD at the scene to do a full analysis of the room, top to bottom. He needed clues about the killer.

"He struck right under our noses while we chaperoned a bunch of fuckin' lawyers, mutually masturbating one another," Stokes grumbled. He had a way with words. Or at least he thought he did.

"It sure looks that way, but this time at least, we're at the crime scene before anyone else can screw it up," replied DiMeglio.

He turned to Evans. "Georgia, reach out to the crime lab in Quantico and get them to send someone right away. For now, Brad and I will supervise the locals and let the coroner remove the body. Let's make sure nothing else is touched. We'll get all the photos we can. The lab can take more when they're here. We'll try to hold off the locals beyond what they need to do to preserve the scene. But our guys need to get here as soon as they can."

Lane arrived and entered the room, straining to look past the gathered police officers to see the body.

"Carla," DiMeglio ordered, "you can't come in here. It's an active crime scene. Please wait in the hallway."

She reluctantly obeyed and waited outside.

"Doctor, can you estimate a time of death?" asked Stokes.

The Miami medical examiner responded, "Hard to say. My guess right now is he's been dead for fifteen to twenty hours. There's almost no decomposition, but the rigidity puts it at about that time frame. I'll know more after an autopsy. But from what I see here, with the suicide note, it looks like an intentional OD on Lexapro."

"Don't judge a book by its cover, doctor," suggested DiMeglio. "We suspect he was murdered by a serial killer we're hunting down who likes to murder lawyers. Criminal defense lawyers in particular."

The medical examiner smiled. "You know what they say about a dead lawyer, Agent DiMeglio?"

He did, but answered, "No," unable to ignore the grin on Stokes' face.

"A good beginning," answered the medical examiner.

"Best lawyer joke ever!" added Stokes, still smiling.

For DiMeglio, it didn't seem so funny when a body lay before him.

Before DiMeglio could stop him, the medical examiner picked up the empty pill bottle with the end of a pencil, looking at the label. He sensed DiMeglio's negative reaction but continued in a serious tone, "The thing is, Agent DiMeglio, the prescription label says it was filled over a month ago." He dropped the bottle into a clear evidence bag. "To kill yourself with Lexapro, you'd need to take a lot of pills. So unless he didn't use the Lexapro regularly, he would not have had enough to kill himself. Regardless, we'll get to the exact cause after the autopsy."

"Doctor, please leave the empty bottle here. I want my lab to look at the crime scene before anything is removed. They'll be here in a few hours."

The medical examiner did not appreciate the request. "That's not proper protocol, agent. I'll take into evidence whatever I damn well please, and I'll take it anywhere I want to take it. Your people can come to my lab, and we'll tape off the scene so they can do all the examinations they'd like. This is my crime scene, and everything in it is in my custody. I want as few people as possible handling the evidence until I have it safely in my lab, including anyone from the FBI."

Sighing in disappointment, knowing the medical examiner was correct, DiMeglio replied, "Fine, have it your way.

But I intend to hold you and anyone who handles the evidence responsible for any screw-ups. That's a promise."

Not moved by DiMeglio's warning, the medical examiner ignored the comment and calmly went back to inspect the scene and gather evidence. DiMeglio left.

"So, what happened?" asked Lane as the two walked down the hall.

"An overdose on something. He was a lawyer at the convention. And a good one. He fits Dick's profile. But, unfortunately, Dick toyed with us while he murdered Haynes. He played us for fools."

"Won't cameras reveal who entered the room? Don't hotels have them in all the hallways?"

"We'll check on them, Carla, and maybe even find something if we're lucky. Dick's already murdered lawyers in hotels and knows how to avoid the cameras. I suspect it will be the same here."

"So this one was an overdose, huh? It seems Dick murders his victims in a fashion akin to how criminals are executed. So an overdose doesn't fit."

"No, I suppose it doesn't. It could be a variation on lethal injection. I don't know. What I know is we have another dead lawyer, and we're no closer to Dick than we were before this poor bastard was murdered. Somehow, we need to up our game. And quickly."

CHAPTER THIRTY-FIVE

The Cause of Death

BARcelona, Radisson Hotel, Miami Beach, Florida

Sitting at a table in the BARcelona restaurant in the Radisson, DiMeglio was having lunch alone, reviewing his notes. The police report confirmed that the crime scene was scrubbed clean. Just like all the others. His lab team from Quantico found nothing. Whoever was killing these lawyers knew how to leave no trace. They either had police training or were self-educated. That wasn't hard to do. The internet, particularly the Dark Web, had plenty of how-to texts and videos on wiping crime scenes clean.

His phone rang. It read, MDME, as in Miami-Dade Medical Examiner.

"Agent DiMeglio," the doctor said, "it wasn't the Lexapro that killed Haynes. Not enough was in his system. But we did find enough fentanyl to kill five men."

DiMeglio immediately assumed the killer administered the fentanyl by simply swapping legitimate tablets with fentanyl-laced replacements. The killer didn't even need to be there when Haynes took his regular dose of Lexapro. An easy crime scene to clean since it required no effort at all once the killer planted the pills. Just wipe for prints.

He called Stokes. "Brad, do you have the hallway video of the four days Haynes had the room yet?"

"No, Chief, I'm working on it. It seems the system has been having problems lately. I'm not surprised."

"Nor am I. Let's get the names and contact info for all the hotel workers who had reason to go into the room. Check who cleaned the room each day and anyone who delivered room service. Make sure you cover anyone who needed to work on anything in that room."

"Will do, Chief. And I'll also look at any footage that shows Haynes working the convention floor. We'll know about any meetings he had. Maybe the techies can help us find him in the tapes with facial ID. I'm on it, Chief."

"Thanks, Brad. Contact me immediately if you get any leads."

He then called Lenoir Peters and told her to book flights for his team to come home.

CHAPTER THIRTY-SIX

Candid Camera

BAU Headquarters, Quantico, Virginia

After three days back in Quantico, they added Haynes' photograph to the board, "Fentanyl OD" written beneath it.

As DiMeglio stared at the board, hoping some inspiration would hit him, Stokes walked in.

"Chief, we have something here," he began. He set his laptop in front of DiMeglio, and pressed the play button on the screen.

The video was a montage of footage from the hallway in front of Haynes's room. Most of it was unexceptional, with visits by housekeepers and room service for breakfast.

"You said the cameras were malfunctioning."

"That's what I was told, but the tapes, they told a different story. The clerk who claimed there were problems with the system is being questioned by the Miami-Dade PD now."

Stokes pressed pause. "OK. Here it is. Watch closely." He pressed play.

The segment showed a man entering the hallway at 1:00 in the afternoon, the convention's second day and the day before the closing banquet. The day the medical examiner confirmed Haynes died.

Stokes hit pause. "OK. Now watch that guy. When he checked in, he insisted on the adjacent room. How he knew it would be available, I have no idea. But it was. So he was lucky. Before checking in, however, he sat in the lobby, appearing to be reading a local paper. A closer look at the lobby video shows him checking out those in the crowd wearing lanyards with name tags from the conference. I'll show you that footage later. But it would have been easy for him to identify Haynes."

Stokes hit play, and the two watched the man enter the room next to Haynes.

Stokes fast-forwarded to later that evening. The time stamp on the footage showed the man leaving the room at 7:00 p.m.

"That's him leaving. He checked out, putting the charges on a stolen credit card. So that's a dead end. There's only one reason someone checks out the day they check in. They're finished with whatever they needed to do."

"Do we have any footage of him entering Haynes's room?"

"No, at least not from the hallway. But he had the adjacent room. That allows easy access outside camera coverage."

"And just about any amateur can pick a lock on an adjacent room door," DiMeglio observed.

"He was no amateur, Chief. That's probably how the man swapped the pills," Stokes concluded.

"Were you able to identify him?"

"Yep. Quantico got his name from Interpol. Antonio Ricci. He's a suspect in some relatively minor crimes in Italy, where he lives. Loan sharking, shakedowns, and stuff like that. Nothing that the local police see as violent. But it's Italy. So God only knows what he's done. He entered the states a couple of days before Haynes died and returned the next day after he checked out of the hotel. So he's probably back in Italy. A quick trip."

"Italy?" wondered DiMeglio. "Why would someone from Italy come here to kill a local attorney?"

"And I know your next question, Chief. What's the connection between the killer and Haynes?"

"And the answer is…?"

"So far, none. As far as we can tell, he came and went and never had a prior connection with Haynes. We'll keep digging. It may be pure coincidence, but it sure seems odd. The only one who can answer your question is Ricci."

CHAPTER THIRTY-SEVEN

Questioned Coincidence

Command Post Sports Bar, Quantico, Virginia

After a long day in Quantico, Stokes and Evans would often stop at the Command Post Sports Bar before going home, particularly on Thursdays when it was Ladies Night and drinks for women were at half price, and Stokes liked the chicken wings. The bar, decorated with military memorabilia, was small and informal. It was a place where they could talk openly. Stokes ordered his usual Budweiser and a plate of buffalo wings, extra hot. Evans ordered a gin and tonic and fried pickles. She liked them but also loved how Stokes thought they were disgusting, particularly when she dipped them in catsup. Annoying him was a game she enjoyed.

"Georgia," Stokes said as the server brought their drinks and food, "have you noticed anything odd about Chris and Carla?"

Sipping her drink, she calmly replied, "If you mean are they having an affair, of course they are," replied Evans.

"What!? You knew?" Stokes was shocked.

Evans smiled. "Like most men, Brad, you're the last to know. Women can sense it. It doesn't get by us." She dipped a pickle into the sauce. Stokes frowned.

"How do you eat those things?"

"I'll buy you a beer if you try one. And they're much better for you than those chicken carcass parts you eat."

"Yeah, right. I'll pass on the pickles."

After eating a couple of wings, sauce covering his fingers and mouth, Stokes continued, "So he's doing it again? How can he be so fuckin' stupid? Another affair with a team member? You'd think he would have learned in New Orleans."

Evans handed him a napkin.

"She's not a member of our team, Brad. He's human. Let it go. And lower your voice. We don't need rumors spreading around here."

"Let it go?" he whispered. "Really? Why are you so supportive of something that could cloud his judgment? It could ruin his career. Has he hit on you, too?"

Evans leaned in toward Stokes, clearly angry at the comment. "Brad, if you ever insinuate that again, I'll take that little black ass of yours and rip you a new one. You understand?" She was serious.

"OK, Georgia, OK. Calm down. I'm just upset. That's all I'm sayin'. Have another pickle." Her anger faded as she pondered what he said.

"What do you mean, it might cloud his judgment?" She slowly dipped a pickle, making sure it had lots of catsup scooped up with it.

"Nothing." He shook his head as Evans slowly ate the pickle and gently dabbed off the catsup on her lip.

"Don't give me 'nothing,' Brad. What's on your mind?"

"OK. Hear me out. I may be nuts, but have you noticed that Carla's not around whenever a text comes from Dick? She vanished from the Miami convention only to turn up outside the room where we found the dead lawyer."

The server brought them a second round of drinks. As regulars, they didn't need to ask. And the bartender wanted to make sure Evans got a second drink before happy hour ended.

Evans sat back in her chair with disbelief in her eyes. "Wow, Brad, you have quite the imagination. So you think Carla is the killer because she wasn't around when Chris got texts? Neither was the Pope. Does that make him a suspect?"

"I'm just sayin', Georgia. It seems a little odd. Look at the facts. Chris opened the case after she pushed him. She interviewed him on *60 Minutes* and used a new murder to blindside him. She finagled getting embedded with us. And now she's trying to suck him dry, in more ways than one, on all he knows about serial killers. That's all she wanted to talk about when we were on the road chasing windmills. Who knows? She could be playing with all of us. It just seems odd to me that she is so conveniently missing when Dick sends a text."

"So? Do you want to suggest it to Chris?" She grabbed a chicken wing off Stokes' plate. They looked too good not to try one. He gave her a napkin, smiling.

"No. Not yet. I first want to see if there's more to it. But don't dismiss it, Georgia. Something tells me Carla is more than just a reporter."

"Be careful, Brad. If you're wrong, anything you say to Chris could ruin your relationship with him. As well as any future you have with the Bureau. You're expendable. He's not."

CHAPTER THIRTY-EIGHT

Foreign Affairs

BAU Headquarters, Quantico, Virginia

"Do you like to travel, Agent DiMeglio?"

"It's part of my job, Dick."

"No. I don't mean on the job. I mean, for fun. Do you like to travel for fun?"

"Occasionally."

"Where have you been outside the United States, Agent DiMeglio?"

"Not many places. Canada, Mexico, and some islands."

"You've never been to any place in Asia, Africa, or Europe?"

"Nope."

"You mean you never even visited your heritage in Italy? I should think you still have family there."

"Never been."

"And you don't have family there?"

"Nope. None that I know of."

"Do you speak Italian?"

"No on that one, too. My parents always wanted me to speak English and be American, not Italian. Do you speak Italian?" DiMeglio hoped to get another hint.

"I speak many languages, Agent DiMeglio. Unlike your parents, mine wanted me to be a global citizen. What your parents did to you was sad. You should see the world."

"What do you want today?" DiMeglio had enough of the small talk and more of Dick's riddles. Dick was trying to get under his skin. He refused to take the bait.

"Nothing. I was just curious if you like to travel. You should always make sure your passport is valid. You never know when you'll need to make a trip. It needs to be good for at least six months before you travel outside the United States. Did you know that?"

"I gather you're going global now. Right?"

"Haven't I already done that?"

The bubbles vanished, and the sixth session ended.

DiMeglio called out to his EA, "Lenoir, get Georgia and Brad in here right now." DiMeglio wrote on the pad on his desk, "Where?" and "Multilingual."

The two arrived, taking their usual positions over his shoulder to view the incoming texts.

"Geez, sit down. Dick's gone. But I just had a conversation with him. Unless he's trying to confuse us, he's planning another murder. This time overseas. My bet is it's in Europe. Asia is too far away. My gut tells me it's in Italy after what we saw in Miami. Logically, we'll find Ricci there as well. For all we know, maybe he's Dick. Not sure why I feel this way. Just a hunch. But we have to go to Rome."

He called his EA back into his office and told her to get tickets to Rome for him, Stokes, Evans, and Lane.

DiMeglio and his team knew it was common for serial killers to change the geographic areas where they found victims. By moving around, they put law enforcement on its heels, mix up jurisdictions, and keep the police constantly chasing them, often after leads in places the killer never intended to go. It was just part of a serial killer's game to keep the police confused.

"Now you've got us chasing him on hunches, Chief?" asked Stokes.

"We've gone with hunches countless times, Brad," interjected Evans.

"I think that's what he was hinting at in the texts. He loves leaving hints and riddles. I think he's telling us the next murder is in Italy."

"So we're supposed to cover an entire country, Chief? That's nuts."

"No. Not all of Italy. If he's consistent, he'll be looking for a prominent attorney known nationally or internationally. Since he seems to enjoy killing at hotels, let's keep with the fishing analogy and see if there is another convention."

"I'll look into it," Evans offered.

"This one just feels right. OK?" said DiMeglio.

"You're the boss, Chief."

CHAPTER THIRTY-NINE

Compromising Principles

Headquarters, Federal Bureau of Investigation,
Washington D.C.

When DiMeglio's EA told him that the Director wanted to see him and Frattarola immediately, he knew he was in for a tough meeting.

"Rome? Are you serious?" said Kinston as DiMeglio and Frattarola sat at Kinston's desk. "On what basis do the two of you want me to justify these expenditures? If the killer is in Italy, let the Italians deal with him." Kinston was not enamored with DiMeglio taking his crew and Lane to Italy on what was admittedly a hunch. And a very expensive one at that.

"I understand your reluctance, Director Kinston," responded DiMeglio, "but the murders are taking place in the United States, so we need to lead the efforts to apprehend the killer." DiMeglio looked at Frattarola, who was sitting in front of the Director's desk, looking worried. "Every clue leads us to Italy," he continued "At this point, we understand enough about how the killer thinks to make this call. If we're wrong, we'll know relatively quickly. But if we're right, we'll be positioned to track him down quickly."

Kinston was very pleased with DiMeglio and Frattarola's work on the PR front and knew that any risk of interrupting that program needed to be avoided. But he needed some fiscal discipline.

"How long is 'relatively quickly,' Chris?" pushed Kinston.

"I can't be certain, but I'd say we'll have a good idea within a couple of weeks and, assuming all goes well, catch the killer within a month or two."

"And what about all the work Julie does to keep you on the circuit? Are we supposed to drop all of that?"

"I will have to cancel some bookings. Or maybe we can do them remotely," suggested Frattarola.

"Sir, I can't do both. Sorry, Julie. Once we're in Italy, I won't be able to predict our schedule, and the time difference makes appearances on talk shows impossible. At best, I might be able to do an occasional press interview on the phone, but anything else would be impossible."

"I suppose we can try that," offered Frattarola.

"Director Kinston, we're close to solving the case, or at the very least, getting critical information we can use for a full profile," she added.

"And if they solve it while Ms. Lane is with them, that's a PR coup we can exploit. The press will eat it up. If Chris is right that he'll have an idea if he's on the right track in a few weeks, I can probably keep everything on hold."

DiMeglio frowned listening to Frattarola. "Let's be clear. This is about finding a killer. It's not about PR spin for the

Bureau. While I'm more than happy to see the BAU's successes recognized, we will not spin this using Lane as our spokesperson or allow her to create some banquet for the press to 'eat up' as Julie put it. Just let me do my job."

Kinston, somewhat taken aback by DiMeglio's reaction, responded, "OK, Chris, follow your hunch. This is your case and area. PR will not interfere. But please try to keep it short. My gut tells me two months is too long to figure out if you're going in the right direction. If this goes south, I don't want a public spectacle of the FBI chasing windmills." Looking at Frattarola, he added, "And I'll be expecting you to prevent that from happening!"

CHAPTER FORTY

Mile High Club

Delta Airlines, Somewhere Over the Atlantic Ocean

Lane strengthened DiMeglio's hunch that Rome would be where they'd find Ricci when she told the team that a lawyer's conference was scheduled in the city. That was too convenient for Stokes.

Then they saw that Anthony Barlow, an American defense lawyer, was a keynote speaker. In his latest case, he defended Ronald Baker, a North Carolina shopping mall shooter who shot sixteen people, killing nine. Barlow got a mistrial in the first round. The retrial resulted in a hung jury. After they had incarcerated his client for three years and two failed prosecutions, the judge granted Barlow's motion to set bail on the condition Baker wear an ankle monitor and remain at home. While the district attorney prepared for the third trial, Baker ignored the conditions and robbed a local convenience store, shooting and killing the clerk. In the showdown that followed with the police, he too was shot and killed.

When DiMeglio was told about the Baker case, it all fell into place for him. Barlow was certainly someone Dick the Butcher would target. Stokes continued to believe too many of the leads they received were a collection of very odd coincidences. The others thought it was serendipity and consistent with Dick's hints.

"Have you ever been to Italy?" Stokes asked Lane as the plane leveled off at 30,000 feet en route to Rome. He made sure he sat beside her. DiMeglio and Evans were two rows behind them. The flight wasn't crowded, so the two of them, as well as Evans and DiMeglio, could share four seats and raise the armrests to be comfortable. Lane was on the aisle seat, and Stokes was two seats over from her, leaving the window seat empty.

"Actually, yes," responded Lane. "My maiden name is Michelotti. My family came from Italy two generations ago and settled in the states. They were olive growers. Now they grow avocados. But we kept our roots and visited many times. In fact, I was there just before I interviewed Chris on *60 Minutes*."

"You're married?" Stokes responded with obvious surprise.

"I was. We got divorced after a little over a year. We just weren't meant for one another. He was a jock that never really grew up. We married right out of high school. He wanted a pretty stay-at-home wife while he hung out with the boys. After being kept in housewife prison for a year, I told him we were done. I moved on."

"How did he take that?"

"He didn't care. Just shrugged it off. No doubt he figured he'd find another bimbo to make him waffles."

Lane waved to the flight attendant and asked for a vodka on the rocks. The attendant told her drinks would be there shortly.

"If he was such a jerk, why did you keep his name?"

"Really, Brad? Do you think a reporter who wants to be remembered would have a name like Michelotti? Everyone would spell it wrong, and no one would pronounce it right. So with my former husband's name in hand, I went off to college and became a journalist. I've never looked back since."

"How did you pay for college?" Stokes wanted to get an idea of her finances.

"That's a pretty personal question, Brad. But if you really want to know, I was lucky to have parents who could pay and help me out."

"So they did well with avocados, huh?"

"Yeah, they mostly made avocado oil. So they went from olives to avocados and did quite well. Not every farmer makes their money on cattle. So if you really must know, my family is well off and I've been blessed with the freedom to pursue my dreams. Getting rid of my deadbeat husband was among my better moves."

"Does Chris know you were married once?"

"I've never told him. Why would he have to know that?"

"C'mon, Carla. The two of you are carrying on with one another. You think it's a secret?"

She blushed. "Well, yes. I did. So did Chris. Have you or Georgia said anything to him?"

"It's not our place to do so. But I will tell you this. Georgia and I think the world of Chris. He's the best agent the BAU has, but unfortunately, he thinks too much with the head between his legs. The last girlfriend he had on a case turned out to be a murderer."

She let his crass remark pass as just another inappropriate comment from Stokes and replied, "He told me about her. That's how he got Sully."

"Yeah. Talk about weird. He talks to that damn dog as if it understands."

"So I've seen. So what are you trying to tell me, Brad?"

"Don't play him, Carla. He's important to us, and he could have been booted out of the FBI with the trouble he got himself into in New Orleans. His relationship with you could have the same result if things go wrong."

"Nothing is going to go wrong. I won't hurt Chris, Brad."

The cart arrived, and Lane took two bottles of vodka and a glass of extra ice. Stokes took a beer. The attendant offered them each a bag of mixed nuts. They both turned her down. They handed their credit cards over, since being in coach, drinks weren't free.

"Can I ask you something else, Carla?"

With a sip of her vodka, she responded, "Sure. I can hardly wait."

"Why are you so fascinated with serial killers? I get that you're writing a story about them, but that's all you seem to want to talk about. You drove me crazy with all the questions while we were on the road." He insisted to Evans that there was more to Lane than she let on. She had some other motive to be digging so deep.

"Reporters ask questions, Brad. It's no more than that, really. I find the idea of killing an innocent person you don't know very curious. That's why I'm writing this story."

Stokes leaned toward her to shorten the distance to her seat. "Curious, Carla? Really? Don't you think collecting dead bodies is more than a curiosity?"

Taken aback by Stokes' tone, Lane took a good drag on her vodka before replying, "I meant no disrespect, Brad. Just that it's something I'd like to understand. And Chris better understands how serial killers think than anyone."

Stokes leaned back in his seat, still looking at Lane. "Has he told you how serial killers actually get sexual gratification from murdering their victims? Some even have sex with them before they kill them. Or worse, even after they're dead." Stokes honestly believed that if he could get a rise out of Lane, he'd have enough evidence to talk to DiMeglio about her.

"He did, Brad," she replied, becoming visibly uncomfortable, pouring the second bottle of vodka into her glass. "But Chris doesn't think Dick falls into that category." She was clearly ill at ease with the direction Stokes's questions were taking them. She pressed the call button to ask a flight attendant for another vodka.

Stokes noticed her shift in demeanor, but her breathing didn't change. Despite wanting another drink, she remained calm, as most serial killers do when confronted or under pressure. Or she remained calm because she had nothing to hide.

"Perhaps Dick is different, Carla. But you think that the killer's vendetta against lawyers must get him—*or her*—off in some manner. No?" He looked for a reaction. None.

The flight attendant came down the aisle with the dinner cart. Their choices were some sort of chicken in a sauce, white fish, or pasta. They both chose the pasta. Lane asked for another vodka. Stokes ordered a bourbon. He was done with his questioning and needed something stronger than a beer to help him sleep on the long flight.

"Brad, why are you asking me all these questions?" She poured another vodka into her cup of ice. "I'm just trying to learn as much as possible, so I can write an accurate article. I'm not the one who is supposed to understand the mind of a serial killer. You, Georgia, and Chris are supposed to do that. Not me."

The drinks cart arrived, and the flight attendant again charged their credit cards and gave them both two bottles. He gave Lane some more ice. Stokes said he'd drink his neat.

I might be looking into the mind of one right now, thought Stokes.

He finished his pasta and bourbons in silence, put on the eye covers provided by the airline, and fell asleep. Lane looked behind her and saw that both Evans and DiMeglio were asleep. She watched movies and stayed awake for most of the flight. The flight attendant kept her supplied with vodka. Six hours into the flight, she finally fell asleep, awakening with a splitting headache two hours later as they began their descent into Rome.

CHAPTER FORTY-ONE

Finto Benvenuto

Leonardo da Vinci–Fiumicino Airport, Rome, Italy

Jeff Mangold, the FBI's foreign attaché in Rome, met DiMeglio and the team after it took them an hour to clear immigration and customs at Leonardo da Vinci–Fiumicino Airport. It was 11:30 a.m. DiMeglio's EA recommended taking the later flight out of JFK, so they arrived late in the morning. That way, she told him, their rooms were more likely to be ready when they got to the hotel.

Mangold and DiMeglio trained together as new agents in Quantico. Each was happy to have a reunion. Mangold, however, differed from DiMeglio. While both were dedicated agents, Mangold liked to mix up his job with some good times. That got him in trouble for partying on duty in the States. After too many reprimands, he ended up in Rome, looking after FBI interests in Italy. There wasn't much going on, and he had a lot of free time on his hands. He was looking forward to working on a real case with DiMeglio.

"Chris, good to see you again, and welcome to Italy! How was the flight?"

"It's good to see you too, Jeff. It's been too long. The flight was fine, but this airport is one of the worst I've ever seen.

Total chaos getting through immigration and customs. No organization at all."

"Like I said, welcome to Italy. If you're looking for organization, you came to the wrong place. You need to go to Germany for that. In Italy, it's all about *la dolce vita!*"

"So I hear. No doubt that pleases you!" joked DiMeglio. "I'm looking forward to seeing how hard you work. You know what they say about the foreign offices," DiMeglio said with a grin. "So, how's your Italian?"

"I'm learning. I can order a drink in a bar and ask a woman what brings her there. That works for me."

"Jeff, you'll never change. That's gonna get you in trouble again."

"True, but I hear you're not in line to get the award for good behavior." Stokes could see DiMeglio bristle from the comment.

"Well, he just got the Medal for Meritorious Achievement," interjected Stokes. "Do you have one of those?"

"OK, Brad. Let it go. Jeff, let me introduce you to my team."

After introductions and explaining why his team included a reporter, the five took their bags and walked out of the crowded terminal. DiMeglio felt safe but noticed Mangold's constant head movement checking his perimeters. Clearly, he was uncomfortable in a crowded place. DiMeglio lightly nudged him, as if to say "what's up?"

"Chris, the truth is we're not welcome here. Most of what we do is work with local police and federal authorities—the

Carabinieri. They lead the game and rarely listen to us. But they can be excellent partners when we need them, as long as you choose the ones you can trust. And from what I've read in the briefs, it sounds like you'll need them."

"We will."

The five stood at the curb outside arrivals, waiting for their ride. Evans, Stokes, and Lane were all looking at their phones, catching up on texts and emails.

"Do you have the right one to trust, as you put it? That doesn't sound very promising."

"Nobody's perfect, Chris. Especially here in Italy. Angelo Torchia is an Inspector in the Italian Carabinieri. *Ispettore* in Italian. He's the liaison assigned to work with you. He's a good cop. Hard-nosed. He sometimes goes off book, but they all do here."

"My kind of guy," observed Stokes. Stokes was not one to go "off the book" very often, but he kept it under cover when he did. He looked forward to meeting Torchia.

"And Chris," Mangold whispered to DiMeglio, "don't tell Torchia or any other cop that you've got a reporter with you. They hate publicity and the prospect that some of their shit is exposed. If you want their cooperation, keep your reporter friend in your pocket." DiMeglio nodded and made a mental note to tell the team.

An unmarked black Fiat E-Ulysse SUV pulled up to the curb. Even with luggage, it sat eight comfortably.

"Nice wheels, Jeff," remarked Stokes.

"We have two of them. It's electric and goes like a bat out of hell. We use them for dignitaries." Then, with a smile, Mangold added, "But since none are in town, I grabbed one for you!" Mangold took the front passenger seat next to the driver. DiMeglio and Lane took the second row, leaving the middle seat empty. Evans and Stokes took the third row.

After the driver put everyone's luggage in the trunk and pulled away, Mangold began, "Let's make a quick stop at the office so you all can sign some paperwork. Your rooms aren't ready anyway, so let's make good use of the time. Then we'll swing by the Carabinieri station to check out weapons. Except you, of course, Ms. Lane. The Carabinieri won't allow civilians to have weapons. So we'll let you wait in the car. Then we'll drop you all off at your hotel. You'll need some rest. How's that sound for a plan?"

"We could use a shower. That includes you, too, Brad," observed Evans with a smile. Stokes didn't smile back.

Jeff continued. "We have our first meeting with Torchia and his Carabinieri buddies at eight tomorrow morning. So you'll have the balance of today to relax and get a good night's sleep."

"Thanks, Jeff. But I don't need to rest, and we can skip the weapons. I can't imagine needing one here. I'm also the only one who needs to meet Torchia for now. The team can stay back at the hotel. I'll have plenty of time to introduce Torchia to them later." He was still working on explaining why Lane was on his team.

"Passing on the weapons is your choice, Chris. But I doubt the killer you're looking for shares your affection for nonviolence. Not in Italy. Remember, you're in a country where almost 10 percent of the population is allegedly involved in organized crime. Rubbing one another out is a parlor game around here, and they don't like the police. At least the honest cops. It's sometimes hard to tell them apart. And us? They don't particularly like us. We're foreigners intruding on their turf. So I always carry."

"We'll be fine, Jeff."

"As long as we don't drive!" remarked Lane. The traffic was heavy, and all the drivers seemed to disregard any semblance of laws or courtesy. Worse, the moped riders wove in and out of traffic with abandon. It was nerve-racking for anyone not familiar with it. But such behavior was the norm for Rome's drivers.

"Yeah. That's why we hire local guys like Raphael to be our drivers," replied Mangold. Raphael cut off a taxi and swerved around a couple of mopeds. "And they obviously don't teach defensive driving here! You know what you're doing, Raphael, right?"

"*Nessun problema, Signor Mangold. Non ho mai avuto un incidente. Record di guida perfetto!*" he replied, never taking his eyes off the road. Lane decided just to close hers.

"If you don't mind, Chief, I'd rather have a weapon. Is that OK with you?" Stokes asked.

"Me, too," added Evans.

A smiling Mangold concluded, "So it looks like you'll have protection anyway, Chris."

Shaking his head, DiMeglio responded, "All I need is a shower and a shave. And a decent meal. It was a long flight, and the Bureau's policy that we must suffer riding in coach didn't make it any easier."

"Yeah, being a field agent can be a bitch too, and coach is no better," smiled Mangold. In truth, his posting in Rome was about as cushy a job in the FBI as one could hope to get. But it was not a career builder. Mangold had burned too many bridges to be on the rise.

"And once we're settled, I want to meet with Anthony Barlow," DiMeglio said.

"No problem, Chris. We're one step ahead of you. He's meeting us tomorrow for lunch at his hotel. You'll all be staying there as well, by the way. Somehow, even though it's way over Bureau expense limits, your EA got you in. So you better be nice to her."

"Believe me, Jeff, Chris knows where his bread is buttered and treats Lenoir like the goddess she is. He'll be sure to thank her when we get back, assuming we survive driving through the traffic," commented Evans.

"*Nessun problema, signorina. Record perfetto!*" said Raphael as he veered around yet another moped and exchanged middle-finger salutes.

"Jeff, let's make it a private room for lunch. I don't want to be seen. Not yet, at least."

CHAPTER FORTY-TWO

A Reluctant Victim

Uliveto Restaurant, Cavalieri Hotel, Rome, Italy

Over sandwiches in a private room at the hotel's Uliveto restaurant, DiMeglio and Mangold laid out the plan to Anthony Barlow. Stokes also attended, declining an invitation from Evans and Lane to do some sightseeing before the hard work began.

"Let me get this straight," Barlow growled. "The FBI wants to use me as bait to catch a serial killer?"

"That's about right," responded DiMeglio.

"And you expect me to believe I can be protected by the very police force I see foul up cases time and time again? Just like you did in Miami."

"Mr. Barlow, we deeply regret what happened in Miami," responded DiMeglio.

"Justin Haynes was a friend of mine, agent. Shit, he and I played a round of golf at Trump's Doral course the day before he was killed. I got to see it all. The smoke bombs and the rest. While you were supposedly protecting us, Justin was murdered. Nice job. I'm not sure I need that kind of protection."

"Actually," interjected Stokes, "you were on our list in

Miami as a potential target. So your reputation precedes you in Rome."

Anthony Barlow was in Italy's posh Rome Cavalieri Hotel to speak at a conference of European criminal lawyers. Marie Létisse had been a featured speaker at past events. Home of La Pergola, the only three-star Michelin restaurant in the city and owned by Hilton, it was a far cry from the highway hotels Hilton had in the United States. The Cavalieri was part of Hilton's Waldorf Astoria collection and sat on a hill overlooking the center of Rome. Amid a residential setting of wealthy homes, it was quiet and secluded. Its rooms were rich in Italian design, and the spa required reservations weeks in advance.

Barlow's visit was his way of writing off a vacation under the guise of a business trip. His practice was in Wilmington, North Carolina, where he opened his firm twenty-five years earlier after a ten-year stint as a prosecutor. That was a typical career path for defense attorneys. Like most in his league, he was comfortable in front of a camera and presented himself confidently, even when he represented a defendant as guilty as sin. His reputation in North Carolina was impeccable despite the times he skirted around the truth in trials. As a Black lawyer, he was very effective in the South, where Blacks and other minorities often dominated juries. Whites could usually avoid service through favors. But he also appealed to white jurors, often struck by his gentlemanly looks and demeanor. Barlow was not a man who would take orders.

The speaking engagement was a common scam the IRS virtually never catches. That Barlow was staying in Rome for ten days when he was only speaking on one of them should have been all the tax authorities needed. DiMeglio would have liked to turn Barlow in to the IRS on his return to the States but had better things to do than be drawn into a tax accounting battle.

"Mr. Barlow, we're admittedly playing a long shot. We believe that the man who killed Haynes is in Rome. His name is Antonio Ricci. But we cannot find him. If he is the serial killer targeting defense attorneys, a prospect like you in his own backyard may be too much for him to resist. If someone else is directing him, the lure is the same. We also received a series of texts from someone claiming to either be the killer or who is intimately involved. We have credible evidence that Rome is a likely location for an attack. And your successful track record matches the likes of those who were previously murdered. We want to use you as bait to drag Ricci out into the open and take him into custody." DiMeglio saw no reason to be subtle.

"And how do you plan to do that, agent?"

"We already have the room next to your suite and the one immediately across the hall. We're leaving the other room adjoining yours empty and available in case his plans include using that room to stage his attack. He did that in Miami and Los Angeles."

"What happened to the attendees already in the rooms

you now have? I heard the hotel sold out weeks ago."

"We made them offers they couldn't refuse," interjected Stokes.

"I guess you're the comedian in the group, huh?" observed Barlow.

"That's enough, Brad. If you agree to cooperate, Mr. Barlow," DiMeglio continued, "your room will be wired and have cameras installed except in the bedroom and bathroom. The empty adjoining room is not wired in case the killer scans it. We don't want to be discovered. We will monitor the hallway and your room from both of our rooms."

"Thanks for my privacy," Barlow sarcastically responded. "Exactly how much is this costing the American taxpayer, agent?"

"A lot," responded DiMeglio. "And not with your help, I suspect, since I'm sure you're writing off this entire trip." He couldn't resist the comment and the chance to rub the lawyer's scam in his face. Barlow's shrug made it clear he didn't give a damn what DiMeglio thought.

"We'll have agents in the lobby as well," continued Mangold. "We know what Ricci looks like, although we suspect he'll be disguised. He might get by us. But he won't get to you. We'll arrest him before you're in any danger."

"As if you can guarantee that? I don't think so. And if I don't want to cooperate?"

"Then you're on your own, and we hope you enjoy your vacation and time in Rome," concluded DiMeglio.

CHAPTER FORTY-THREE

Setting the Trap

Room 420, Cavalieri Hotel, Rome, Italy

Barlow was reluctant but knew he had no choice. Still, as he saw it, if he helped catch his friend's killer, all the better for his public relations image and marketing.

Evans and Lane shared a twin deluxe room on the hotel's first floor, the cheapest room available. DiMeglio and Stokes shared a similar room, although DiMeglio spent most nights in room 420 across from Barlow. He couldn't stand the snoring by Stokes. Unfortunately, the arrangement didn't allow trysts with Lane. Such luxuries, like private accommodations, in the already stretched FBI budget were out of the question.

After three days, with the adjoining room still empty and no sign of Ricci, DiMeglio wondered if Kinston's fear of a wild goose chase might be correct. His team was exhausted. And exhaustion causes mistakes. That's something DiMeglio could not afford.

Barlow, despite being asked to stay out of too many public places, made a point of networking every afternoon at the Tiepolo lobby bar and going out into the city with different people each evening. It was as if he wanted to challenge DiMeglio and his team. The conference was all about business for Barlow, and networking was his priority. A potential death threat did not slow him down. After all, the FBI had his back. For two nights, DiMeglio had him followed when he left the hotel to go to clubs but stopped when he took a gamble that murdering Barlow out in the open was not the killer's pattern. To the killer, it was personal, and death had to be administered one on one.

At 10:00 on the third evening and the last day of the conference, DiMeglio and Mangold drew the overnight shift in the room across the hall from Barlow. It was a rainy night, so most of those attending the conference remained in the hotel, partying in the lobby bar and under the outside canopied area overlooking the pool.

By now, the room was a mess. They kept the Do Not Disturb sign on the door, so the service staff never saw their equipment. Same for the adjoining room next to Barlow. Four days of ordering room service and skipping any cleaning took its toll.

"I'm not sure, Jeff," DiMeglio confided to Mangold. "Three days and nothing. Tomorrow is the last day of the conference. This may be another fuckin' dead end. Dick may be baiting us yet again. Just like he did in Miami."

"But he killed someone in Miami. And waited for the last day to do so. You've made a career of going with your gut and getting it right. Maybe Dick is just being careful.

He could even be attending and impersonating a lawyer. He could be right under our nose."

"I doubt it. No one in this group behaves like a loner. Everyone seems to know one another. I've learned from this case that even at the international level, criminal defense attorneys seem to be in a club of mutual admiration."

"Yeah. Like flies to shit."

"So no, Dick is not here."

DiMeglio's phone rang. It was Evans, sitting in the lobby, observing people mingling in the bar. It surprised her to see someone checking in at such a late hour. Per the plan, the desk clerk texted Evans from his check-in computer, knowing he had to stall anyone who asked for either of the adjoining rooms.

"Chris, a woman is checking in and wants one of the two adjoining rooms."

"A woman?!"

"Yeah, my reaction too. And the one at the counter sure as hell doesn't look like a killer. She can't be over 110 pounds. She's about five foot four, maybe five, brunette. Good looking. As instructed, I assume the clerk is holding her at the reception desk with an excuse that he needs to see if the room she wants is ready. She appears to be getting impatient. What do you want to do?"

A woman!? thought DiMeglio. If Evans was right, the woman she described couldn't possibly be the killer. The nature of the murders needed more strength than she likely had. Or so he thought. DiMeglio concluded she was not acting alone, recalling the reports from Los Angeles on the mystery woman who met Paul Stafford at the bar.

"Let her have the room. I suspect she'll have a friend arrive soon enough."

"OK. It's your game, Chris." She texted the clerk to give her the room.

"Well, well, it appears the plot has thickened," observed Mangold, eyes glued to the monitors, waiting for the woman to appear in the hallway.

They picked her up again on the cameras when she left the elevator on the room's floor. Evans' description was a good one. She was very attractive. Was the plan a honeypot with her seducing Barlow? Was she going to poison him? But she didn't need an adjoining room to carry out such a plan. Why then did she insist on the room? DiMeglio made a mental note to check on adjoining room reservations at the murder scene in Los Angeles. While it was a dead end for any evidence in Miami, the possibility of using adjoining rooms in three hotels was a pattern. And finding patterns was how DiMeglio profiled serial killers.

The two noticed she scanned the hallway before entering the room to make sure no one saw her. They also noted that she was alone in the elevator and pulled her own luggage, so no bellhop accompanied her to the room.

She entered, the door closed, and the waiting game began.

Barlow came upstairs just at 11:00 p.m. and went into his room. The cameras had seen nothing suspicious in the hallway or his room since the woman had checked in. Just a bellman delivering ice to Barlow's room as he did nightly. Everything appeared secure. DiMeglio decided not to tell Barlow about the woman, not wanting to spook him. He was the bait.

Like he did every night, Barlow put ice in a glass, poured himself some bourbon, and relaxed on the suite's couch to watch television and check his phone. He often got calls from the States since the time zones made it six to nine hours earlier there, depending on where in the States the caller was located. However, Barlow kept any verbal conversations brief since the FBI was listening. If he had something more to say, he texted, and, of course, he used Signal. DiMeglio regretted that the cameras in the room didn't make out his phone's screen. He made a mental note to install some overhead cameras next time. An hour later, Barlow made his way to the bedroom, bourbon in hand, and closed the door behind him.

True to DiMeglio's suspicion, at 1:30 a.m., a visitor arrived, quietly knocking on the door. The man was about six foot two, tall and muscular like an athlete. His hair was jet black and reached his shoulders. DiMeglio immediately recognized it as a wig. If you saw him in the street, you'd probably peg him as a rock star or a drug dealer. He had no luggage and was dressed in jeans, a dark shirt, a leather jacket, and a baseball cap pulled down to hide most of his face. He bore some resemblance to Ricci, but it was hard to be sure. The woman greeted him at the door without saying a word.

"Georgia, get Carla and come upstairs and go to the adjoining room. Brad is there now. Leave one of the local police in the lobby." His next call was to Torchia, asking him to join them in the room. DiMeglio wanted eyes on him, so he did nothing that might disrupt the plan.

Torchia arrived in minutes. He had been at the bar. A knock on the door interrupted them. It was Lane.

"I told Georgia and Brad I wanted to be with you. So they sent me over."

That did not please DiMeglio. It was not what he ordered Evans to do. He'd have a word with her later. Now across from Barlow's room, the four watched the drama unfold on the monitors and wondered what, if anything, would happen next.

DiMeglio turned to Torchia. "Angelo, if something is going down tonight, it will happen soon. I've got my team in the room next to Barlow's. If we smell anything going on, they'll enter from the side, and we'll go in through the front door. I don't want anyone to be hurt. Got it?"

"*Ti capisco,*" he responded.

"This is exciting," offered Lane. "My first bust!"

It was now 2:00 a.m. Barlow was in bed, presumably fast asleep. The four of them sat and watched the monitors, waiting to see Barlow's killer arrive.

CHAPTER FORTY-FOUR

Catching the Prey

Room 423, Cavalieri Hotel, Rome, Italy

At 2:30 a.m., with Barlow fast asleep, DiMeglio, Mangold, Lane, and Torchia watched as the adjoining door from the woman's room opened into Barlow's suite. She and the man entered. He was no longer wearing his wig. Evans and Stokes saw the same thing on their monitors. The woman was carrying a small bag. DiMeglio finally got a good view of the man's face. It was Ricci. That's all he needed. Waiting any longer might put Barlow in danger.

"Go," he texted to Evans and Stokes as he, Mangold, and Torchia entered the hallway, Lane following behind. DiMeglio told her to stay in the hallway until they secured the room.

When the two FBI agents entered from the adjoining room, guns drawn and loud orders to freeze and raise their hands, the woman and Ricci were stunned in disbelief. They did as ordered.

DiMeglio, Mangold, and Torchia arrived seconds later. "Bind 'em," ordered DiMeglio.

Stokes holstered his weapon and put plastic ties on Ricci's hands, now behind his back. Evans did the same with the woman. Torchia and Mangold kept their guns trained on the suspects. Once they were bound, DiMeglio motioned for them to sit on the couch. Torchia and Mangold holstered their weapons.

Barlow came into the room in his bathrobe, groggy and confused. "Son of a bitch, you caught them!" he exclaimed with a genuine sense of relief. "Thank you."

"Go get cleaned up and dressed," ordered DiMeglio. Barlow dutifully obeyed and retreated to the bedroom, closing the door behind him.

To make sure no one tripped up on technicalities and opened up defenses exploited by lawyers like Barlow, DiMeglio turned to Torchia. "Give them their rights." This arrest had to be by the book.

Torchia dropped a piece of paper on each of their laps. It included the mandatory warnings detained suspects are entitled to in Italy:

> *You are being temporarily detained. You have the right to:*
> - *Appoint a lawyer and receive legal aid if you can't afford a lawyer.*
> - *Get information regarding the charges raised.*
> - *Have an interpreter.*
> - *Remain silent.*
> - *Access documents on which the temporary detention is based.*

- *Inform the consular authorities, as well as your family members.*
- *Access emergency medical help.*
- *Be brought before the judicial authority for the confirmation of the arrest or temporary detention within 96 hours.*
- *Appear before a court to challenge the legality of the temporary detention order.*

Unlike in the United States, nothing needs to be said verbally. In Italy, even if a suspect demands a lawyer, questioning can continue and, more important, they can be detained for ninety-six hours before they can fully exercise their rights. That's four days without a lawyer, plenty of time to sweat out confessions, even from those who are innocent. In that window of opportunity, Italian authorities are unrestrained in asking questions, often to the point of coercing what they want. That part is not unlike the methods used in the U.S. if a person does not demand a lawyer. DiMeglio understood the rules and intended to take advantage of them.

"Angelo, tell them both to stand up."

"*In piedi. Entrambi!*"

Ricci and the woman calmly rose, looking at DiMeglio with disdain. "*Non ho niente da dire.*"

"He says he has nothing to say," responded Torchia.

DiMeglio turned to Ricci. "Do you speak English?"

"*Come ho detto, non ho niente da dire,*" he responded.

"Again. He says he has nothing to say."

"And you?" DiMeglio asked, looking at the woman.

She said nothing.

"Yeah, I figured as much." DiMeglio started patting Ricci down, retrieving his wallet, phone, some keys, and a small notepad. Evans did the same with the woman but found nothing.

"Tell them to sit down." They both did so before Torchia translated the order.

DiMeglio opened the small bag the woman carried into the room. It was filled with latex gloves, rags, and a couple of bottles labeled as cleaning fluid. They'd later be tested. One turned out to be ammonia, and the other ether.

"So you're the one who cleans up the mess?" DiMeglio asked the woman. She did not respond.

"Or she's the mystery woman from the Los Angeles hotel where Stafford jumped," offered Evans.

The woman stirred in her seat. That confirmed her role as far as DiMeglio was concerned. They were a pair. That also explained why everything was wiped clean. DiMeglio concluded Ricci was the killer, and the woman was his house-keeping accomplice and, sometimes, bait for his targets.

DiMeglio, sitting in the chair across from the couch, turned to Ricci. "Well, let's at least see what we have here," placing the phone, keys, wallet, and notepad on the coffee table between them.

DiMeglio took the ID from the wallet and continued,

"Antonio Ricci. I have to say I'm surprised someone like you would carry their actual identification." No reaction from Ricci. DiMeglio emptied the rest of the wallet on the coffee table. Some Euros and a few credit cards, all in Ricci's name. Another surprise for DiMeglio. This guy was hiding in plain sight.

Reaching for the notepad, he watched for a reaction from Ricci but saw none. Once he opened the notepad, he understood. It was empty.

Next, he tried the phone. It was locked. On a hunch, he held it in front of Ricci's face. Sure enough, facial recognition was enabled and unlocked the phone. A bit of good luck. That got a reaction from Ricci. He was not happy.

"Why don't we start with your recent calls?"

Ricci stared at DiMeglio with disdain.

While a few recent calls had names associated with them, most were only numbers or showed the caller was "unknown." As DiMeglio scrolled through the list, he saw that some repeated themselves several times. There were no active voicemails, but in the deleted voicemails, there were many.

He looked at Ricci. "Well, won't you look at that, Antonio? You forgot to delete the voicemails after you listened to them. A pretty common mistake, my friend. People don't really know how to cover their tracks, particularly stupid ones like you. I'll bet your voicemails tell quite a story. But we'll get to that later."

Ricci's breathing was getting deeper. His face reddened. He was obviously upset. The woman looked confused.

DiMeglio moved to the texts. But the messages were in Italian, as he suspected he'd find with the voicemails. So he'd have to get someone to translate them. That would take time.

He opened the Signal app. He found the list that Signal provides to users identifying who among their contacts also uses Signal. That gave DiMeglio a lead to possible co-conspirators. He turned the phone to face Ricci so he could see the list.

"Looks like you have a lot of friends on Signal, Antonio. Care to tell us who they are?"

"*Vaffanculo*," he responded.

"You don't need to translate," DiMeglio noted to Torchia. Even in Italian, he knew "fuck you."

DiMeglio turned to Evans. "Get the ID and notepad to Quantico ASAP. See if they can make something of them. Leave the phone here. But copy down all his contacts on Signal first and send that list to Quantico as well. We need to run them down one by one. If anyone else is involved, they're likely on that list."

"That is our evidence, agent," objected Torchia. "You will not take it anywhere."

DiMeglio remembered he had the same jurisdiction problem in Miami. But unlike Miami, where he could trust the medical examiner, he recalled Mangold's admonition about trusting anyone, including Torchia.

Seeing DiMeglio's reaction, Mangold interceded, "And I suppose you have the same level of experts we do in Quantico to analyze the evidence, Inspector? So why not take advantage of our expertise? We want to help." While his distrust of the Italian police could not have been more ingrained, he knew being confrontational with him would lead to more problems than solutions.

"We are more than competent enough to handle the evidence, Agent Mangold," replied Torchia calmly. This wasn't the first time he'd disagreed with foreign law enforcement. "Let me remind you that you are in my country to assist us. We are not here to take orders from you. I cannot allow you to remove evidence of a crime committed here in Roma. If we need your help, we'll ask."

DiMeglio was resigned that neither he nor Mangold could win the argument. "Fine, Angelo. Just understand that I will hold you personally responsible if anything—and I mean anything—happens to the evidence."

"*Ti capisco.* Of course I understand," responded Torchia derisively. "I would make that same threat to you."

"Guys, we're on the same team. Let's keep that in mind. I'm sure no one wants to make mistakes," interjected Mangold, wanting both DiMeglio and Torchia to tone down the rhetoric.

Ignoring Mangold's comment, Torchia continued, "Now, I'll also take our two suspects in for further questioning, Agent DiMeglio."

"As the saying goes, they have ways to make them talk," offered Stokes.

"That's enough, Brad," interjected Evans.

"Angelo, for now, I'd like them to stay with us," DiMeglio responded, hearing Mangold's message and changing the tone of his voice. "I have an idea I'd like to play out." He turned to Evans. "Georgia, move them to the room across the hall. Take Carla with you. Make sure no one is in the hallway when you do so, and make sure the Do Not Disturb sign is on the door. Don't let anyone but the three of us in. We won't have much time before others who may be involved find out Ricci and his girlfriend failed."

Torchia did not object, deciding to let DiMeglio play out his plan.

"Angelo, let's bait a trap and see if Dick calls. If no call comes in, then Ricci and his girlfriend may be our serial killers. But, on the other hand, if Dick does call, we know they are dupes in a much bigger game. Then you can have them and do whatever it is you do to suspects. But for now, I ask for your cooperation."

Torchia could have overruled DiMeglio since Ricci and the woman were apprehended on Italian soil, but he obviously appreciated the new tone of respect and decided to allow DiMeglio to play out his game. He also liked the strategy. Torchia knew he'd eventually get to be alone with the prisoners. Losing a day of interrogation wouldn't matter. Not with his techniques.

"OK, Agent DiMeglio, let's play out your game. But one day only. In twenty-four hours, they're mine. *Comprendere*?"

"*Comprendiamo*," responded Mangold.

CHAPTER FORTY-FIVE

My Obituary

Room 423, Cavalieri Hotel, Rome, Italy

Barlow returned from the bedroom, ready to return to the conference's closing day as if it was just another day. "So you got the killers, huh?" The sun was shining after a day of rain. The guests were waking up. "Another notch in your belt, agent? And where are they?" he asked.

"Never mind where they are. The two are not talking, and my gut tells me others are involved. This is an international operation, and I doubt a two-bit hood from Italy and his girlfriend could pull this off. And we still need to figure out how the lawyers they want to kill are picked."

"Really? That seems obvious to me," said Barlow, sitting on the sofa across from DiMeglio. Torchia was on the balcony having a cigarette, and Stokes was at the desk, checking his phone for email. Mangold was making a pot of coffee in the kitchenette. "It's a vendetta, pure and simple," Barlow continued. "He wants to change the system. Get rid of the lawyers and put suspects behind bars, regardless of their innocence. It's his own personal Inquisition. He wants lawyers to answer for the clients they keep free. It couldn't be more obvious than that."

"Like clients who then kill again, Mr. Barlow?" asked Mangold. "That might be a damn good reason for a vendetta."

Barlow ignored him. "I suggest you question the dead lawyers' clients or the families of their victims, Agent DiMeglio." With a look toward Mangold, he added, "And tell your lackey to dispense with criticism of my profession. We're the only ones who keep folks like him and you from trampling constitutional rights."

"We've already started with those connections, Mr. Barlow," responded DiMeglio, ignoring his comment directed to Mangold. "And sometimes what may seem obvious can lead to a false path. Either way, I assure you we don't need your advice on investigating a case."

"Yeah, just like your job performance in Miami. Why don't you also tell Justin's widow how good you are?"

DiMeglio let the comment go by without comment, ending the conversation. The tension in the air was palpable. Mangold returned and handed DiMeglio a cup of coffee, sitting in the chair next to him. He didn't offer Barlow a cup. Stokes, in the kitchen, poured himself a cup and returned to the desk and his phone. Torchia, in from the balcony, made himself busy brewing an espresso. He wanted nothing to do with the pot Mangold made. As far as he was concerned, drip coffee wasn't coffee at all.

Barlow broke the silence. "So, when are you going to go public about their attempt to kill me? If you don't, I will. No more lawyers just doing their job should die."

"Whether or when we go public, Mr. Barlow, is our decision. And if you do so on your own, you'll be interfering with an ongoing investigation. That will put you behind bars. So I respectfully suggest you keep quiet, just like the next dead lawyer we're going to make others believe is you."

"Huh? What does that mean?"

"We need others, if there are any, to believe the duo succeeded. So why don't you write your obituary that we'll all get to see in the news?"

"Seriously? That's about as amateur a move as I've ever heard. You've been watching too many episodes of *CSI.*"

"Maybe. But we need time to sift through the evidence we now have. And your death will give us a day or two. I suggest you start writing, Mr. Barlow."

"But we don't even know how they were going to kill me! Nothing I've seen gives us a clue about their plans. So how am I supposed to describe my murder?"

"Mr. Barlow, you're a criminal defense attorney. I have no doubt your imagination can come up with a plausible lie. After all, that's what you do for a living. So sit down and start writing. You're not going anywhere."

"You can't keep me here unless, of course, you're arresting me. And since you have no grounds to do so, I'm free to leave."

Mangold jumped in again. "Really? Consider yourself a material witness that we can't let go because we fear for your safety," suggested Mangold.

"That's bullshit, and that also isn't grounds to keep me. I know what you can and cannot do to me, Agent DiMeglio."

Torchia, espresso in hand, joined in, standing behind DiMeglio to make eye contact with Barlow.

"But you don't know what we can do, Mr. Barlow. You're in Italy now. Not the United States. And you go by our rules. We can detain you for days if we want to. And we don't need a reason, particularly with a foreigner."

"Yeah, I bet you can. That must really help with your tourism, Inspector."

"OK. OK. Let's all calm down," interjected DiMeglio. "In the end, we're on the same side. So yes, Mr. Barlow, you are free to leave and say whatever you want. But if others are involved, and they don't get word you're dead, sooner or later, they'll come looking for you. So if you want to be safe, you'll do as I ask. At least for now. I can't force you to, Mr. Barlow, but if you go, I promise you we will lift any protection and leave you to the wolves."

"You might just be comfortable with them, Barlow," suggested Stokes from the desk. "Do you like to be a sheep in wolf's clothing?"

"It's a wolf in sheep's clothing, you putz," responded Barlow.

"Nah. I'd say you're more a sheep than a wolf. I got it right."

"Myth has it Romulus and Remus, newborn wolves, were

abandoned on the banks of the Tiber River when Roma was founded," added Torchia. "Roma was named after Romulus."

"Nice to see you know your history, Inspector," responded Barlow, still seething.

"It is part of our education. It is from those wolves that Romans gain their bravery and fierceness in battle."

"And maybe their disregard for individual rights?" Barlow rhetorically asked. "This is ludicrous!"

"Ludicrous, Mr. Barlow?" responded Torchia. "Just give me a reason to show you how being a wolf is how we deal with sheep like you."

DiMeglio interjected, "Enough, already. Let's move on. And we can dispense with the historical allegories."

Back to Barlow, "If you want to stake your life on your beliefs and leave, that's fine. We'd all like to go home on the next flight. You'd then be in the excellent hands of Inspector Torchia and his cadre of Italian Carabinieri. Would you prefer that, or do you want to follow my suggestions?" DiMeglio could see Torchia bristle at the insult.

"Fine," responded Barlow. He walked to the dining area table, opened his laptop, and began typing.

CHAPTER FORTY-SIX

Dead on Arrival

Room 423, Hotel, Rome, Italy

The early wires broke the news that a lawyer was found dead in his room at the Cavalieri Hotel, reporting that the cause of death was under investigation but that there appeared to be no signs of struggle or suspicious foul play. His name was being withheld until they could notify his relatives. The rumors didn't take long to circulate at the hotel, as guests surmised that the dead lawyer must be Barlow, the irrepressible attendee who missed that morning's closing session.

As the morning progressed and they waited for a call from Dick, DiMeglio asked Torchia to scroll through the Signal messages on Ricci's phone and look for some pattern that would connect him to anyone else who might be in on the scheme. Torchia said they were mostly small talk. But quite a few were to and from a contact named "Sasha." Torchia noted they had an apparent romantic overtone. DiMeglio concluded Sasha was not only his accomplice but also his girlfriend.

"Do you see any pattern around the dates of the past murders?"

"It's hard to tell," replied Torchia. "I'm not that familiar with all the dates, but his messages with Sasha are shorter and more impersonal around some dates I do remember."

"Unfortunately, that's nothing more than circumstantial," noted Stokes.

"Perhaps that's true in your country, agent. But we convict on a lot less here in Italy."

"I'm not surprised," Stokes replied. "But all we have on Ricci and Sasha is breaking and entering. They weren't carrying any weapons. Had they succeeded, this would have been their first murder in Italy. So we don't even have enough for mere suspicion."

"Murder was their intent, Brad," added Mangold.

"Yeah," replied Stokes. "But this time, they didn't succeed. So as of now, they're just a couple of bungling burglars. If we have any chance of breaking this case, we need to connect them to the murders in the States. Then we can charge them and get them extradited."

"Agent Stokes, if you want to keep them in custody, I can charge them with whatever you'd like. I can make sure it's days before they see a lawyer. That is not a problem. But first, I have a talk with them."

"That will all come soon enough, Angelo," DiMeglio said. He couldn't help but wonder how much easier his job would be if due process were abandoned and he had free rein like Torchia to suspend an individual's rights for four days. Recalling Mangold's warning, he wasn't sure Torchia would tell him what the texts actually said if it suited Torchia's purposes to use them against the suspects or to advance his career. So he decided to have Mangold assign someone at the FBI offices in Rome to translate the messages and put them into a format he could sort and better analyze. Perhaps he'd see patterns that could be added to the board.

CHAPTER FORTY-SEVEN

Speaking Up

Room 420, Cavalieri Hotel, Rome, Italy

Evans and Lane sat silently with Ricci and the woman, now presumed to be Sasha. Lane was typing on her laptop. Evans, bored, was scrolling through news and other social media sites on her phone. The two exchanged small talk but nothing about the case.

After two hours, Ricci broke the silence, "*Voglio un avvocato.*"

"Sorry, I don't speak Italian," responded Evans. "Can you say it in English?" Of course she was lying and knew "*avvocato*" meant lawyer and assumed he wanted one. She and Stokes found it humorous that the word "lawyer" in Italian was so close to "avocado," a fruit they both hated. As Stokes liked to put it, lawyers, like avocados, are ugly, thick-skinned on the outside, slimy on the inside, with nothing but a giant pit at their core.

"He says he wants a lawyer," translated Lane.

"That's right, I want a lawyer," Ricci repeated in English.

"Oh, so you speak English, Mr. Ricci! Why didn't you say so earlier?! It would have made getting to know you so much easier." Evans delighted in tormenting suspects, particularly this one.

"I want a lawyer, too," added Sasha, taking Ricci's lead.

"Wow!" responded Evans. "You speak English, too? How convenient! Now we can all have a friendly conversation."

"Get us lawyers," Ricci demanded.

"As much as I'd love to grant your wish, I'm afraid I'm not acquainted with any lawyers in Rome. Are you, Carla?"

"Sorry. No."

"Damn. So I guess the two of you are out of luck. But when I get a chance, I'll see if I can find someone who knows a lawyer. That may take some time. Why don't we talk while we're waiting and get to know one another better? Won't that be nice?"

"Fuck you."

"And *vaffanculo*, too, Antonio," responded Lane. Evans didn't ask for a translation. She got the gist of the message.

"Suit yourself, Antonio," responded Evans as she looked at her phone. She had a text from DiMeglio.

She turned to Lane. "Chris says we need to turn these two over to Torchia. It seems he won't wait longer because the security in the hotel isn't adequate. Maybe he'll get a call from Dick before then. But Angelo is taking custody." She noticed Ricci raise his head, not hiding his concern.

Sensing Ricci's discomfort, Evans asked, "Who is Dick, Antonio?"

Sasha looked at him as if to say, "Tell them."

"I have to go to the bathroom," he responded. "And I'm hungry." Evans typed on her phone back to DiMeglio. Within a minute, Stokes appeared.

"You have to go to the bathroom, huh? OK. Stand up and follow me." He led him into the bathroom, leaving the door open. Evans stood behind him, gun drawn and trained on Ricci. After cutting off his zip cord, Stokes gave him a shove toward the toilet.

"Can I have some privacy?" Ricci asked.

"Just do your business and put your hands behind your back when you're done."

"Do anything funny, Antonio, and I promise you I'll blow your head off," added Evans. He did as he was told. Stokes zip-tied his hands again, and Ricci returned to the couch.

"How about you?" Evans asked Sasha.

"No. I'm just hungry."

"I'll give you some water. You'll have to ask Inspector Torchia for anything more than that."

Stokes left and returned to Barlow's room. Six hours later, the Carabinieri arrived and took Ricci and Sasha into custody. The team called it a night. Barlow agreed to stay in his room until DiMeglio gave him the green light to leave, the reality finally sinking in that his life might depend on cooperating with the Bureau.

CHAPTER FORTY-EIGHT

Pulling Strings

Room 420, Hotel Cavalieri, Rome, Italy

Mangold called DiMeglio early the following day, waking him from sleep.

"C'mon, old boy, time to rise and shine! I've been in the office for more than an hour. Jet lag still getting to you?"

"I guess. It's been a long few days."

"I hear you. What exactly are you looking for, Chris? If you want all these texts translated and put into a spreadsheet, it will take weeks. By then, any element of surprise you have in faking Barlow's death will be gone, and you'll have another lawyer or two on your dead man's list."

A soft knock on the door interrupted the conversation.

"Hold on. Someone's at the door."

Through the peephole, DiMeglio could see Lane carrying two coffees and some pastries on a tray. He opened the door, put a finger to his lips, and held up his phone to ensure she said nothing. Lane understood and put the tray on the table. He locked the door.

"Sorry, it was housekeeping. I told them to come back later. This room is a mess."

Mangold chuckled. "I bet it is."

"Anyway, my ploy may already have taken too long," said DiMeglio. "There's been no word from Dick, and he usually likes to brag right after a kill."

Lane handed DiMeglio his double macchiato. She took a sip of her cappuccino and a bite of a croissant. She offered one to DiMeglio, but he waved her off.

"So we may have all we'll get with using Ricci and Sasha as bait," he continued. "Regardless, I want to see if there are any patterns around the dates of the other murders and whether there are suspicious messages from someone other than Ricci or Sasha near those dates. I don't want to let others destroy evidence or cut off connections once they find out my ploy failed. I'm trying to figure out if Ricci or Sasha is Dick or if we're dealing with another person."

"What does your gut tell you?"

"That Ricci and Sasha are puppets. Someone else is pulling the strings. While the two are pros, they're just not smart enough to undertake a global killing spree. They obviously don't have the personal finances to pull it off. They're just thugs. There's something more to this vendetta that motivates Dick. I doubt Ricci or Sasha gives a damn. All they want is to get paid."

"OK, I'll send my assistant Elena over as soon as she gets in. She can take a real look rather than just translate and transcribe the texts. I trust her. So can you. Let's see if she can find something, and then you can take it from there."

"Can't you send an agent with some training? How is your assistant qualified?"

"Because she's Italian, Chris. And if I've learned anything while I've been here, it's that Italians understand Italians. We don't. Just trust me. She'll be better than any agent. I know what I'm doing."

"Quickly, please," replied DiMeglio, hanging up.

Lane came over to him. "I've missed you."

He pulled her to him. "I've missed you, too." They fell back on the couch, the Do Not Disturb sign still on the door.

CHAPTER FORTY-NINE

Codebreaker

Room 420, Cavalieri Hotel, Rome, Italy

Two hours had passed since Lane left the room. Mangold's assistant arrived at DiMeglio's room and was reviewing the texts on Ricci's phone, sitting in a chair. DiMeglio was at the desk on a Tauria call with a techie named Rob Polk, stationed in Quantico. Tauria was the latest in secure calling options. It was virtually impossible to hack with its 256-bit AES encryption. Polk insisted he and DiMeglio use Tauria when he heard that Dick the Butcher was technically savvy. DiMeglio didn't care what app they used. He just wanted answers.

"We have his phone," he told Polk. "There are a bunch of contacts and text exchanges with people around the times of the murders. One or more of them may be Dick the Butcher or someone involved with the killer. I don't think this is an enterprise by just the two suspects we have in custody."

"OK," Polk replied. "There are some things we can try, even with Signal. Whether any of them will work depends upon how sharp the other user is on blocking tracking methods available on the app. It sounds like this Ricci character is not the sharpest tool in the shed. So we might get lucky. What kind of phone is it?"

"An iPhone," replied DiMeglio.

"Shit. That makes this harder. iPhones are tougher to crack than Androids. And Apple closely guards its encryption algorithms, rarely cooperating with us. But they're not foolproof. What kind of phone do you use?"

"An iPhone. Why?"

"Because that will make it easier for me to give you instructions, since you already use the same phone."

DiMeglio snapped his fingers at Mangold's assistant, motioning for her to give him the phone.

"OK. Now what do I do?"

"Go to the home screen and open the Signal app. Its icon should be on the face of the phone. You may have to scroll through pages depending upon how many apps he has."

"Already there. Like I told you, we scrolled through it earlier."

"Right. Sorry. OK, on the app, click the owner's picture in the upper left-hand corner. It may just be a letter in a circle."

"Done."

Mangold's assistant started making herself an espresso, pointing to her cup, silently asking DiMeglio if he'd like one. He gave her a thumbs up.

"Open the settings," continued Polk. "Go to 'privacy' and then to 'advanced' at the bottom of the page."

"Hold on. One step at a time." Polk repeated his instructions, slowly, one step at a time.

"OK, I'm there." It was the first time DiMeglio ever looked beyond his phone's general settings, let alone the settings for Signal. He made a mental note to do so on his own phone to be certain he had the maximum protection available.

He accepted the espresso and waited for the next instruction.

"Is the feature labeled 'always relay calls' checked? If the button is on the right and the left side is green, that means it's active."

"It's green."

"Deactivate it by moving the switch to the left."

Polk explained that the option, if active, masks a user's location during calls by routing the calls through random servers around the globe that prevent tracking. But because it makes verbal calls less dependable with annoying dropped conversations, many experienced Signal users turn the relay option off. Doing so now won't help with the past calls, but Polk explained it might open a chance to geolocate a caller if DiMeglio can get someone to talk to him on the phone.

DiMeglio was not optimistic about that. "That's not likely to happen," he said. "Whoever Dick is, he has refused to communicate on anything other than text."

"That's savvy. He knows that tracking oral conversations is easier. So deactivating relay calls is likely a dead end but keep it off, anyway. Now close Signal and go back to the home screen."

"Done." The assistant was looking at her own phone, listening intently and mimicking what DiMeglio was doing.

"Click on the settings icon for the phone. Now click on his name. It appears at the top. Then click on 'Phone Numbers.' What do you see?"

"His name, some email addresses, and a phone number."

"Just one number?"

"Yes."

"OK, another dead end. Let's try something different. Go back to the home screen, scroll through the apps, and see if you can find one called 'Phoner,' 'Burner,' or 'Hush.' They're the most popular burner number providers."

"Burner phone number providers? Are you serious?"

"Agent DiMeglio, you have no idea what's out there for the taking."

"Found it. Phoner."

The assistant came over to watch DiMeglio. She did not have the app on her phone.

"Open it, and who is that with you walking in the background?"

"Don't worry. She's fine. Works for the Bureau here in Rome."

"Alright. What do you see on the screen after opening Phoner?"

"A label that says, 'Phone Numbers' and some sort of balance information with credits and stuff."

"Good. That's the home page. That tells us nothing we need to know, but it's where we have to start. Click on the message icon on the bottom."

"OK. It shows a telephone number and a bunch of messages."

"Does the telephone number have a pull-down menu?"

DiMeglio clicked on the number.

"Wow. It's a list of a bunch of other numbers."

"The list is the telephone numbers he's used as burner phones."

The assistant and DiMeglio looked at one another in disbelief. "Are you saying you can turn an iPhone into a burner phone by getting other numbers?"

"Exactly, agent. You should know that."

He didn't. And he didn't appreciate the insult. DiMeglio really hated techies.

"Open any of the numbers while you're in messages. Do it with a few of them," instructed Polk.

DiMeglio browsed through four of them. "Holy shit. There's a long string of texts under each one of them."

"Somewhere in all those strings is your killer, Agent DiMeglio. You're wasting your time looking at the texts on the number that came with the phone. I doubt the killer would be stupid enough to use it. I suspect he used a host of burner numbers to better shield his identity. It's those you want to translate."

"But why so many numbers?"

"My guess is he goes to a new number after each murder, trying to cut off or complicate the connections."

"So if this phone has a long list of numbers, does that mean Ricci is Dick? Wouldn't he be the one who used the numbers?"

"Sure, he used them, but he's not necessarily the killer. It's more likely the killer let him get the numbers. That made him even more difficult to track down. If he and the actual killer are smart, they keep changing numbers and using some way to tell one another when a new number is being used. They might do that in an old-fashioned way. By calling one another on a landline or from a phone booth. That way, it can't be traced. That's why, in the old days, the mob only used phone booths."

"But why not just buy a bunch of burner phones and throw them away when you're done with them?" asked the assistant.

"Good question. The only answer I can give you is they're either lazy or can't get enough of them. Or they might just be enamored with the technology of turning an iPhone into a burner. One downfall of technology addicts is they constantly adopt the newest tech without thinking old school might still be better."

DiMeglio kept scrolling through the numbers. "Damn, there are dozens of numbers and hundreds of texts. This will take forever, and we don't have that kind of time."

"Dozens? Wow. It makes me wonder how many lawyers this guy's killed. If he's switching numbers after each murder, Dick the Butcher is one badass serial killer."

"Yeah. That's what I'm worried about. I can't help but wonder if he's been on this vendetta for years."

"OK. Let's see if we can make your job a little easier. Start with the most recently used number. That might include texts for the latest plan to murder someone. But Signal is as tough as it comes, and we have little chance of hacking into his iPhone in any quick order. Even if you figure out the last number used, it's a burner, and combined with Signal is probably a dead end. Regardless, start sending texts to the contacts listed with the burner numbers, one at a time. If you're lucky, you'll get a response that helps you find who you're looking for."

"Again, I don't have the time for that."

"I can start doing it," offered the assistant.

"Sorry. That's the best I can suggest. And it's actually worse, Agent DiMeglio."

Frustrated, DiMeglio sarcastically responded, "Please stop keeping me in suspense."

"If Dick is very savvy, as you suspect he is, he changes physical phones as well, so the connection to an app like

Phoner is more difficult to cross reference, particularly with Signal. It sounds like this guy didn't do that, but you may have even more phones and more numbers to check."

"So we're screwed, and you're effectively telling me this phone is a worthless piece of shit."

"Maybe. But right now, it's the only piece of shit you have. So start texting while I think about other ways to fool someone on Signal."

DiMeglio hated the way techies loved to string him along to show their superior intellect. He didn't have the time for such games and replied, now derisively, "Why don't you enlighten me with something I can use rather than give me tutorials on how Signal is impossible to break?"

"Then bring me over there and let me work with the locals. That's the only way you'll be assured they don't fuck up the evidence."

Polk was on a plane that afternoon.

CHAPTER FIFTY

Lady Macbeth

Poolside, Cavalieri Hotel, Rome, Italy

Ricci's phone pinged at 4:00 p.m. when DiMeglio and Evans were sitting by the pool getting some fresh air. The caller ID was masked. DiMeglio grabbed his pad.

"Really, Agent DiMeglio?" the text began, "Did you think I'd fall for some amateur trick and tell you where I am? How many of those numbers did you use for texts, foolishly thinking I'd fall for it?"

But you just did. And it's time to push.

"I have a question," DiMeglio typed. He hesitated a bit, wondering if he could force Dick to confirm or disclose something important. He'd done his homework and Dick the Butcher was not the only murderer in Shakespeare. He took a breath and asked, "Should I actually call you Lady Macbeth? That seems more fitting. She used others to commit murders she couldn't. Isn't that a more appropriate name for you?"

He waited for a few seconds to let that sink in.

"Let me read a short piece from *Macbeth*," continued DiMeglio. "It's from Act I, Scene 5, 'Come, you spirits that tend on mortal thoughts, unsex me here, and fill me from the crown to the toe top-full of direst cruelty.' That was Lady Macbeth's revelation that she wanted to be a man. Is that why you want to be called Dick?"

Silence.

He pushed for more. "And you're in Italy, aren't you?" knowing it was speculation but supported by some evidence and his assumptions.

Bubbles. Then none. Then bubbles again.

"Kudos, Agent DiMeglio. But I think you've known I am a woman for some time. But I still prefer Dick." The quick admission surprised DiMeglio. It was the first mistake she'd made. Now DiMeglio was ready to bait the trap.

"And I suspect every text you've sent uses a burner phone to keep us at bay. You must have quite a collection. Am I right?"

He paused, hoping for a sign that she was going to reply. Seeing nothing, he typed, "And we'll learn more once Ricci and his girlfriend talk."

The bubbles returned.

"Oh, my, how your imagination runs, Agent DiMeglio. So full of questions and conclusions. Such hopes to trick me! Be careful what you assume. But I must compliment you on tracking down Antonio and Sasha. They were such obedient soldiers. And you even saved the life of a lawyer, to boot. Well done. I'll deal with him later. Please let him know."

"Jesus, Chris, what a fucking psychopath!" remarked Evans.

"Show me a serial killer who isn't, Georgia," DiMeglio replied.

With Ricci gone, DiMeglio feared that Dick, aka Lady Macbeth, would go dark like many serial killers do when they fear the police are getting too close. If she went dark, any chance of DiMeglio catching her would be nearly impossible. He needed to keep her active, even if it meant risking another lawyer's life.

"Yes, Antonio and Sasha in custody is a problem," she typed. "Italian police have a way of loosening the tongues of suspects, even if they're innocent."

"Now that your assassins are out of commission, Lady Macbeth, and will soon talk, why don't we stop this cat-and-mouse game? Just come in. You know I'll eventually find you."

"Come in, Agent DiMeglio? Why would I do that? It's more interesting to have you chase me. And frankly, it will take you years to find me. Assuming you ever do. By that time, I can get others to carry out my mission."

"So you don't do any of this yourself, Lady Macbeth, do you?"

"Agent DiMeglio, do not call me Lady Macbeth. I told you I don't like it." He could sense her anger in the text. "We agreed you'd call me Dick when we started talking. He is the character I admire. If you want to continue our conversations, you'll call me what I want to be called."

DiMeglio returned to his question. "So, Dick, you don't do this alone, do you?"

"As for doing all this by myself, Agent DiMeglio, I'm much too old for that. Execution of my plan is a game for the young."

DiMeglio wrote on his pad, <u>older</u>. While getting under her skin could be useful, pushing too far could scare her away. He'd made his point, and it was time to move back to her rules.

"How long have you lived in Italy, Dick?" Another gamble.

"C'mon, Agent DiMeglio, I'm not going to make it easier for you."

He wrote, "<u>Lives in Italy?</u>"

"So you're just the financier of this murderous operation? Is that about right?"

"Let's just call me a facilitator, Agent DiMeglio."

He added, "<u>Money</u>."

"Where will you find your next assassin, Dick?"

"Who says I need to find one, Agent DiMeglio? What makes you think Antonio was my only soldier?"

"Damn, Chris. Could she have a network?" asked Evans. "Were there others working for her who killed the lawyers?"

DiMeglio wrote, <u>Network of assassins</u>.

"We've talked long enough, Agent DiMeglio. I'll call again soon."

"Wait! I'm fascinated that you are a woman. It's very unusual for a woman to be a serial killer. Here's a photo and a link to a post regarding a very famous one. Did you ever read about her?" He attached a link to a photo of Aileen Wuornos, a serial killer sentenced to death for six of the murders she committed.

If Dick opened the link to the photo or the PDF, the metadata returned to his phone would give DiMeglio Dick's IP address and possibly the location of the closest cell tower to Dick's phone or even her phone itself. It was a trick suggested by Polk. But would Dick take the bait?

She didn't open the link or the file. "Yes, I've heard of her. I think Charlize Theron played her in the movie about her life. Pity no one wanted to appreciate how the rapist she killed deserved to die. But as much as you'd like me to, I don't need to open anything."

The ploy didn't work.

"I'm tired, Agent DiMeglio. We'll talk again soon."

"Why don't you leave me with a number where I can call you?"

"C'mon, Agent DiMeglio. I'm not stupid enough to fall for your tricks!"

Yes, you are.

"Then when can I expect to hear from you again?"

"Soon, Agent DiMeglio. We have so much more to talk about."

The seventh session ended, leaving DiMeglio with an ominous feeling that more murders were ahead if she wasn't stopped soon. Murders that needed to happen if he hoped to catch her.

"Chris," Evans said, "I have an idea."

CHAPTER FIFTY-ONE

Bank on It

Room 420, Cavalieri Hotel, Rome, Italy

The team gathered in the room across from Barlow's.

On the speakerphone, Torchia said that the pair were not talking. Yet. "I'm working on them," he reported.

With the conference over, Barlow returned to the States, saying he'd hire his own bodyguards and wanted nothing more to do with the FBI. That was fine with the team, particularly Stokes. DiMeglio warned him that Dick said she'd "deal with him later." But he was arrogant, lacking any sense of appreciation that DiMeglio and his team had saved his life. At least for the time being.

"If she is financing this operation, she's got a lot of money," began Evans. "And she's tech-savvy. So I'll bet she does online banking or at least uses online resources to monitor her investments. And even more so if she's older."

"So what's your point?" asked DiMeglio.

"Let's canvas the banks in Italy and see if significant withdrawals were made online around the dates of the murders. There could be a pattern. And patterns are what we want to see. It's another long shot, but they've been working for us so far. Whoever she is, she's had to move a lot of money."

"Do you have any idea how many banks there are in Italy, Georgia?"

"No. But I'll bet we can narrow that down by culling out the smaller ones and then, from the rest, identify which banks wealthy people likely use. My guess is that there's only a handful."

"That's true," offered Torchia over the speaker. "But they are very secretive. We have a long history of protecting wealthy families since the Medici. So they won't easily cooperate."

"Something tells me, Angelo, that you can get over that problem," concluded DiMeglio.

CHAPTER FIFTY-TWO

Fact Patterns

Poolside, Cavalieri Hotel, Rome, Italy

Dick texted the following day while DiMeglio was enjoying a macchiato on the patio overlooking the pool. It gave him time to be alone in the morning to think. DiMeglio was not interested in small talk when he got the text from Dick and immediately made that clear.

"Dick, let's stop the charade. You live in Italy, don't you?" It was yet another guess, but a calculated one DiMeglio wanted to confirm. If he were wrong, Dick would deny it.

She didn't respond. But she didn't deny it, either.

"I still don't understand why you're killing innocent lawyers. So let's have an honest conversation."

"Agent DiMeglio, why are you so angry?"

Bubbles as Dick typed some more.

"But to be honest," she continued, "I don't care if you are angry with me. Italy is a big place. Lots of cities. Lots of places for me to live. Even assuming you might narrow it down to a province or even a city, that will take you years. In the meantime, more lawyers will die the deaths they deserve."

He wrote <u>Italy!</u> on his notepad.

"I wouldn't count on that, Dick."

"So, Agent DiMeglio, what else has your profiling determined?"

Good, she's curious. Now she might make some more mistakes.

"You're wealthy. Otherwise, you could not hire the killers you use. And you're socially connected. That's no surprise. It comes with your wealth."

"Age?"

"My guess is 60, probably older. Your views on lawyers and obsession with Shakespeare put you in that age range."

"Why older? Maybe I'm younger."

"Young people don't care about lawyers and have never read Shakespeare. They're more interested in posting TikTok videos and reading *Harry Potter*."

"Anything else?"

"Your English is very good for an Italian. But my assumption is that you are either not Italian or were educated in England or the United States. But most likely the States, given the often informal nature of your texts."

"Perceptive, Agent DiMeglio. But I'm not impressed. That sounds like pretty basic stuff."

"Perhaps it is, Dick." But she didn't deny any of it. Each time he added to the board, the more he learned. He recognized he was disclosing more than he usually would with a suspect. Still, he had a growing respect for Dick's intellect and decided disclosure would keep the conversations going, piquing her curiosity to learn more.

"But I will find you, Dick. One step at a time."

"Perhaps, Agent DiMeglio. But until then, one lawyer at a time."

On his notepad, he added, <u>Educated in U.S.</u>, <u>Connected</u>, and <u>Older</u>. More additions and confirmations for the board.

The eighth session ended.

CHAPTER FIFTY-THREE

Nightmares

San Francisco, California

Two days passed before Charlotte Williams, a defense law-yer in San Francisco, was found in an alley off Mission Street, raped and bludgeoned to death. As DiMeglio and Lane logged on to the San Francisco Medical Examiner's website to virtually inspect the body and autopsy results, the gruesome nature of the murder struck him as out of character until he read the police report. Stokes, Evans, and Mangold opted out of viewing the body. "Been there, done that," said Stokes.

The two were in Barlow's room. DiMeglio convinced the hotel to let him keep it as an active crime scene.

"Williams defended a serial killer named Charles Stimpson," DiMeglio told Lane. "I remember that one well. It wasn't my case, but he was someone you'd never forget. They don't get much worse than that sick bastard. He was accused of killing prostitutes after he raped them. Allegedly, he killed over thirty in and around San Francisco. When he was done with them, he'd leave their bludgeoned bodies in alleys, cut up and bleeding, so the rats could have a meal on the remains. He enjoyed taking bodily parts as souvenirs and leaving notes that sometimes had the victim's last words."

"It looks like Dick wanted Ms. Williams to experience the same death. Pretty sick."

"Yeah, pretty sick."

They virtually inspected the body on the computer. DiMeglio used the trackpad and keyboard arrows to move and zoom in on the camera when he wanted a closer look. The only thing lacking in reviewing an autopsy virtually was the smell of formaldehyde and embalming agents used to preserve the bodies. And the oppressive atmosphere of death. At first, Lane was repulsed, but after a few minutes, she couldn't take her eyes off the horror. She'd seen crime scene photos but never anything as graphic as the brutality Williams endured.

It was clear the killer did a thorough job of brutalizing his victim. Williams' face was unrecognizable, with a crushed skull and grossly swollen eyes. Most of her hair was gone, presumably torn from her head. The top and bottom rows of her teeth were crushed, and her jaw shattered. She was covered with bruises and had been violently raped. As was Stimpson's trademark, her nipples had been cut off and taken from the scene. Her remains were grotesque, indicating a horrifying death. Despite it being on a computer screen, for DiMeglio and Lane, it was all too real. It made DiMeglio sick to his stomach. He was amazed that

Lane stayed through it all despite her ashen look when the sheet was lifted from the body and the camera zoomed in. Their review took over an hour. After that ordeal, the two decided they needed a drink and headed for the hotel bar. They remained silent in the elevator, processing the horror they'd just seen.

Once at the bar with drinks ordered, Lane started the conversation. She ordered a double vodka martini with three olives. Belvedere. DiMeglio ordered an Irish Manhattan. Lane told the bartender to make his a double, too.

"Chris, how the fuck did Williams get Stimpson off?"

"I don't recall the details, but I do remember the outrage in the press when he was released. I assume it was on some technicality. Or he got out on bail. I don't remember any trial."

"Jesus, this stuff is really sick. How do you deal with what we just saw? I assume you've seen a lot, but until today I couldn't imagine how horrible it was. Doesn't it get to you?"

"Over time, Carla, you learn to block it out. But you never get over it. I have occasional nightmares. There's just so much you can erase from your mind. I'm sorry you had to see that today."

"That's OK, Chris. To tell you the truth, I found it fascinating. It was horrible, for sure. But something about it made me want to understand how someone like Stimpson thinks. How can anyone be so brutal?"

DiMeglio excused himself and went to the bathroom,

where he vomited, a response that was not uncommon for him when he saw the work of the more sadistic serial killers. When he returned, the two sat in silence for several minutes before ordering another round for the two of them. Then, breaking the silence, he said, "He sure was one of the sicker ones, Carla. Even I can't handle some of it. When I excused myself to go to the bathroom, it wasn't to take a piss. I got sick to my stomach. That's a common reaction I get after seeing the bodies or some of the physical evidence. I try to convince myself that it's just part of the job. But it never gets easy."

She put her hand on the back of his. "It has to take its toll eventually, doesn't it?"

"I'll let you know when that happens." He took a good draw, finishing his first Manhattan as the second round arrived.

"Whatever happened to Stimpson, Chris? Did he kill again?"

"No one knows. The FBI never investigated his string of murders. It was all a San Francisco operation. But after he was released, the murders stopped, and he never reappeared. At least not in San Francisco. There were reports of similar murders in Oregon and Iowa, but no one put them together. Others speculated he was dead. But for all we know, Stimpson is still out there roaming the streets, planning to kill more prostitutes."

"Like other serial killers still on the street?"

"We can't catch them all. Especially the ones who kill people no one else cares about. Like prostitutes. When they go missing, no one gives a shit."

The bartender brought them another round. "This one's on me," he said. He could tell they needed it.

"At least you care," Lane said. "Even for defense attorneys who get bastards like Stimpson off. I agree those charges deserve a defense and no one, particularly the lawyers who defend them, deserve to die by the act of some psychopath like Dick, but at times I do find it hard to have sympathy for some of them."

DiMeglio, looking at his glass, said, "And what makes them worse than anyone else just trying to do their job? There are countless people we don't like. That doesn't mean they deserve to die. Not even whores and defense lawyers."

He took another sip of his drink, looking down at the glass in contemplation.

"Chris, is it time to tell the public about the possibility of a serial killer out there murdering criminal defense attorneys? It broke my heart when I saw what he did to Charlotte Williams. You need to let people know. They have the right to take precautions."

"You're right. It may be time. Let me think about it."

Lane waved to the bartender for the check.

"Let's take our drinks to the room. Let me take your mind off what we had to look at today."

CHAPTER FIFTY-FOUR

Pictures

Room 423, Cavalieri Hotel, Rome, Italy

The phone call from Polk came in as DiMeglio sat on the room's balcony, enjoying lunch and the view. Though DiMeglio knew he'd get tough questions when he filed the team's expenses, he was enjoying his time with Lane. And neither Evans nor Stokes objected.

"I may have something for you, Agent DiMeglio."

It had been a week since Barlow left. DiMeglio feared he'd soon have to call it quits and return to the States. There was little reason to chase windmills, something he could leave to Mangold and Torchia. And his EA told him the Bureau brass were balking at the costs. Polk had been working with the local crime lab, trying to hack into Ricci's phone, all to no avail. Dick the Butcher knew what she was doing. Even if one or more of the calls logged into Ricci's phone were from the killer, there was no way to trace it. Ricci and Sasha never talked and now had lawyered up. It was one dead end after another.

"I'll take whatever you've got."

As DiMeglio listened to Polk's idea, Lane joined him on the balcony, gently massaging his shoulders as he talked. He put Polk on the speaker, letting him know Lane was there.

"First, we looked at the significant location folder on his phone. iPhones keep track of where you've been. It's buried deep in the systems folder so few people even know how to find it."

"Can you get to your point? I'm growing tired of the tutorials."

"OK, sorry. It doesn't matter since he turned it off, but it does show he was pretty savvy, so we tried something different that even fewer users know about."

"Please spare the suspense."

"Ricci had quite a few photos on his phone," Polk continued. "Anyone with a phone today is obsessed with taking photos. He had over a thousand. So I reverse searched them on Google."

"Reverse searched?"

Lane kissed DiMeglio on the neck and sat down to have lunch.

"Yeah, it's something most people don't know, including criminals who use Signal. Signal strips metadata from photos sent through it. So there's no information stored in the photo."

"Can you say that in English for me?"

"Sure. When you take a photo with your phone, the camera automatically saves the date, time of day, exposure used, and the picture's location. It's all hidden in the background unless you know how to see it. And most people don't know and they don't care. They never look. That's why so few people know about it."

"OK, so how does Signal come into this?" He was getting frustrated with the nerdy language.

"The guys who invented Signal knew about the metadata. So they programmed Signal to strip it from any photos, making them untraceable. Dead ends."

"Hold on, you're telling me photos have their metadata removed when sent via Signal. So, wasn't the data missing in the photos on his phone?"

"Very good, agent. You're learning. Yes, the metadata is removed from any photos he received via Signal. He probably got a lot of the photos as an attachment in a Signal message and saved them. He may have even stripped the data from other photos he took, thinking that would make them untraceable. My bet is it was a combination of both, and this putz thought he was safekeeping all the photos."

"Once again, you're more frustrating than informative. You said you might have something for me. Stop wasting my time if it's just to tell me you've found another dead end."

"Humor me, Agent DiMeglio. I assume you're at or already on your computer. If not, log on and tell me when you're online and have access to your email."

"Hold on. I'm eating lunch." He motioned for Lane to get the laptop.

A minute later, he was logged on.

"OK. I'm online." Lane was watching over his shoulder.

"I'm sending you a photo," instructed Polk. "One that is stripped of all metadata, just like you'd get in a Signal message. Tell me when you get it."

It popped into his inbox almost immediately.

"Got it."

"Open the email, but do not open the attached photo."

"Got it. Now what?"

"Open Google. Click on 'Images.'"

"Done."

"On the right side of the search bar is an icon of a camera. Click on it."

Lane pointed to it, although DiMeglio already saw it and clicked.

"OK. Now I see a box telling me to drag or copy a photo into it."

"Right. Now drag the photo directly from the email into the box."

Instantly, Google showed the attachment and dozens of other photos identical or similar to it.

"What am I looking at?"

"Agent DiMeglio, when we did that with Ricci's photos, the overwhelming majority are pictures of places in Tuscany. That pattern repeats itself time and time again. He's from Rome. He doesn't own any property in Tuscany. And no relatives there either, as far as we can tell. His girlfriend, Sasha, isn't from Tuscany. So why so many pictures from Tuscany? Either he has a lot of business there or is a tourist obsessed with photographing locations in Tuscany. Somehow, I doubt he's a tourist, and he has no known business interests there, but I bet he knows Dick the Butcher. Perhaps that's a stretch, but the coincidence of an assassin visiting the same area so often when he has no ties there makes that stretch logical. So that left me with one plausible conclusion. Dick the Butcher lives in Tuscany."

"Wow. Sorry I insulted you earlier."

"That's OK. We're used to it. But I have more."

"You live to string me along, don't you?"

"Yep. You have all the fun out in the field. We at the lab sit in stuffy, closed rooms with white walls. We never get to see the road. So this trip is special for me. But that doesn't mean I'm not going to make you earn it."

"Yeah, I heard. Your lab's motto is 'Make 'em earn what we learn.' Touché to you. Now spill it."

"Thousands of photos were generated when we reverse-searched all the ones on his phone. It would have taken us forever to cull through them for some common threads that narrowed the search. So we developed a new algorithm. It took us a few days to perfect it. But now we have it. Are you ready for the results?"

"I can't wait."

"Your killer is somewhere in the Chianti hills outside of Florence—or more properly, Firenze, the name Italians use for the city. In Siena, Firenze, or somewhere in between. The algorithm pinpointed it by unique aspects surrounding the area, including rivers, types of trees, roads, buildings, towns, and more. In fact, one road appears in an inordinate number of his pictures. SR222—the Chiantigiana road. It winds south from Firenze to Siena. Locals tell me it's the most scenic drive in Tuscany. Dick the Butcher lives on or near that road."

"How certain are you?"

"Not 100 percent, but close."

"And how far is it from Firenze to Siena?"

"About seventy kilometers. That's just over forty miles."

Lane sat down, looking at DiMeglio as if she'd just received her first Christmas gift. They'd finally gotten the break they needed.

"But there's even more, agent. I've asked Quantico to send over a Stingray. Once I get it and set it up, we can all go to Firenze and begin the search. It should help us zero in. We're close, Agent DiMeglio."

"Stingray?" asked Lane.

"I thought the Bureau no longer used the Stingray," added DiMeglio.

"Sort of," replied Polk. "Officially, we don't use 'em. The one we use is a new generation. Top secret. We have a special contract with L3Harris Technologies in Florida, the manufacturer. We don't want the public to know about it. You can thank me later if this works."

"I'll do a lot more than that!"

DiMeglio's EA made travel plans to move the team to

Firenze. On receiving DiMeglio's update, Kinston remained doubtful but agreed to support the plan once Frattarola reminded him that if the team was homing in on the serial killer, the positive spin they'd get in the press once she'd been apprehended was well worth the investment.

CHAPTER FIFTY-FIVE

Firenze

Hotel Nuova Italia, Firenze, Italy

Two days before the team departed for Firenze, the *Washington Gazette* ran an article written by Lane and approved by DiMeglio on the investigation and the possibility that a serial killer was hunting defense lawyers. She did not name those who may have been victims and wrote that it was too early in the investigation to confirm the connections to a single killer. Another reporter's name, not hers, appeared on the byline. DiMeglio didn't want reporters to track her down and possibly discover she was in Italy. Her article mentioned the killer's penchant for quoting Shakespeare, but it did not disclose "Dick the Butcher" or the twist on suicides. DiMeglio agreed to let it run only because he appreciated Lane's desire to warn the public. He did not want any facts of the investigation revealed.

A frenzy of responses from international print and broadcast media followed. State bar associations speculated on who was murdered, irresponsibly releasing a long list of lawyers who died under suspicious circumstances. When asked to comment, the press office of the FBI issued the standard statement that it does not comment on active investigations. DiMeglio ignored any inquiries to him. Some media outlets reached out to Lane, remembering her interview with DiMeglio on *60 Minutes*. At DiMeglio's instructions, she did not make herself available.

"Let the *Gazette* respond to inquiries. We've fed the story enough," said DiMeglio. "We need to find the killer."

"Chris," suggested Lane, "I think that's a bit naïve. The *Gazette* reporter does not have the answers. So not giving information to them will create issues and increase the curiosity from the press. Let me talk to them."

"Carla," interjected Stokes, "remember you have a nondisclosure agreement and if Chris doesn't want you talking to them, then you don't."

"I want our team members and whereabouts to stay confidential," DiMeglio added. "That's why we told both Kramer and Barlow if they said anything, they'd face possible charges of interfering with an active investigation. While they both knew such a threat was hollow, they agreed to comply. We don't need to have the investigation made more difficult. Police departments in Los Angeles, Chicago, New Orleans, and Paris were also told not to comment. So far, they're complying. I need you to as well."

Lane sighed, knowing there was no purpose in continuing the argument.

Once in Firenze, the team checked into the Hotel Nuova Italia, close to the train station and within walking distance to the city's center. The Nuova Italia was not as posh as the

Hotel Cavalieri; this was no longer a stakeout to protect a potential victim, so the team was back on the FBI budget plan. At under €200 per night, it cost a fraction of the Cavalieri, but provided what they needed. Everyone had their own room. A separate room worked as an office, complete with a Do Not Disturb sign hanging from the door and instructions to the management that the room was not to be serviced. Breakfast was free. Stokes especially liked that. The hotel was known for its service as well. So given some places they stayed on other assignments, the team was happy.

The only people outside the team who were aware of their move to Firenze were Mangold and Torchia. DiMeglio stressed the need for secrecy and made Torchia promise not to tell anyone else in the Carabinieri.

"Angelo, I need your assurance that you will tell no one and that there will be no leaks. If Dick discovers where we are she may shut down her communications with me."

"You can trust me, Agent. I will tell no one. Unless I have to for your own protection."

DiMeglio took little comfort in Torchia's assurances but had no choice but to trust him.

The plan was to set up surveillance operations in the seven-seater Fiat Freemonts they rented in Firenze. DiMeglio rented three different-colored SUVs from three various local rental car agencies. The cars looked like any other SUV rented by a tourist or owned by a local. He wanted to avoid suspicion, and three cars allowed them to rotate vehicles on the trips. To further minimize the possibility of discovery, they planned to stagger the times they ran the route and occasionally use different side roads.

As further cover, when the team checked out of the hotel in Rome, they booked flights back to the States so Dick would think they were no longer in Italy, hopefully giving her a sense of security. Evans thought the fake return was unnecessary and believed Dick was too smart to fall for it, but DiMeglio insisted they err on the side of caution and cover as many contingencies as possible. If they were getting close, they needed to take every precaution.

The Stingray was no bigger than a toaster, with switches and dials on its face. It looked like an old-style radio and fit comfortably in Polk's lap as he relaxed in the back row of the SUV. There was plenty of legroom.

DiMeglio had never seen the device. He was amazed at how small it was.

Stokes drove, and Evans sat in the front passenger seat. Lane and DiMeglio were in the SUV's second row of seats. Polk was behind them in the third row. A condition of the Bureau releasing the new generation Stingray to DiMeglio was that no local authorities could see it in operation. As far as the FBI was concerned, it didn't exist.

"What does that thing do?" asked Lane.

Polk answered, "It's essentially a device that mimics a cell phone tower. If a Stingray is near a cell phone, it fools the phone into thinking it is a cell tower so the phone routes calls through it. That lets the Stingray operator—that's me—grab information from phones within its coverage area, including location and metadata. While it works even if a phone isn't in active use, we prefer a conversation or text exchange to home in on our target. I'll spare you all the technicalities, but with a connection that lasts, I can pinpoint the exact location of a call source. That's how we can locate the phone and, presumably, the user."

"But I thought Dick the Butcher was too smart for this kind of thing. Wouldn't she just block it?" asked Lane.

"That, Ms. Lane, is why the new Stingray is cloaked in secrecy. In fact, it may be the most protected surveillance device in the world. Blocking it can be done, but that requires a caller to, at the very least, use what's called a VPN, a virtual private network."

Polk then explained that a virtual private network allows a user to access the internet via a public network, like one that might be at a Starbucks. It mimics a phone connected to a private network with all the protections that thwart hackers.

"We think Dick the Butcher is using a public network because she would not want to risk getting identified at her residence or office, even with the blocking technology we assume she has. Instead, she can move around using different public networks and give herself an escape route if needed. Public networks are all over Italy. She might use a VPN, but I think that's unlikely. Most people don't do so and mistakenly believe that Signal has automatically disabled spoofing just like it has stripped metadata. We'll soon see how smart Dick the Butcher really is."

"Indeed," volunteered Stokes, intently staring at Lane in the rearview mirror. "My bet is she's smart, but she's slipping. In the end, they all do." He saw no reaction from her.

They began their surveillance route on the second day in Firenze. As the team wound down SR222 each day, they understood why it was called one of the most beautiful drives in Tuscany. The ride rolled through vineyards filled with grapes and fields filled with olive trees, giving them a sense of true Italy as a primarily rural country. Big cities like Rome, Firenze, and Milan don't reflect Italy's actual lifestyles. One picturesque village after another dotted the roadway with lots of places to stop for the views. Stokes particularly liked the ride with its blind curves. And when Polk told him to take some side roads, he enjoyed it even more. The curvier and narrower, the more Stokes enjoyed it. Evans complained he drove worse than Raphael, Mangold's driver. But no one else wanted to drive. So Stokes, as he got more familiar with the roads going back and forth from Firenze to Siena, became as aggressive a driver as any Italian.

During most of the drives, the team sat silent until Polk instructed Stokes where to drive. On the first few trips, he mapped the route on the machine, noting where the cell towers were and those areas where the signals were weak.

He also made notes on the public Wi-Fi locations along the way. Most cafes and hotels had them.

Polk entertained the team with some history about the Stingray. On the third day, he explained, "The Stingray was first used in 2013 to locate a drug deal going down in a parking lot in Tallahassee. The defense attorney could not understand how the police pinpointed the location of a drug deal when they had no informants. When he asked the prosecutor for information, they refused. A judge then ordered that they disclose the information. The prosecutor folded and cut a deal that allowed the defendants to go free on probation with no time served. Free drug dealers were more important than letting the defense bar on to the fact that police had such a device."

"I guess one could say you wanted to hide how law enforcement invades privacy rights without a search warrant," observed Lane.

"I disagree," Polk said. "I concede that a lot of cases may have been dismissed rather than disclosing that the Stingray was used, but we've also gotten some great intel that we used to find other ways to get the evidence we need without disclosing the use of a Stingray. To this day, the FBI will not officially acknowledge it has any of the devices. But the truth is we use them every day."

"Carla, let me again remind you of your NDA," added Stokes. "You can never mention the Stingray in anything you write. You understand that, right?"

"Yes, Brad, I understand that. To be honest, I bet everyone knows you have them and use them to catch the bad guys. My guess is it's all over the internet. But if you want me to keep your little secret, that's fine. It's not part of my story anyway, although the FBI secretly using surveillance devices is intriguing."

"Intriguing or not, Carla, you can never report on it. You need to clearly understand that," continued Stokes.

"Enough, Brad," interjected DiMeglio. "She gets the message." With the tension in getting so close to their target, he didn't need discord within the team.

"So, what's next?" asked Lane.

Stokes observed from the driver's seat, "We keep driving along this road, hoping Dick contacts Chris, doesn't use a VPN, and still believes in the Tooth Fairy. Then we have a few minutes to grab the data, geolocate the caller, and swoop in with the cavalry."

"Except we're not going to swoop in," cautioned DiMeglio. "We'll identify the caller and determine if their location is temporary. If it is, as we suspect it will be, we'll follow them until we see where they end up. We've got one stab at this, and I want to be certain we've found Dick the Butcher, not some other messenger in her cadre. Once we have that, and after we put the Stingray back in its box, we'll call in the troops."

"The Carabinieri, Chris? Can you trust them?" asked Evans.

"We have no choice, Georgia. This is their country. They have jurisdiction. So if this works, they'll think we're some kind of mystics able to see into the minds of killers. It's critical, however, that we do this by the book."

CHAPTER FIFTY-SIX

Jell-O

Santa Elisabetta, Firenze, Italy

Day after day, Stokes drove the team along the 40-mile road back and forth in a rented SUV.

They'd been in Firenze for six days with no word from Dick. The beautiful countryside along the daily road trips had worn off. Boredom was setting in for the entire team. Seeds of doubt on Polk's speculation that Dick the Butcher was in Tuscany were rising within the team. The only excitement for DiMeglio was the nightly trysts with Lane.

So DiMeglio decided to ignore the FBI's budget and treat the team to dinner at Firenze's Santa Elisabetta, a Michelin two-star restaurant housed in the historical Byzantine Pagliazza Tower, an ancient structure completed in 544 AD. Sitting in the restaurant was like going back in time to the reign of the classic Italian dynasties and the Renaissance.

They were seated at one of the seven tables in the restaurant. After getting cocktails and menus, Lane observed, "All this technology has me confused."

"It has us all confused, Carla," responded Evans. "We always seem to be one step behind the bad guys. The old tools like wiretaps and bugs are fast becoming obsolete.

Instead, we have to work with internet apps intentionally built to prevent surveillance."

"Or Stingrays," commented Stokes.

"The worst offender is Apple," added Polk. "Their obsession with privacy and encryption makes hacking a criminal's communications virtually impossible. They act as if we're the enemy, not the crook."

"And any twelve-year-old knows more about technology than any agent in the Bureau," added Evans. "Brad and I miss the old days."

"Yeah, now we drive around all day," responded Stokes. "Don't get me wrong, I love the drive, but we need some action."

"Guys, can we just enjoy dinner without talking shop?" asked DiMeglio. "We're in a great restaurant in the middle of one of the most historical cities in the world. The Renaissance surrounds us! And you want to talk about technology and bitch about wishing we were still in the past? Even our good friend Shakespeare warned against embracing the past."

"And no doubt you have a quote to share, Chief," offered Stokes.

"Indeed I do. 'To mourn a mischief that is past and gone is the next way to draw mischief on.' *Othello*. Act I, Scene 3."

"Wow! You just pulled that out of the air?"

"I wish I could say I did," responded DiMeglio, turning to Polk, "but the whole old-school crap came up when we first tried to figure out if we could hack Signal. That got me thinking, and I armed myself with the quote. You walked right into it, Brad!"

"And now we're probably going to endure the quote on the office wall!" responded Stokes.

"All I need is the poster!" DiMeglio picked up the menu, while the others chuckled.

"But I'm not totally opposed to dwelling on the past. The menu says this tower was a women's prison in the 12th century. Its name, 'Pagliazza,' comes from the word 'straw,' or 'paglia' in Italian. It means 'beds of the prisoners.' So letting the FBI pay for such a wonderful dinner can't get more appropriate! We should savor that sweet revenge!"

"And I bet Jeff sure as hell expects us to have a good time," laughed Evans. "He had to pull a lot of strings to get us this reservation. So enough with the work bullshit. Let's have a fun night and eat like kings!"

"And queens," added Lane.

Evans suggested they all have the nine-course *Chef Experience* tasting menu, but at nearly €400 per person, DiMeglio vetoed that idea. Even he had to exercise some restraint with the FBI's money. They settled on the five-course *Trace of Innovations* tasting menu for half the price. Except for Stokes. He elected to go à la carte and ordered ravioli. While the others were enjoying prawns, amberjack, stuffed pasta, and turbot, Stokes was eating run-of-the-mill pasta. Halfway through the dinner, the chef brought Stokes a second helping, saying he certainly didn't want Stokes to go hungry. He was getting a kick out of an American like Stokes, stuck in a food rut.

Over three bottles of wine, DiMeglio kept the dinner conversation away from work with comments on the meal, artwork in the restaurant, people they'd met at the various stops they made on the daily route, and the history surrounding Tuscany. It was all pleasant and light until Stokes brought them back to his nostalgia for the past while they waited for dessert.

"Chief, I appreciate the dinner. Sort of. The ravioli was great. And I'm sure you all enjoyed the weird stuff. But even you admit it was a lot easier when we didn't have to deal with all this internet shit."

"C'mon, are we really going to get back to that? We haven't even had dessert," protested Lane.

Supporting Stokes' comments and ignoring Lane's objection, Evans added, "Not to mention all the paranoia over privacy." The wine loosened everyone's tongues.

"Right, Georgia!" replied Stokes, taking the opportunity to reopen the discussion. "Take this Signal and Stingray crap. It's as if anyone can hide in plain sight. Without hackers and sci-fi gadgets, we're virtually helpless."

Polk frowned.

Stokes quickly added, "No offense intended. But I'm not that old, and I can still remember when the only way bad guys could hide was by using random phone booths. Like the scene in *Goodfellas* when the De Niro character calls a friend from a booth outside a diner and finds out his buddy, played by Joe Pesci, has been whacked. That was a great example of the reality of the day. Not only couldn't calls be traced, but we couldn't listen to anything. Now that was real security. If Dick and his crew were really smart, they'd go old school."

"And where, Brad, will they find a phone booth?" asked Lane. "They're just as much a relic as the art in this restaurant. Except we like the art. All the bad guy needs today is a cell phone and an app."

"You have a point, Carla," observed Evans. "I think our job is getting harder as criminals get smarter. Smarter than us."

"Georgia," interjected DiMeglio, "so far, all that technology can't replace our intellect and intuition. They're not smarter than we are. Piece by piece, we still break down criminal enterprises, and we do it every day. Better than anyone, including those criminals you think are so smart."

The server brought dessert before Evans could respond.

"*Mousse al Finocchietto, geletina di Lampone, Lampone giallo e granite di Bergamotto* for everyone," he announced. "Including you," he added with a sly grin as he placed a serving in front of Stokes.

The break let Evans calm down from the comment

DiMeglio made. "OK, let's put this conversation to rest again and enjoy this wonderful dessert. I'm not sure what it is, but it sure looks good."

"Carla, you speak some Italian," interjected Stokes. "What does that translate to?"

"Whipped raspberry gelatin. But a lot better than my mom's Jell-O version. Even you'll enjoy it, Brad!"

CHAPTER FIFTY-SEVEN

Par for the Course

Casentino Abrezzo Golf Club, Poppi, Italy

Two days after the dinner at Santa Elisabetta, Mangold called. DiMeglio was enjoying his afternoon routine at Caffé Paszkowski on the Piazza della Repubblica. He found the spot shortly after they arrived in Firenze. A three-minute walk from the hotel, it was a place where DiMeglio could be alone and find the solitude he needed to think. In addition, for less than €3.00, DiMeglio could get a good macchiato. The café also served pastries and other sweets to accompany the coffee, an indulgence DiMeglio enjoyed. Were it not for Mangold's caller ID, he wouldn't have answered his phone and allowed invasion of his private time.

"How's it going?" asked Mangold.

"It's dead here. Not a single call."

"You still think Rob was right?"

"I do. It makes sense. We just have to be patient."

"So do you think she's on to you being in Firenze and not back in the States?"

"I doubt it. My guess is she's just playing the game. Time is on her side, so she'll be patient. And planning her next murder. So she'll be silent until she thinks our guard is down. That's predictable behavior."

"Or she could check sources to see where you are."

"True, but there's nothing we can do about that. It's her game. We can only play it and hope Kinston does not lose his patience. My biggest fear is he'll call an end to this."

"I understand. Listen, I'd like you to meet someone from Tuscany who might be helpful."

"OK, who?"

"Marchese Giamani de' Conti, one of the last marquis in Tuscany. Of course, titles today are only ceremonial, but those from the old noble families are highly respected and very well-informed. He goes by Gino. But let him give you permission to call him by that name. Otherwise, he's the Marchese. Conti's heritage goes back to the era of the Medici. They ruled Tuscany with an iron fist from the fourteenth to eighteenth centuries. They were also the bankers to the Pope. So they had it all. The Contis were under their thumb but were nonetheless independent and wealthy from wool and sheep. From the 1300s, generations of Contis made uniforms for the Italian and French armies, sometimes even when they were at war. So they know diplomacy."

"Sure. Set it up. Sounds like an interesting guy. The team can do without me for one day. And besides, I could use a break and some fresh air." DiMeglio was bored and needed something to bring some variety to his routine. The excuse to give the team a day off was convenient.

"He is very interesting, Chris, and someone you'll never forget. So how's your golf game?"

"Golf game? It's as bad as ever. What's that got to do with anything?"

"Conti loves to play golf. They say he's more open in conversation while he's playing a round. I'll set up a day for the three of us to play."

Two days later, DiMeglio, Mangold, and Conti were set to tee off at the Casentino Arezzo Golf Club in Poppi, Italy. The two-hour drive for DiMeglio was over the Tuscan hills along curving and narrow roads. He rented a Fiat 500 Cabrio, a small compact that was easy to drive, although fitting into it was tricky for someone as tall as DiMeglio. But he knew that most of the roads barely fit two cars, so oncoming traffic could make your stomach turn. The smaller the car, the better. With a small 61-cubic-inch engine that put out only 69 horsepower and a maximum speed of just over 100mph, it was a far cry from his Dodge Charger back home. But the Italian roads are not built for muscle cars.

Despite the beauty of the countryside, it was not a relaxing drive as it meandered through fields of grapevines and olive trees, one storybook village after another. Regrettably, he'd become numb to the beauty of the countryside after so many drives along the Chiantigiana Road. With a six-speed manual transmission, DiMeglio had to concentrate at every turn. One bad turn, and he could careen down a cliff or hit oncoming traffic head-on. By the time he got to

Poppi for the 10:00 a.m. start, DiMeglio was physically and mentally exhausted. It gave him an appreciation of Stokes' driving skills.

"I hope the rented clubs will work for you, Agent DiMeglio," commented Conti as the threesome approached the first tee.

"Marchese, they're more than fine. And please call me Chris."

"I will. And I'm just Gino. I don't need the trappings of nobility on the golf course. I find golf to be a universal equalizer. The rich and poor, the smart and stupid, or the mean and kind can play well. Or they can stink. Excellence in golf defies hereditary providence."

Conti played a mixed set of Honma Beres graphite irons, Cobra woods, a Majesty Prestigio driver, and a Bettinardi putter, a collection of clubs among the most expensive in the world. His putter alone cost over $400. DiMeglio had never even heard of the driver but imagined that it had to cost more than $1,000. Conti's entire set cost him well into the thousands. And his bag! It was a custom leather bag by Gucci in Italy's red, white, and green colors, with Conti's name embroidered on its side. He was obviously a very serious golfer or someone who liked to flaunt his wealth. Maybe both. Either way, very few players could afford his extravagance.

Mangold was playing a set of Stix, a new up-and-coming brand, purported to be a good buy for the money. His entire set cost him under $1,000. DiMeglio rented a set of

TaylorMade, a middle-market brand. They were fine. His clubs at home were Callaways, which, although higher-end clubs, were a fraction of the cost of Conti's clubs.

Conti looked to be in his late sixties or early seventies, with thick white hair and bright blue eyes. At 6'2" and about 200 pounds, he was in excellent shape and carried his nobility well. He very much looked the role of his royal heritage. The only sign of his age was prominent liver spots on his hands, both of which were the hands of someone who worked hard in tough times. But he was steady as a rock.

Today, they elected to play only nine holes. Conti said he did not have time to play eighteen. He never played eighteen with someone new. Conti had to get to know someone and their game before spending four hours with them. And besides, as he told DiMeglio and Mangold, the course only had thirteen holes. The remaining five were never built when the money ran out.

The first hole was a par three, overlooking a valley dominated by Poppi Castle in the distance.

Conti teed up his ball. DiMeglio was happy to see they were hitting off the yellow tees. They were closer to the hole. The serious players hit off the black tees, adding twenty or more yards to each hole.

"So, Chris, what's your handicap?" asked Conti.

"If I'm being kind to myself, it's about a fifteen." DiMeglio would usually shoot fifteen over par, or an eighty-seven. A good score for a recreational player. On a good day, Mangold's handicap was twenty. DiMeglio knew, however, that most golfers lie about their handicaps and usually shoot worse.

"And what is your handicap, Gino?" asked DiMeglio.

"On a bad day, about a five. But I'm usually under that, particularly on this course."

Shit, I'm going to look like a fool. And this guy is like seventy-five years old!

Conti's swing was perfect, and the ball landed within ten feet of the hole, just what a golfer wants to do, giving him a good shot at par.

Mangold teed up and drove his ball about fifty yards short of the green well to the right but still on the fairway. A decent shot.

DiMeglio gently placed his ball on the tee. He was strangely nervous and intimidated, a feeling he was not used to. A good athlete, he was always up to a competitive challenge. His first shot of the day would establish how he'd do on the course. It had to be on the mark.

His swing was smooth. It felt good. Unfortunately, the ball did not cooperate, and he hooked badly to the left, careening down a hill and effectively out of play. While he could hike down the hill to the ball and try to get it back onto the fairway, it would be a time– and stroke–consuming nightmare.

"Take a breakfast ball, Chris," commented Conti. A do-over. Conti, as the host, was the only one who could make that offer.

With a bad shot out of his system and his nerves calming down, DiMeglio teed up again, took a deep breath, and swung. It was a laser shot to the green that landed a foot closer to the hole than Conti's shot. The three stood in silence, speechless after DiMeglio's first disastrous shot.

"If I were a betting man, Chris," Conti smiled, breaking the silence, "I'd say that first shot of yours was a setup."

"I'm just lucky," responded DiMeglio.

"I bet you are. Why don't we make this interesting and play a skins game? Say €10 a skin? At the end of the game, we can even up with one another. If there is a tie for any hole, the skin carries over to the next one. That work for the two of you?"

DiMeglio knew that if Conti won every hole, which appeared likely, he'd earn nine skins or €90 from them both. So the potential financial hit was low, even for an FBI agent, but he agreed that any wager made the game more interesting.

"Sure," DiMeglio replied, knowing full well he'd owe Conti something by the end of the game. But he was intent on keeping it as low as possible and keep Conti talking. FBI rules prohibited agents from gambling while on duty, but DiMeglio ignored the rule, as he did many times on a golf course. Mangold had no chance of winning a hole and was effectively out €90. He muttered, "I'm just happy we're only playing nine holes."

DiMeglio assumed Mangold would pay Conti at the end

of the game but also knew he'd never see a penny of what Mangold might owe him. That was fine.

Both Conti and DiMeglio parred the first hole. Since no one won the hole, the skin carried over to the next hole, where two skins would go to the winner.

As play continued, the threesome strolled along the course, eschewing golf carts. Conti's condition was excellent, and walking the course seemed effortless to him. Caddies carried their bags.

"Jeff tells me, Chris, that you're hunting down a serial killer in Tuscany."

"Yes, I am, Gino. She's killing criminal defense lawyers."

Conti smiled. "I can't say I blame her. I've certainly had my fill of lawyers. But even the most corrupt among us deserve to live. Right?"

"Right," replied Mangold. "Gino, you've lived in Tuscany for decades. What are your thoughts of a serial killer, let alone a woman serial killer, living in Tuscany?"

Now on the fourth hole, the conversation paused as they approached the green. Conti parred and kept his scratch game going through the first four holes. DiMeglio shot a bogey, one over par, as he did on the second and third holes. Mangold did the same on the second hole, but double-bogeyed the other two. DiMeglio was holding his own, but Mangold had fallen behind. At that point, Conti had all the skins, winning the second through fourth holes. So far, both DiMeglio and Mangold owed Conti €40 through four.

As Conti teed up on the fifth hole, a par four, he pointed in the distance and observed, "Do you see that castle over there? It's the Castello dei Conti Guidi. The Poppi Castle. It was built sometime before 1169. It is now a beautiful museum with a nice café on the property. Within thirty kilometers, you can visit the Castello di Porciano, now a luxury hotel, and in between them are the remains of the Castello di Romena. The Conti Guidi once owned it."

"Part of your family, Gino?" asked DiMeglio.

"No. My surname—Conti—has no connection to the family that owned the castle."

Each had a good drive on the fifth hole and continued their walk as Conti lectured. DiMeglio and Mangold had no idea where he was going with it.

"Italy and Tuscany have a history of violence, revenge, and betrayal. Castles passed hands through battles, many of which were led by the Medici family with the help of a mercenary from Milan named Francesco Sforza. You should visit his castle in Milan. Together, they united Tuscany, ruled the land, and controlled all the castles. They made deals with noble families in Venice, Naples, and throughout Italy. And they made deals with the Pope in Rome. But they kept only those promises that continued to be to their advantage. Otherwise, they broke them, and Sforza and the Medici collected more bodies and property. It is not a part of my heritage for which I am proud. But in that heritage lies a lesson about Tuscany, gentlemen."

Conti chipped onto the green and made his first bogey. DiMeglio managed a par and won his first skin. Mangold double-bogeyed yet again. Conti was clearly unhappy about losing a hole and fell into a mood where talking suddenly stopped. DiMeglio was fearful he'd never learn the lesson, but, as Mangold had instructed him, he remained silent and waited for Conti to renew the conversation. Conti parred and won the sixth hole. DiMeglio did not fare as well, with a double bogey, the same score Mangold managed. In continued silence, the threesome prepared to tee off on the seventh hole, a par five, one of the most challenging holes on the course. Conti's tee shot was perfect. His second shot fell within fifty yards of the green. Two shots later, he parred, and his mood changed. Both DiMeglio and Mangold bogeyed. Another skin for Conti.

DiMeglio took a chance. "Gino, you were about to tell us a lesson about Tuscany."

"Ah, yes, I was. I apologize for being so quiet. But as you can see, I take golf seriously and get upset when I play poorly. I've yet to master the ability to just enjoy the game and the beauty of the outdoors," he concluded as he waved his hand toward the horizon.

The valley was indeed inspiring. The rolling hills and quaint villages offered yet another tranquil scene. DiMeglio was beginning to understand why Italians were so dedicated to enjoying life. How could they not do so with so much beauty surrounding them? Yet, in the equally idyllic vista in

Chianti, the blight of a serial killer stained that tranquility.

"I only wish I could play as poorly as you do, Gino!" interjected Mangold, already eleven over par with two holes to go.

"Chris, the lesson is simple. Memories in Tuscany are long. Revenge is woven into our fabric. If your killer is a woman, that would not surprise me any more than if your suspect were a man. In fact, the women of Tuscany are far more expert in exacting revenge than men. *Dietro ogni uomo intelligente, c'è una donna ancora più intelligente.*"

"Behind every smart man, there is an even smarter woman," Mangold translated.

"And women in Tuscany appreciate the expression far better than men that revenge is a dish best served cold," added Conti. "Tuscan men want revenge quickly, then forget. Tuscan women are more patient in seeking justice and never forget."

"You know everyone in Tuscany, Gino," offered Mangold. "Can you see anyone here vengeful enough to pull off the murders I've told you about? No amateur could have pulled them off. The killer is smart and well organized, and most likely very wealthy. If you were making a list of suspects, who would be on it?"

Conti birdied the eighth hole, and both DiMeglio and Mangold did worse. Another skin to Conti. As they approached the final hole, Conti answered Mangold's question.

"I honestly don't know, Jeff. There are thousands of

wealthy Italians in Tuscany. Men and women in the fashion, marble, gold, wine, olive oil, and cheese industries have made Tuscany one of the most prosperous regions in the country, and there is no sign of decline. The money keeps pouring in. It would be impossible to create a list of suspects you could manage."

Conti teed up and hit a dead-center drive. DiMeglio's drive fell ten yards shorter. Mangold hooked his to the left.

"But if your killer is a woman, your list might be more manageable. She is most likely to be in the wine or olive oil business. Maybe fashion. Men dominate the others. So perhaps you have a few hundred suspects. You can probably narrow that down by identifying the ones whose wealth is high enough to afford the game they are playing. Much of the country's wealth is tied up in land and fixed assets. Not many people have substantial cash on hand. So look for someone who does."

"We're looking into that," responded DiMeglio.

Conti and DiMeglio hit the green in three strokes. Mangold made it on four.

As Conti lined up his putt, he added, "I've been thinking about Jeff telling me she likes to quote from Shakespeare. Is that true?"

"It is. She took her name, Dick the Butcher, from *Henry VI*."

Conti parred the hole and, as he picked up his ball, said, "Then I suggest, Chris, that you remember Shakespeare's

King Lear: 'Come not between the dragon and his wrath!' She will not stop. You'll be next on her list if you get in her way. If she is a vigilante, it's not because she wants to change anything. That's not the nature of Italian matriarchs. She kills out of revenge. It's personal for her. That makes her very dangerous. So be very careful."

"We'll be careful," responded DiMeglio.

Conti finished his round at par with thirty-six strokes and eight skins. DiMeglio parred the eighth and bogeyed the ninth for a forty-three on the nine holes and one skin. Mangold came in with a fifty with two more bogeys and no skins. In the end, DiMeglio and Mangold each owed Conti €80, and Mangold owed DiMeglio €10, a debt DiMeglio would never see paid. Conti owed DiMeglio €10 for the one skin DiMeglio won. So DiMeglio was out €70 to Conti. After lunch at the clubhouse, where small talk dominated the conversation, Conti's driver arrived, and the marquis stood to leave, quite satisfied with his performance.

"Chris, do you own a tux?"

Perplexed by the question, DiMeglio replied, "I do, but not here in Italy."

"Rent one. Or better yet, buy one. I'll send you the name of my tailor."

"I'm sorry, Gino, what am I missing here?"

"Just get a tux. I'll explain why later."

With that, Conti left.

CHAPTER FIFTY-EIGHT

False Alarm

Hotel Nuova Italia, Firenze, Italy

On the seventh day in Firenze, Dick the Butcher finally reached out to DiMeglio at ten in the evening. The team had retired to their rooms. DiMeglio was alone in his, waiting for Lane to show up. In Washington, it was four o'clock in the afternoon. That was fine since it afforded darkness along the Chiantigiana road and less likelihood of discovery if Dick had eyes on the route.

"Agent DiMeglio, how was the flight home?"

DiMeglio noted it appeared she bought the story that they were in the States.

"It was fine, Dick. Just give me a minute. Let me get off another call."

He was stalling for time. When the call came in, DiMeglio texted the team. It would take Stokes ten minutes to pull the SUV out front, assuming he was dressed and not already in bed. The entire team could be on the road twelve minutes after the call came in. They'd been following that routine for days. Texting took time, so stalling was not that difficult, and DiMeglio could text while he was on the way to the SUV.

His phone pinged.

"I admire your tenacity in trying to make me trip on something. I suppose if you try enough times, I might give something away. We'll see."

As he walked, DiMeglio kept typing. "Dick, we will find you. You understand that, right?"

"Perhaps."

Stokes pulled up to the hotel just as the ninth session ended. But the session was over. No further contact by Dick. DiMeglio texted the team to stand down. Stokes returned the SUV to the garage. A frustrating false alarm. But at least Dick reached out.

CHAPTER FIFTY-NINE

High Society

"So I heard you got the tux."

"Yes, Gino, I did. And your tailor isn't exactly a bargain!"

"Ha! In Italy, great fashion comes at a price. No doubt you'll look magnificent in it."

"So now maybe you'll tell me why you sent me shopping?"

"Chris, the wealthy in Tuscany take great pride in our history, particularly as the birthplace of the Renaissance and haute couture that puts Milan to shame."

"OK. But what does this have to do with my buying a tuxedo?"

"You said you think your killer is a woman in Tuscany's high society. If such a killer is here and as wealthy as you seem to think she'd need to be to orchestrate her vendetta, then chances are she is hiding in plain sight. I told you to buy the tuxedo so you can join me this week at the Pitti Immagine, the international fashion show that takes place in Firenze at a medieval fortress called La Fortezza. It attracts everyone who is anyone in Tuscan society."

"And you think our killer will attend?"

"Chris, if you're right in how you've profiled her so far, I'd bet on it."

"OK, but showing up will tip her off that we're here in Firenze. We've tried to keep that secret so she doesn't know how close we are."

"Chris, don't be naïve. If she is who you think she is, she knows you're here. Tuscany can't hold a secret. And besides, if you can actually meet your killer, it's worth letting the cat out of the bag, as you like to say in America."

"And how do you suggest we do that at the event?"

"That's part of the challenge, Chris. While there is the venue where all the models strut down the runway in new collections from Gucci, Ferragamo, Pucci, Cavalli, and others I've never heard of, most of the hoi polloi goes to the sideshows organized by the top fashion houses. So we'll have to do the circuit. You up for that?"

"I am, but why not split up my team so we can cover more?"

"That's up to you, Chris. But you need someone local to cover the parties with you. Someone like me who will know everyone there and who can introduce them to you. Otherwise, you and your team will be like fish in the ocean. You won't have a clue who is who, let alone who matters."

"And how do you propose to introduce me?"

"How about, 'Good evening Ms. whatever your name is, I'd like to introduce you to my friend, Christopher DiMeglio. He's an American who works for the FBI. Quite a fascinating fellow.' It's the truth, of course. And it will get the rumor mill flowing."

"Or get Dick running."

"Perhaps, but I suspect she's not going to back down. Tuscan women never back down. And the chance for you to look at her eye-to-eye and see if you see something behind the coldness of her stare may get you who you're looking for."

"OK. When?"

"Tomorrow night. My driver will pick you up at 6:00. Be on time. It's going to be a long night."

CHAPTER SIXTY

Bar Hopping, Firenze Style

DiMeglio and Evans met Conti in the hotel lobby. He and Conti agreed that he should bring Evans and that Conti would bring his American wife, Betsy. A foursome was better cover. Somehow, Evans managed to find an incredible gown that made her look the part of someone who would fit into the fashion crowd.

"Is that a Versace?" asked Conti's wife.

"I have no idea," responded Evans. "I bought it in some shop Gino sent me to. I plan to return it tomorrow."

The foursome hit their first party to see the Ferragamo collection at the White Room in the Palazzo Pitti, a magnificently ornate venue completed in 1776 by Lugano artisans Grato and Giocondo Albertolli, two of the most prolific architects of Firenze's golden era. As the night progressed, they visited one historical building after another, all designed by some of the greatest architects of their time. It was a tour of some of the most impressive fashion and Romanesque, Gothic, and Baroque architecture in the world. Before long, either the champagne or the whirlwind tour made it impossible for DiMeglio to tell a Pucci from a Gucci or a Cavalli from a Scervino. They toasted with Dom Perignon and Tattinger in Baccarat crystal at the For-

tezza da Basso, Odeon Cinema, Piazza Santa Croce, Pala-
gio di Parte Guelfa, the Salone dei Cinquecento in Palazzo
Vecchio, and more. DiMeglio was careful not to drink too
much. The same could not be said of the others, including
Evans. DiMeglio had ever seen anything like it. Those they
met were the beautiful people of Italy. High fashion and
even higher net worth.

Evans, staggered by the jewelry adorning the women
present, took note that many were far younger than their
male companions. Some women, however, were clearly
among the older aristocracy. The deference offered them by
others and their sophisticated demeanor signaled not only
their wealth, but also their stature in the hierarchy among
those attending.

Conti was in his element. Ever the perfect host, he intro-
duced DiMeglio and Evans to one self-titled royal after
another, not saying anything about what Evans did. He
simply described her as DiMeglio's companion. He liked to
leave a little to the imagination of those to whom he intro-
duced them. He knew that would elicit questions and give
DiMeglio a chance to size up the potential suspects.

"Marchesa," he'd say time and time again, "please let me
introduce you to my good friend, Christopher DiMeglio.
Chris is with America's FBI. He and his companion, Georgia Evans, are here to see why Firenze is the center of the
fashion world." Other introductions were to a contessa, prin-
cess, lady, or duchess. Or whatever title the icon wanted to

be called. It amazed DiMeglio how Conti and his wife could remember the right honorifics for so many people.

After an introduction, some would respond, "Thank you, Gino. It is a pleasure to meet you, Mr. DiMeglio and Ms. Evans," in tones that made it clear that they really had no interest in knowing more about either one of them. They didn't seem impressed at all that DiMeglio was with the FBI. Evans assumed many of them didn't even know what the FBI was. But most they met were far more curious.

"The FBI. Really?" remarked one contessa. "That's quite interesting. Why would someone from the FBI be interested in fashion? I thought you preferred to hunt down criminals."

Evans replied, "Yes, Contessa, we do that, but, when we're lucky, we get to meet wonderful people like yourself." Evans, forever the charmer, thought DiMeglio. That's why he brought her with him. She had a way of communicating to other women and making them comfortable. And it gave him more time to observe their responses.

"Oh! And you're with the FBI, too?" one asked Evans. "Gino didn't mention that. Typical man. He seems to think most women are arm candy. I'm amazed Lady Betsy puts up with him!"

"Well, Duchess, that's our little secret, isn't it. We know what they want and how to manipulate them. Men, on the other hand, just want to raise their fists and show their muscles." Evans had them eating out of her hand.

Another asked if they were looking for criminals in Italy or if they were just on vacation.

"We are," replied DiMeglio. "Our work can take us all over the world."

"And what kind of criminal are you looking for, Mr. DiMeglio?" asked another.

To DiMeglio's chagrin, Gino, feeling the champagne, jumped in, "Why they're looking for a serial killer! And guess what? They think it might be a woman from Tuscany!" If given the chance, DiMeglio would have never been so specific. He already thought the idea of attending such a public event was risky, particularly with the press in the room. The last thing he wanted was a local scare generated by Italian newspapers notoriously known for sensational reporting. Crime in Italy wasn't just a problem, it was a passion.

"Oh my," another replied on hearing why they were in Italy. "That's very upsetting." After the third time Conti mentioned serial killers, DiMeglio took him aside and asked that he stop doing so.

"As you wish, Chris. I'm just trying to help you root out your killer if she's here."

"I appreciate that, Gino. But in law enforcement, telling less is sometimes best." He would have liked to tell him to shut the fuck up and stick to improving his golf game.

Another asked who the serial killer was killing. Still others asked why DiMeglio and Evans thought a woman was the killer and how they decided she might be in Tuscany. Questions from the dozens they met that night seemed endless.

With each introduction, DiMeglio looked for signs. A nervous response when Conti said his name. A sweaty handshake. A look of surprise in their eyes. Or a look of disdain as well. Anything that might be a tipoff. And he listened to them carefully. While he'd never heard Dick's voice, he had come to know how she articulated her thoughts in texts. He listened for conversation that was similarly precise. But most of all, he hoped to look into the eyes of someone who knew him and who would see that the game was near its end. He'd seen the look of serial killers when they're caught. A combination of disbelief and acceptance.

They finally got back to the hotel at 2:00 a.m., exhausted.

"So, Chris, do you think we met Dick tonight? I couldn't tell one marchesa, duchessa, and contessa from another. I can't believe how many people Gino knows."

"That was impressive. I'll give him that. But he ran his mouth off too much. We didn't need to tell anyone that we're in Italy searching for a serial killer. Within days, it's going to be in the press. That will make our job harder if it causes Dick to go into hiding. We're quickly running out of time."

Still feeling the champagne, she ignored DiMeglio's concern, responding, "And the wealth. My god, Chris, some of those women wore jewelry that even Jeff Bezos couldn't afford!"

He decided being serious with Evans would get him nowhere. "Somehow, I doubt that. But to answer your question, I don't know if I met her. A dozen or more of them showed signs that made me wonder, but none stood out over the others. I just don't know."

"Well my gut says we met her."

Before they got to the elevator, his phone vibrated.

CHAPTER SIXTY-ONE

The Reveal

A chill ran down his back as he read the text. Evans stood behind him, hand on her mouth in disbelief.

"Well, Agent DiMeglio, I must say it was a pleasure meeting you tonight. Perhaps we'll see one another again soon."

Bubbles.

"In the meantime, I have work to do. And you have to deal with the next dead lawyer. I'll make it easy for you and keep it close to your home."

Evans asked DiMeglio, "What are you going to say to her, Chris?"

"I'm not sure." All he could do was stare at the phone. His heart was racing. Just like it always did when he felt he was close to capturing a killer. "I have to be careful. She's obviously not spooked by meeting me. But I wonder what game she now wants to play since she knows we're here. She's got to be scared."

"Why? She's a psychopath, Chris. I doubt she's scared at all."

"Maybe. But psychopaths are sometimes unpredictable, Georgia. When backed into a corner, they strike like a caged animal."

"What do you mean by that?"

"I mean she may decide her best defense is to rid herself of us. She said she was going to keep it close. We may very well have gone from hunter to prey, Georgia."

"Then why did you expose yourself and put us all at risk?"

"Because, Georgia, that is exactly what Gino and I hoped would happen. We have her attention. She's come out. And now we'll see what she does next."

"Like kill us? I'm not sure I share your confidence in the plan! That assumes you even have a plan. Why won't she just go into hiding?"

"That could certainly happen, but I doubt it. We're too close. And she's shown nothing that tells me she's a quitter. Quite to the contrary. She wants to rub it in our face every chance she gets. Tonight is no different. We need to get everything we can on the women we met. She's made a fatal mistake. We just have to be patient."

"We're in Italy, Chris. Looking into everyone we met tonight could take weeks. We don't have that kind of time!"

"It won't matter. My bet is she comes out in the open before then."

"Jesus, Chris, I hope you know what you're doing." Looking at DiMeglio's phone, Evans asked, "So are you going to answer her?"

He put the phone in his pocket.

"No."

CHAPTER SIXTY-TWO

Dark Skies

Hotel Nuova Italia, Firenze, Italy

Washington was a decidedly target-rich environment for Dick. With over 25,000 lawyers, Washington, D.C. has one of the world's largest number of lawyers per capita. The only U.S. city higher is New York. Italy ranks number four in the world with 310,000 licensed lawyers, or one per every 200 Italian citizens.

"She said she'd keep it close to your home," offered Stokes. "Assuming she didn't mean she'd kill one of us, my guess is the next lawyer must be in or near Washington, D.C. That's our headquarters; nothing could be closer than that."

"So we've resorted to guessing?" asked Evans.

"Georgia, it's as good as it's going to get," replied Stokes. "Either she's going to kill someone near us or near our home. I don't think it's just a guess."

"I agree with Brad," said DiMeglio. "It's a long shot, but not a bad supposition. And there are more than enough famous criminal defense lawyers to target in the District. Unfortunately, that means it's nearly impossible to help whoever Dick's next victim is going to be."

"And we'll have a new assassin," added Stokes. "Ricci is

still in custody with Torchia in some dark hole near Rome. God only knows what Torchia is doing to him. So we not only can't identify the next victim, we have no idea who is going to kill him."

"Or her," added Evans.

While it was late afternoon in the States, his team tried to notify local authorities as best they could.

"Chris, we've warned the airports to be on the lookout for any flights coming into Dulles from Italy. But there's no reason to be sure the assassin will come in via Washington or even from Italy. Most likely, he or she is probably already there. And there are other airports with easy connections as well. So we'll probably have a dead end with the airports."

"Let's cover them the best we can, Georgia," replied DiMeglio. "Right now, some poor bastard is a sitting duck and as good as dead. Shit, the assassin or assassins could be from any country." It frustrated the team that a murder was about to happen, and there was nothing they could do about it.

"We've asked the local bar associations to send out a cautionary warning to its members, but that won't happen for hours," continued Evans. "Hopefully, some of them will read it, but I doubt it will reach enough or change their behavior. We cannot make them all lock their doors and hide."

"Should we notify the broadcasters? They could do a piece on the news. I can also have the *Gazette* put something in the paper as well," suggested Lane.

"No. We don't want to cause panic," responded DiMeglio. In part, he didn't want to give too much away to Dick. He needed her to keep operating, even if it cost the life of another lawyer. "I'm afraid all we can do is wait. Warning and writing about it will only feed Dick's desire to lord herself over us. I don't need any more of her shit. In the meantime, some poor schnook in Washington is about to be murdered and we can't do a fucking thing about it."

CHAPTER SIXTY-THREE

Deadlines

Caffé Paszkowski, Firenze, Italy

Two days had passed since Dick's call after the fashion show. With the pressures from Kinston to find a solution or move on, DiMeglio was mulling over his conversation the night before with the Director, trying to enjoy his afternoon routine of a macchiato at Caffé Paszkowski. Alone and without Lane.

"Chris, it's been nearly two months since you've been in Italy," complained Kinston. "And all you have is a hunch from a technical assistant that your killer is somewhere in Tuscany and that you might have met her at some party in Italy. Even you have to admit that it's getting a bit thin for me to justify devoting FBI money and personnel to chase what's increasingly sounding like a pipedream. You need to get results or come home."

It was also becoming clear that despite Frattarola's urging that Kinston let DiMeglio continue the search, she too was becoming concerned that it had all become a futile search for the Holy Grail.

"I'm sorry," concluded Kinston, "but you have two more

weeks. That's it." So now he had a deadline and needed results, not more problems.

Stokes and Evans knew DiMeglio enjoyed the occasional solitude, so he was not likely to welcome any interruption. But they knew of no other way to ensure they had a private moment with him that would not raise Lane's suspicion if he told her he was meeting with them.

They found him sitting at a table by the window overlooking the piazza, observing strolling tourists stop to take photos of the Renaissance-style buildings bordering the square and the Colonna dell'Abbondanza, a tall column topped with a statue of Abundance, the Goddess of Fortune. He enjoyed watching parents mind their children riding the modern merry-go-round, a feature in stark contrast to the history surrounding it. Although maybe not the most beautiful piazza in Firenze, it worked for DiMeglio.

"Chief, you have a minute?" interrupted Stokes. "Sorry to bother you here. But Georgia and I would like to run something by you."

DiMeglio sighed. "Sure. And I hope this is important."

"It is," responded Stokes.

"Then have a seat."

"Before we begin, Chris, I just want to say I don't completely agree with Brad. He's probably chasing ghosts with this idea. But I agreed we'd run it by you. Like you've always said, never reject an idea." She could see an "Et tu Brute?" expression on Stokes' face but wanted to deflect DiMeglio's potential anger should he react badly to Stokes' suggestion. Which she knew he would.

"Well, you have me intrigued. Order some coffee." DiMeglio waved to the server. "And have a pastry if you'd like." A few pastries DiMeglio ordered were in the basket on the table.

Evans ordered a cappuccino. Stokes, an American coffee.

"Geez, Brad," observed DiMeglio as the server left to fetch their order, "don't you ever venture into something you can't buy at a McDonald's?"

"Chief, just call me a patriot. If it ain't American, I don't want it."

"OK, Brad, I'm listening." While needling Stokes was always entertaining, DiMeglio wanted to hear what he had to say that Evans described as chasing ghosts. And not appreciating interruptions at the one time of day he could be alone, he wanted this over quickly.

Stokes explained his theory that Lane was suspiciously absent whenever Dick called. That she started the entire hunt for the killer with just two murders. She was also Italian, and she had a perverse fascination with serial killers. "Too many incredible coincidences, one after another," Stokes suggested.

Emotionally, DiMeglio wanted to reject Stokes' idea immediately, just as Evans thought he would. Stokes' idea was clearly a reach. But DiMeglio's training was not to reject any theory without first dissecting it. Nor was the irony lost on him that if Stokes was right, DiMeglio backed his way into the same nightmare he had in New Orleans. So he sat quietly, trying to sort it out in his mind.

The coffees finally arrived, and Stokes broke the silence.

"Are you mad at me, Chief?" Stokes remembered Evans' warning that DiMeglio might not take the idea well. But Evans agreed that his theory needed vetting with DiMeglio despite the risk.

"Not at all, Brad. I appreciate your honesty. My first reaction is that it's a stretch and not something I ever considered. First, she doesn't have that thing about money. Second, I doubt she knows the kind of people who could pull something like this off. Georgia, what do you really think?" As always, her opinion meant a lot to DiMeglio.

"I must say, I thought it was screwy when Brad first mentioned it. But, on balance, I'm still not convinced. She just doesn't strike me as a killer."

"Some of the nicest-acting people have been serial killers," Stokes interrupted.

Evans frowned at the interruption and continued, "My initial impression was she's just an aggressive reporter who can be a real pain in the ass, but I've come to like her in the last few weeks, and while I still don't think Brad's right, we can't reject it. So we must put it to rest, or she must go on the board. That's the rule."

"So Brad, do you have any idea how we can figure it out?" asked DiMeglio.

"It seems pretty simple to me. Just make sure she's with us next time Dick calls."

"That's one approach. But what makes you so sure, Brad, that if you're right, she's the one texting? Dick's not acting alone." He paused, took a sip of his macchiato, and added, "In fact, Brad, if we're speculating, Carla could have been planted on the team to feed information back to Dick and disinformation to us. When money isn't an issue, anything is possible. While she may not be the killer, she may be an accessory."

The two were shocked at how clinical DiMeglio seemed to be once he accepted that the idea was worth discussing, however preposterous he might have thought it was. They were talking about a woman he was sleeping with, and not some stranger. But despite that, DiMeglio was business first. Always. His lack of emotion was consistent with his approach to all cases.

"I did wonder about her being an accomplice and not Dick," replied Stokes. "But it seemed too coincidental that she was missing whenever Dick gave us the next clue on where to go. So I rejected that idea. But someone is the puppeteer in this story, and I agree the puppet master is not acting alone. I don't necessarily think she's capable of hiring assassins, let alone paying for them, but I'm not willing to dismiss it. She does have money, Chris, and reporters meet all sorts of shady figures. You may be giving her too much leeway. Regardless, I do believe she's very possibly the one texting. She's a journalist. Her writing skills are excellent. The texts reflect that."

"I'll give you that, Brad," responded DiMeglio.

"Look, guys," interrupted Evans, "let's keep our eye on the ball. Carla's going nowhere and if she is Dick, we'll know soon enough. But within two weeks, we've got to find out who is behind all of this. Or we pack our bags and go home with nothing. I'll concede it could be Carla, but we're in no position to make assumptions."

"OK then, we set it up. We do this by the book. Georgia, I don't want you to let Carla out of your sight while we're on the clock. And the moment I get the next call from Dick, I'll alert the two of you first. You then find Carla. If you can't find her, we've perhaps confirmed her role."

"Chief, I hope I'm wrong," said Stokes, seeing the concern in DiMeglio's face, however clinical he could be. It was one thing to have a serial killer on the team. It was entirely another thing if the team leader was once again sleeping with her.

CHAPTER SIXTY-FOUR

Death's Name

Hotel Nuova Italia, Firenze, Italy

DiMeglio's alarm went off at 7:00 a.m. Lane had already left and gone back to her room. The two of them continued the charade of hiding their relationship, even though Stokes and Evans obviously knew about the affair. Lane never told DiMeglio that Stokes said he and Evans knew about it. Lane continued coming to his room almost every night after the team called it a day. She'd then return to her room early and feign she had a good night's sleep when the team met for breakfast.

That night, she asked if something was bothering him as they finished enjoying one another in bed. She could sense he was distant. After his conversation with Stokes and Evans, DiMeglio wanted to ask Lane why she was strangely absent whenever Dick called, but he could not do so. If Stokes were right, asking her would not get an answer, and it would alert her she'd become a suspect. That might shut her down. He had to play the game, so he assured her nothing was wrong.

"Prove it," she said as she leaned into him for more. It was the most dissatisfying sex DiMeglio ever had, not so much because she had become a potential suspect, but over the guilt he felt at not being honest with her.

After a shower, he dressed in his usual casual way, in khaki pants and a collared buttoned shirt, and made his way to the restaurant. He was in no rush before he began their daily routine of driving back and forth along the Chiantigiana Road. He arrived just after 9:00 a.m. His team was waiting for him. He could see in their eyes that the night had not been calm.

Lane pushed her phone to him as he sat down.

"From my editor. It made the wires about two hours ago."

The article in the *Gazette's* online edition read:

HAS THE SHAKESPEARE KILLER STRUCK AGAIN?

Nathan Hunter was found dead today on the tracks at the NoMa-Gallaudet train station. His body was discovered just after midnight, and the police currently have no witnesses. He was struck by a train pulling into the station, but was probably dead before the train hit him. The conductor says he saw the body lying lifeless on the tracks when he tried to stop the train.

Hunter was a highly respected criminal defense attorney in the District. He was known for taking on some of the worst defendants who prowled D.C. streets, often getting them off only to have them later commit more crimes, including murder.

While a dead lawyer in a train station might be explained in several ways—suicide, accident, or just plain bad luck—we ask: Was Nathan Hunter the latest victim of the Shakespeare Killer, known for his fascination with the Bard of Avon, in his quest to murder criminal defense lawyers around the world? Or is Hunter's death just a mere coincidence?

We contacted the FBI, but they declined to comment. More on the story as it develops.

DiMeglio turned to Lane, clearly angry. "Did you write this!? It has no byline."

Taken aback by his aggressive nature, she responded, "I promise, Chris, I didn't write it. I assume an editor wrote it as soon as he saw the police blotter."

"And out of nowhere, he assumed a dead lawyer in Washington must have been the work of our killer? You alerted him to the threat, didn't you?" His tone was clearly accusatory.

"Yes," she admitted, upset with DiMeglio's anger, but not about to accept the blame for doing anything wrong. "I saw no harm in that. You had already notified authorities and the bar association, so I saw nothing wrong with alerting my editor. He wrote the piece. I was asleep in bed." Neither DiMeglio nor Lane noticed the raised eyebrows of the other team members at her comment about being in bed.

"Carla, I specifically said not to notify the media. Did you not hear me?"

Evans broke the tension as DiMeglio and Lane continued staring at one another.

"Poor bastard," commented Evans. "There's nothing we could have done."

DiMeglio wasn't ready to let it go. "You broke our protocol. You should have never warned your editor."

"I didn't think I was doing any harm. And all along, you know I've been keeping my editor informed."

"And did you come up with the name?"

"What name?"

"The Shakespeare Killer."

"No, Chris, I didn't. I told my editor about the killer's fascination with Shakespeare, but the name came from him. Not me."

Still unrelenting, DiMeglio continued, "And what if he inadvertently said something about our still being in Italy, Carla? Then what? Just how much have you told him?"

"C'mon, Chris, any secrecy of our being in Italy was blown by attending the fashion show. My editor understands confidentiality. You know I have been keeping him informed." Tears began welling up in her eyes. DiMeglio realized he was pushing too hard. He made his point. This was a side of DiMeglio she had not seen. Had she known the ultimatum DiMeglio received from Kinston and the revelations on her from Stokes and Evans, she might have understood his behavior.

DiMeglio turned to Evans and Stokes.

"NoMa is one of the worst sections of the District. Why the fuck Hunter would be there can only be because Dick's assassin took him there. Son of a bitch."

Evans joined in, relieved that DiMeglio had moved on from attacking Lane. "Guys, we need to get this bastard now. She's killed enough." Turning to Stokes, she added, "Let's get on the road. I'm sure Dick will reach out to Chris so she can crow on her latest murder. The only good news is because the murder was in D.C., she has no idea we're in Italy and maybe only miles away from where she lives."

"The Shakespeare Killer, huh?" commented Stokes. "I like it."

Twelve minutes later, the blue SUV pulled out of the hotel parking lot and headed down the Chiantigiana road.

CHAPTER SIXTY-FIVE

Just Desserts

Chiantigiana Road, Radda, Italy

The team meandered along the southern route from Firenze toward Siena as they had so many times, passing through Strada, Greve, Panzano, Castellina, Fonterutoli, and Quercegrossa.

"OK, let's stop at Enoteca Nuvolari for lunch," announced Lane. Lunch at a bistro in or around Siena had become part of their routine. Lane usually chose the spot off Open Table. At this point, it seemed they'd had lunch in just about every restaurant on the route. Still, there was one favorite— Enoteca Nuvolari on the Chiantigiana road in Castellina, near the il Borgo di Vescine, a former fortress and now one of many quaint villages along the route.

"Good idea, Carla. Let's see our friends at Nuvolari. I'm in the mood for pasta, and for you, Brad, they have that plate of cold cuts," said Evans.

At 12:30 p.m., Stokes parked in the lot beside the restaurant. He welcomed avoiding the ritual of finding a parking space, a real chore in most of Italy.

Like most of Europe, lunch was the main meal of the day. It was usually heavy, and people near Siena did not differ from most Italians.

Massimo Furini warmly greeted them and showed them to an umbrella-covered table in the courtyard. A meal outside—alfresco—is a tradition in Italy that they all enjoyed. Somehow, the fresh air made everything taste better. Even Stokes agreed. Furini was a real talker and loved to practice his English on American visitors. This was their third stop at the restaurant, but they never let on to him what they did. Instead, they held to a cover story that they were a film crew scouting sites for production. When they told that to Furini, it took no time before the manager, Bartolo Gentile, and the chef, Carlo Lombardo, joined him in the welcome, wanting their restaurant and adjoining B&B to be part of the movie. DiMeglio's team found it fun to play the role of movie studio executives.

Lane ordered the Pici Cacio E Pepe, a thick spaghetti with cream and pepper sauce. Stokes got his usual, the Gran Selezione di salumi chiantigiani Platter, a selection of Tuscan meats and cheeses. It was as close to cold cuts as he could get. All he needed was a loaf of rye bread and a good mustard, neither of which was available. DiMeglio, Evans, and Polk split a Bistecca ala Florentina, the Tuscan variation of a T-bone steak served very rare and more than enough for three people. In virtually every restaurant in Italy, you could order the beef however you wanted it—rare, medium, well, whatever—but it didn't make any difference. It always came rare. Very rare.

They were in for a long lunch.

An hour later, when the meal began winding down and coffee was served, Evans and Lane went to the ladies' room. A few minutes later, DiMeglio's phone rang. Dick the Butcher appeared on the caller ID. That was the first time she identified herself with a caller ID. With her talents in technology, DiMeglio assumed it was intentional. But why?

"Are you enjoying a nice evening cocktail?" Dick typed. It was 7:45 p.m. in Washington.

DiMeglio looked at Stokes.

"It's Dick. Get to the car. I'll stall as long as I can." Stokes left, with Polk following behind. DiMeglio waved to Furini for the check. Rather than wait, he left enough cash on the table to cover the bill and an extra tip, something appreciated in Italy where tipping was optional, and most Europeans were too cheap to leave anything extra.

As he walked to the car, DiMeglio typed back, "Dick, you have a real knack for calling me when I'm in the middle of something. I'm in the office late. Can you give me a few minutes and call me back? Or stay on this line, and I'll get back to you." It was risky to suggest she hang up, but the team needed time to get on the road and set up the Stingray.

"I'll call back." The session abruptly ended, with DiMeglio fearing he wouldn't hear from her.

As Evans and Lane returned to the courtyard, they saw DiMeglio on his way to the car and followed suit, quickly catching up to him. He confirmed the message from Dick.

As they walked to the SUV, Evans and DiMeglio let Lane

get ahead of them. He whispered to Evans, "Was she with you all the time?"

"Never out of my sight."

"Good. Let's hope that addresses Stokes' concerns."

Lane and DiMeglio took their seats in the second row. As Evans fastened her seatbelt in the front passenger seat, she leaned over to Stokes and whispered, "Now, do you feel like a real asshole?"

He whispered back, "I don't suppose she was in a stall. Was she?"

He could see on Evans' face that Lane did precisely that, and Evans didn't have the proof of innocence she needed to end Stokes' suspicion.

"Then she's still on my list."

"Christ, Brad, get over it."

With everyone in the SUV, DiMeglio ordered, "Brad, Georgia, please stop whispering to one another and get the car on the road."

CHAPTER SIXTY-SIX

A Text Too Far

Chiantigiana Road, Quercegrossa, Italy

They drove back to Siena to start the trip, working their way back to Firenze. Within a mile of their passing the Enoteca Nuvolari restaurant, Dick called back. Evans looked back over the seat to watch Polk as Stokes kept his eyes on the road. He could see the three in the rearview mirror, where the eye exchange between him and DiMeglio conveyed DiMeglio's relief that Lane, with them in the SUV, was not texting anyone. Evans looked at Stokes with a grin that read, "Idiot." But Stokes was still uncertain, ever the bulldog who wouldn't let go, remembering the observation DiMeglio made about unlimited money buying anything.

"Keep her on the line, Chris. I need time," Polk pleaded. "And Brad, you can drive faster until I get a hit that ties to the conversation."

"Faster!?" replied Stokes. "There's no such thing as faster on this fuckin' road." He had a point.

"Agent DiMeglio," texted Dick. "By now, you've seen the news from Washington. I bet you already visited the crime scene."

"I'm not going to tell you where I've been, Dick."

"Ah, yes. Of course. Do you enjoy living in Washington, Agent DiMeglio?"

"I do."

"And you would not prefer the Virginia countryside? I'm told it's so much more peaceful."

Polk waved his hand in a circular motion, telling DiMeglio to continue the conversation as they passed through Croce Fiorentina. It was odd that even though Dick could not hear them, they all remained silent as if she could. It allowed DiMeglio to concentrate on the texts.

"The countryside, Dick? Why do you like the countryside?"

A pause with no bubbles. DiMeglio feared the conversation was over. It was always nerve-racking how long it took her to type responses. He concluded she was very careful about what she wanted to say, correcting the texts as she wrote them. That may have explained why they never had typos, even though DiMeglio believed English was not her native language.

"Dick, are you still there? Did you like the name the article gave you? The Shakespeare Killer."

Bubbles.

"So now you assume I live in the countryside. Perhaps I do."

"But do you like the name?"

They passed through Fonterutoli.

"What's in a name, Agent DiMeglio? A rose by any other name would smell as sweet. Don't you agree?"

"*Romeo & Juliet*?"

"Indeed. Act II, scene 2."

"Well, if you don't like it, I'll stick with Dick the Butcher. It's more fitting and better describes what you're doing."

No bubbles. DiMeglio feared he may have angered her, and that she had cut off any further texting.

He tried to shift the conversation back to how she began it. "Italy has a lot of beautiful countryside, Dick. Tell me where your favorites are."

The bubbles returned.

As they passed through Quercegrossa, Polk raised his hand, thumb up.

"Shit," said Evans, "we got her."

"Can you track the call?" asked DiMeglio. There was too much excitement to be quiet.

"Yes, get her to type more. And Brad, slow down."

"Still there, Dick? If you don't want to talk about the countryside, why don't you explain to me why you killed Hunter?" He paused, then added, "I'm sorry, why did you have someone else kill Hunter while you relaxed in the Italian countryside?"

While he feared that being too aggressive might shut her down, he knew enough about serial killers that any defeat was unacceptable for them. They needed to have the last word. She was no different.

"Turn left at the next street," ordered Polk. Stokes obeyed. "And Chris, keep your texts short. I need her to be texting, not you."

"Come not within the measure of my wrath, Agent DiMeglio. It would be good for you to remember that if you want our talks to continue." She was back, quoting Shakespeare. And she was angry.

"Work with her anger, Chris," urged Evans. "That seems to keep her engaged."

A new text appeared. "He died, Agent DiMeglio, because he was just another worthless lawyer who lost any sense of humanity and left killers free to hurt others. He has now paid the price."

"Slow down. Now!" Polk hollered. Stokes abruptly stopped the SUV, causing DiMeglio to drop his phone as the momentum pushed the three in the back forward. Luckily, it was intact after sliding to the front. Evans picked it up and handed it to him. Polk almost lost his grip on the Stingray, now hugging it as if it were his child.

"I said, slow down, not stop! Just go slowly. Chris, get her to type something."

"Sorry," replied Stokes.

DiMeglio, caught up in the excitement, wasn't sure what to type. So he went with something new.

"Dick, why kill him at a train station?" He kept it short.

"She's somewhere up ahead," said Polk.

"The road bears to the left. Should I continue?" asked Stokes.

"Yes. But take it slowly, and Chris, keep her texting!"

"I don't pick the locations, Agent DiMeglio," wrote Dick. "I leave that up to others."

Less than a hundred yards down the road, Polk again yelled, pointing to a building in front of them, "Stop! She is in that building! Park out front." He was pointing at La Loggia Villa Gloria, a luxury Tuscan hotel built in the 1800s. With three buildings and just over fifty rooms of differing standards and sizes, it was modern by Italian means. Hardly somewhere you'd expect to find a murderer.

"Unless she has a room, which I doubt, she's using the public Wi-Fi in the lobby or the restaurant. She might even be in the bathroom, but she's definitely somewhere inside that hotel."

CHAPTER SIXTY-SEVEN

lo scacco matto

La Loggia Villa Gloria, Berardenga SI, Italy

"Evans," ordered DiMeglio, "go inside and see if anyone in the lobby is responding as I text. Carla, you go with her and get to the restaurant. Leave your earbuds in. I'll tell you when I'm sending something or receiving something. Make sure you cover all the public places."

The two left the SUV and hurried into the hotel, unavoidably looking suspicious.

Upon entering the lobby of the main building, they saw that it was relatively small and decorated with Renaissance-inspired paintings and wall hangings, a style common to the area. The hotel maintained the art with its dark and sometimes foreboding images, ironically à propos to the macabre nature of their investigation. Besides the desk clerk and a bellman, there were three people in the lobby. Lane immediately realized all eyes were on them and regretted coming into the lobby so abruptly. Thinking quickly, she cupped her right arm under Evan's left elbow and calmly led her to the front desk.

"*Salve, ha delle stanze?*"

"*Sì, quante persone?*" responded the clerk.

Smiling, Lane drew her arm in, affectionately bringing Evans closer to her, "*Due, per favore.*"

As Lane gave him a credit card, the clerk smiled back. It wasn't the first time he'd checked in a gay couple.

Evans looked around the lobby. One woman and two men were seated, the woman and one man were looking at their phones. The other was asleep in his chair, head tilted back and mouth wide open. The only thing he was missing was a snore.

"I'll meet you in the restaurant," said Evans. Lane nodded, smiled, kissed Evans on the cheek, and let her go. Evans blushed and hurried off. While waiting for the clerk to find a room and give her keys, Lane watched the lobby. Evans arrived at the restaurant, overlooking sunlit vineyards and olive trees. It had tables both inside and out. About twenty people were finishing lunch or enjoying drinks.

DiMeglio spoke his first question to their earbuds.

"OK, I just sent a message. See anything?"

"No," reported Evans, "I'm in the restaurant. It's pretty empty, and has about ten tables with people, a few on the terrace. Half have their phones out, but there's no way I can tell if they're responding to you. There were only two on phones in the lobby. Carla is checking them out."

DiMeglio asked Lane. "Carla, see anything?"

Lane touched her ear to hear DiMeglio. "Just two people staring at their phones, both typing. Doesn't anyone call people anymore?" she whispered.

The desk clerk looked up curiously at Lane.

"*C'è un problema, signora?*"

Lane smiled and shook her head. The clerk went back to his computer.

Dick came back. "OK, Agent DiMeglio, we've had enough for today. Perhaps we'll talk tomorrow."

"Shit, she's cutting me off."

He quickly typed, "Wait, Dick. Why the rush?"

No response. The session ended.

"Don't worry, Chief," said Stokes. "Let's just watch. She clearly does not live in the hotel. Let's see who leaves. And you can send another text. We'll watch for reactions. If we get one, we have her."

DiMeglio quickly relayed the plan to Evans and Lane.

After a few minutes, a well-dressed, handsome older man in the lobby rose and looked at Lane. She smiled at him. He seemed to examine her for an uncomfortably long time (like so many Italian men do with attractive women), nodded as if to say hello, and proceeded outside. Lane followed at a distance, telling DiMeglio the man was leaving the lobby.

The man left the building and began walking toward a row of cars when DiMeglio sent a text. Evans had caught up to Lane.

"C'mon, Dick. Let's keep talking." DiMeglio saw the man look down at his phone.

"Are you there, Dick?" he typed.

The man stopped, stared at his phone, and started typing. A text appeared on DiMeglio's phone. "I said perhaps tomorrow, Agent DiMeglio."

The man put his phone back in his pocket and stopped at the door of a black Mercedes EQS 580 sedan, the auto manufacturer's latest entry into the all-electric vehicle craze. A very expensive car.

"Brad, please tell me you got some pictures of him."

"Yep. He might as well have posed for them. And he sure has a nice set of wheels! That sucker costs north of a hundred grand."

"Send the pictures to Angelo," ordered DiMeglio.

"Already done, Chief," responded Stokes.

Lane and Evans returned to the SUV as the Mercedes pulled out. Stokes let him get a good lead and then pulled out to follow.

The streets near the hotel were narrow, so it wasn't hard to keep a distance. No one was going to pass anyone.

The Mercedes turned back onto the Chiantigiana Road toward Firenze. After a few kilometers, it turned right onto an unmarked road that led off into vineyards.

"Keep your distance, Brad."

The Mercedes turned again, this time to the left. Stokes was too far behind to keep the car in sight without being discovered. By the time Stokes reached the dead end after passing a few dirt roads on either side, there was no Mercedes.

"He must have turned off the road somewhere. Double back," ordered DiMeglio as his phone rang. He put it on speaker.

"His name is Luca Romano," reported Torchia. "And we have loosened Ricci's tongue as well. He admits he knows Romano."

"I thought Ricci and Sasha had lawyered up," interjected Stokes.

Torchia recognized the voice. "They did, Agent Stokes. But they kept talking to us. As you once said to Mr. Barlow, we made them an offer they couldn't refuse."

"Well, we just lost Romano on the road," reported DiMeglio. "Where does he live? What do you know about him?"

"Did Ricci say Romano was Dick?" asked Evans.

"No," responded Torchia. "They claim he's the only one they ever met, but did not believe he was in charge. I'll tell you more in person. We're already on our way to Firenze, but if the pieces of this puzzle fit together properly, your serial killer is none other than the Contessa Sofia Bartolini."

"And she lives where we are?"

"Yes. With Romano, her servant of many years. She's been transferring a fortune to secret Swiss bank accounts near the time of the murders. To more than one external account. That may mean she has more than one assassin working for her."

"Great work, Angelo. Thanks."

"Wait for us to get there. Remember, agent, you are in Italy and must play by our rules. We will arrest her and Romano. While I'll let you question them, they'll be taken into custody by us, not you. Do nothing on your own. Local police will watch the villa. They're going nowhere."

"Understood. You'll get credit for the arrest. Just make sure the locals don't screw up and tip them off. We'll head back to Firenze and meet you there."

"Who the fuck is Contessa Sofia Bartolini?" asked Stokes.

"I think she's a woman Chris and I met a week ago."

"Exactly," replied DiMeglio as he now put a face to the figure of his mysterious serial killer. "She was the one who wanted to know why we thought our killer was a woman."

CHAPTER SIXTY-EIGHT

Royal Conditions

Villa Bartolini in the Chianti Hills, Italy

Back in Firenze, waiting for Torchia to arrive, the team Googled the Contessa. Although records were unclear and little was written about her, they discovered that Villa Bartolini in the Chianti hills had been the primary Bartolini residence since as early as 1451. Such longevity awed DiMeglio. The ancestors of the people who lived in the villa were alive before Columbus sailed to America.

Its seventeen bedrooms and fourteen bathrooms were all part of a residence of just under a thousand square meters—about ten thousand square feet—on fifty-four acres of gardens, vineyards, and olive trees, some of which were believed to be as old as the villa itself. As was common in Italy, the Bartolini family passed the estate from generation to generation. Contessa Bartolini, the current matriarch of the family, lived there, with occasional visits from her son and grandchildren. Her husband, Marchese Antonio Bartolini, died over a decade earlier. The reports also mentioned the death of her two daughters, but not much detail was available. They learned she was an American by birth, born in Cleveland to a wealthy wine-importing family. In Italy, during a summer abroad while attending Amherst, she met the Marchese and fell in love. They married, and she moved to Tuscany to be his wife and raise their children. While she could have taken the title of Marchesa, she preferred Contessa. Since noble titles were technically banned in Italy, those with noble blood took whatever title they pleased for tradition's sake.

The following day, they all arrived at the villa.

When a friendly contact in the local government told the Contessa that the Carabinieri were on their way, she offered no excuses. Instead, she demanded an hour alone with DiMeglio before she would peacefully surrender. She was of Italian nobility—*Nobiltà Italiana*—and protocols dictated authorities honor her request. It's not as though she was going to get away.

"We're giving you one hour, agent," warned Torchia, now in charge of the team preparing to arrest the Contessa and Romano. Two Carabinieri vehicles, one a van that would transport the prisoners, three local police cars, and DiMeglio's SUV lined up in front of the villa. Torchia intended to make a show of it. DiMeglio was certain he was ready to take photos with himself leading the Contessa on her perp walk. "When that hour ends, Agent DiMeglio, we're coming in to take them into custody. Not a minute more. I still think this is a bad idea."

It was sunny and warm and Stokes liked to say, "A fine day for a hanging."

"I understand," responded DiMeglio.

"Do you have the Beretta we issued to you?"

"No. I didn't pick it up. I don't need it. I never carry one in the States and leave my weapon at home in a safe. Needing a firearm is just not part of my job."

"Really? Sidearms are always part of a police officer's job, agent. And the Contessa isn't afraid to kill. So what makes you think you'll be safe with her, let alone with Romano?"

"Because I am not a target. I don't fit the profile of who she wants to see dead. So I'll be fine."

"Profile, huh? So you're willing to risk your life on whether you fit a profile?" He turned to Stokes. "What's that expression in your country about not being able to get someone to do what they should? Something about a donkey?"

"It's a horse. You can lead a horse to water, but you can't make him drink," said Stokes.

"A horse, huh? Horses are smart. Your Agent DiMeglio is acting more like a donkey," responded Torchia as he stepped aside so DiMeglio could walk up the steps and into the villa. DiMeglio recalled Conti's advice that the killer, particularly if a woman, would be dangerous, and he needed to be very careful. He suddenly regretted not having the Beretta, but it was too late now.

As he walked toward the door, Torchia loudly reminded him, "One hour."

Now at the ornate double door into the villa, DiMeglio

could only imagine how Italian nobility, particularly in Tuscany, lived. It struck him how the trappings and gaudy evidence of wealth contrasted with the humble life of his grandfather, who immigrated to the United States to escape the poverty in Italy. He wished his grandfather could see him now on the verge of bringing an Italian aristocrat to her knees. It made the justice he was about to administer all the sweeter.

The door opened, and Luca Romano greeted him. DiMeglio felt a chill run down his back, wishing again that he had the Beretta.

"The Contessa is expecting you."

Consistent with the exterior grandeur, the reception area was more like a museum than a place where one welcomed guests. It was dusty and smelled slightly from the damp wall hangings of ornate draperies and embroidered tapestries. DiMeglio wondered how old they were. Centuries, maybe?

"Please follow me."

Romano brought DiMeglio to a sitting room that overlooked a grove of olive trees, more than DiMeglio could count. The room décor reflected what one would expect from old Italian wealth. DiMeglio suspected masters from the Renaissance like Michelangelo, da Vinci, and Botticelli painted some of the frescoes on the walls.

The Contessa was waiting for him and rose from her chair to greet DiMeglio, motioning him to sit in a chair opposite her. A centuries-old coffee table, probably worth more than everything DiMeglio owned, separated them from one another. The chairs were overstuffed but comfortable with high backs, mahogany wood arms and legs, and blue velvet-like fabric. She sat quietly as DiMeglio soaked in the scene.

The Contessa was pretty much what DiMeglio expected. It was obvious she'd aged well for someone who was now over eighty. He imagined great wealth amassed with little hard work made that possible. Dressed in a simple black dress, her bright white hair, coiffed close to her head with a small bun in the back, made her look more like a nun than a murderer. The pearls on her neck, the diamonds in her ears, and the gold bracelets on her wrists were the only signs that she was far from a nun. She wore a wedding ring with a diamond at least two carats in weight. DiMeglio could see that in her youth, she had been a beautiful woman. He recognized that some paintings on the wall were of her at an earlier age. DiMeglio assumed other similarly regal-looking paintings in ornate frames were of her husband and children. Or perhaps of ancestors.

"Agent DiMeglio, welcome to Villa Bartolini. I hope you find it as beautiful as I do," she said calmly and sat back in her chair.

Romano stood, awaiting dismissal.

"Luca, please pour me my tea. Would you like some, Agent DiMeglio?"

Luca poured the tea and remained standing, pot in hand.

"No, thank you. I don't drink tea."

"Really? Have you ever had Italian tea?"

"I doubt it. Frankly, all tea tastes the same to me."

"We own a farm in the hills north of here, where we grow our own tea. Until the last ten years, tea was something no one in Italy drank. Italy is all about coffee and espresso. But I always liked tea, so we began cultivating it about fifteen years ago. Now it sells out every year. You should try it."

"I don't drink tea." DiMeglio was not interested in small talk.

"Your loss. Is there something else you'd like to drink? Or perhaps you'd like something to eat?"

"No, thank you. And we certainly don't have time for a meal, Contessa."

Disappointed, she responded, "Suit yourself." She took a sip as though she had all the time in the world to have a conversation.

"It's such a pity we have so little time, Agent DiMeglio. I have so much to tell you."

With a nod from the Contessa, Romano left the room. DiMeglio wondered if he might come back with a gun or something else to kill him, but if the Contessa wanted him dead, he'd be dead already. At least that's what he told himself.

"Contessa, why am I here? The Carabinieri are outside. They will be here in less than an hour to take you into custody. We agreed to the hour you requested, but nothing more. So please don't waste time and get to whatever you want to tell me. If you think there is any way I can prevent your arrest, or you can avoid the inevitable by talking to me, you're sorely mistaken."

After taking another sip of her tea, she asked, "So, Agent DiMeglio, what exactly do you think justice is?"

DiMeglio was dumbfounded that she wanted to discuss justice on the verge of her arrest as a serial killer. When caught, most serial killers want to talk about themselves and why they did what they did. Not discussions about justice. But DiMeglio could only play along. He wanted to use the hour as best as he could to learn from her and add it to the profile of yet another serial killer. But his patience was thin.

He sarcastically responded, "Justice isn't murdering innocent people."

"Come now, Agent DiMeglio, humor me. After all, you've solved the case. And I'm not going to escape. You can at least indulge an old woman with some entertaining banter. Perhaps it will even help you understand why innocent people—as you describe them—died."

DiMeglio noticed that even after so many years in Italy, she had never picked up an accent. Yet her Italian seemed perfect. He decided that's what education and wealth get you.

DiMeglio's instincts as a profiler also told him she was a psychopath who wanted to kill any lawyer who successfully defended someone who was guilty and who, once released, continued to commit violent crimes. In her twisted mind, the lawyers, not the criminals, needed to pay with their lives. He wasn't sure there was much more he needed to get from her, but he kept the conversation alive just in case he'd get a nugget or two that gave him insight into her depraved mind.

He replied, "Very well, Contessa. Justice is treating all men—and women—equally."

"Really? Treat everyone equally. Aristotle once said, 'Equals should be treated equally and unequals unequally' when asked for his definition of justice. Do you agree with him, Agent DiMeglio?"

DiMeglio didn't respond.

"You know, Agent DiMeglio, Aristotle was an interesting man. But from the look on your face, I doubt you care. You should read more of his thoughts on justice. Historians say he meant individuals should be treated the same unless they differ in ways relevant to the situation in which they are involved. I think Aristotle would have understood why I treat defense lawyers differently."

"Contessa, what is your point? We don't have much time." DiMeglio did not like to be lectured by anyone. Particularly someone who saw nothing wrong with hiring assassins to carry out a twisted vendetta.

"Be patient. I'll get to it. But first, tell me how justice treats everyone equally."

He was annoyed, but decided to continue humoring her. She obviously had no intention of going off her script.

"Justice ensures equality through due process before impartial juries and judges." He remembered that from one of his classes at Quantico.

"Due process and impartial juries and judges? So far, nothing about innocence or guilt?"

"Innocence is assumed, Contessa. Due process—the presumption that someone is innocent until proven guilty—is how our Constitution works. It's the job of the prosecutor to prove guilt. Not for the individual to prove their innocence."

"And when due process fails, and a guilty man goes free or an innocent man is sent to prison, what then? Has justice prevailed?"

"In the grand scheme of things, yes. The occasional result of the guilty going free and the innocent being convicted is an unfortunate price we have to pay. Freedom does not come free. The alternative is anarchy. Or, in your case, rule by homicidal psychopaths." He couldn't resist the insult, hoping it might get a rise from her and more personal information.

But she showed no displeasure at the comment. Nor was DiMeglio surprised by how calm she was. Eerie calm in tense situations is common among serial killers, particularly when caught.

"Well, Agent DiMeglio, call me what you will. I guess it is of little consequence." She picked up her cup of tea and calmly had another sip. "You really should try some of this tea. It's wonderful. Shall I call back Luca?"

"No, Contessa, I don't want anything. But what you have done is of consequence to me. And it matters to the families of the lawyers you had killed." While he was approaching the end of his patience, DiMeglio remembered his own advice that you can learn something new in every case. Maybe the Contessa could provide something different that would help him profile the next killer.

"I suppose the families feel it matters very much, Agent DiMeglio. So I'll give you that."

She paused as though she wanted to make sure DiMeglio was paying attention. She looked at him and said, "The Shakespeare Killer. I think I like that. *Though she be but little, she is fierce.* From Act III of *A Midsummer Night's Dream*, Agent DiMeglio."

He'd had enough. "Contessa, quite frankly I'm losing interest in your obsession with Shakespeare. You're a murderer. Nothing more. Nothing less. It doesn't matter what you call yourself."

She smiled, calmly took another sip of tea, and responded, "Aren't you the least bit curious about what I think justice is?"

He actually was and responded, "All right, Contessa, tell me. I can't wait to hear the logic of a psychopath."

Still no reaction.

"Justice, Agent DiMeglio, is finding the truth. Without truth, there is no justice, and when the truth reveals a criminal, it must proceed with retribution, deterrence, and, when necessary, incapacitation. Those are the principles upon which justice must be administered."

"You forgot rehabilitation and restitution," responded DiMeglio, again remembering his classes at John Jay.

"No, Agent DiMeglio, I didn't forget. All your words about due process and equality and about rehabilitation and restitution are empty. Anyone who uses those concepts to free guilty men is as complicit as the men they represent. More so when they make it their profession to free guilty men, one after another, relying on your definition of justice, Agent DiMeglio."

"So I suppose you'd return to the Inquisition, Contessa, when a few self-anointed judges decide the fate of those charged with crimes? No need for a trial, let alone a jury. Just tell the truth, as long as it's consistent with what they want to hear, and you live. Otherwise, you die. Right?"

"It would certainly be faster and put a lot of lawyers out of business."

DiMeglio sighed at what seemed to be an unending debate that would provide no closure. "It's going to be time to go soon, Contessa. If there's anything else you want to tell me, please do so now. Before I leave."

His phone rang. The caller's ID read it was Carla Lane.

"You should answer that, Agent DiMeglio."

CHAPTER SIXTY-NINE

Tea and Crumpets

Villa Bartolini in the Chianti Hills, Italy

"Chris, another lawyer has been found dead. This time in Venice. They found a guy named Mario Scarpa dead in his car from carbon monoxide poisoning. He was an Italian criminal defense lawyer. A good one. But that's all Georgia and Brad have as of now. They're talking to Angelo to see what more they can learn, but he seems clueless, too."

"Carbon monoxide?" He looked at Bartolini. She simply shrugged, smiled, calmly took another sip of her tea, and said, "Like a gas chamber."

DiMeglio put his phone on speaker and placed it on the coffee table.

"Was there a note?" he asked.

"I don't know," responded Lane. "We're obviously not at the scene, and Georgia says God only knows how well the locals will preserve evidence."

"They'll eventually find a note, Agent DiMeglio," assured the Contessa.

"Carla, you're on speaker. I'm sitting here with Contessa Sofia Bartolini. Dick the Butcher. The Shakespeare Killer. Lady Macbeth. Pick whatever name you like. I thought you might like to ask her a few questions of your own." He took the chance that the Contessa would open up more to a woman. "If there's at least one thing we can be sure of, for now, this latest body in the canal will be the last the Contessa sees fit to have murdered. The game is over for her."

Bartolini raised her eyebrows. "What, Agent DiMeglio? Do you think I can no longer move forward just because you've discovered me? I can die but once while my cause lives on, even with the Carabinieri on my doorstep."

"That just gives me more reason to see you go to the gallows. I only wish Italy had capital punishment. As for doing more, that requires money. A lot of money. And all your assets will soon be seized. You won't be able to pay anyone else to do your bidding."

She smiled. "Don't you want to hear why I did what I've done, Agent DiMeglio? Or Ms. Carla, do you? After all, you're a reporter. You care about the truth. So do either of you honestly see me as just a vigilante? Is there not a missing piece in your profiling puzzle?"

Of course there was. There were always missing pieces, but DiMeglio knew she was a vigilante. He just didn't understand why. She could have told him in their many Signal discussions, but she didn't even leave a hint.

"Contessa," answered Lane, "we would like to understand."

"Yeah," added DiMeglio, "understanding how a psychopathic mind works is important in my job. So by all means, tell us."

She slipped a beige 8x11 envelope across the table. It had been sitting there since the conversation began. DiMeglio picked it up. Inside was an old newspaper clipping with yellow, ragged edges and ink smudged from hands holding it over the years. It had been read many times.

PITTSBURGH GAZETTE

**Prominent Italian Millionaire
and Family Murdered in the
William Penn Hotel**

Saturday, December 27, 1986
On a complaint from an adjoining room about a stench emanating into the hallway, the body of Marchese Antonio Bartolini, an entrepreneur and successful wine grower from Italy, was found dead on his bed in the suite he rented. His two daughters, ages 12 and 16, accompanying him on a trip to Pittsburgh, were found dead in the suite's other bedroom, both strangled. Preliminary reports show the two girls were also sexually molested. It appeared to be a robbery gone wrong that turned into murder and rape. Police are investigating.

DiMeglio looked up and could see the Contessa's eyes tear up. He almost felt sorry for her, but reminded himself that she was a killer.

"Chris, are you still there?" asked Lane.

He read the article to her.

He wondered how they'd missed this in their research.

But then he saw the date. The Saturday after Christmas. A day when the news is buried and no one pays attention. That's why they missed it.

"The police caught the man who killed my husband and raped my babies. There were fingerprints and DNA evidence. They caught him on cameras in the elevator and lobby. He even confessed when arrested. But his lawyer, a public defender named Geri Clark, got him off because the police failed to give him some kind of warning."

"The Miranda warning, Contessa?"

"Yes, I think that's it. And they mishandled evidence. They even threw out his confession, saying the police coerced it. His name was Michael Johnson. He had been arrested many times before he killed most of my family."

"And what happened to Clark?" asked Lane.

"She committed suicide."

"Right, Contessa. I'm sure she did," replied DiMeglio.

That made for at least one more victim.

"Ms. Carla, do you have any other questions?" asked the Contessa, once again calm. "Perhaps you're more curious than Agent DiMeglio."

"Is that why you're exacting revenge on defense counsel?" Lane responded. "Just for doing their job? Why not kill the defendants? They're the killers."

"I eventually saw that Johnson was taken care of. And I made sure he suffered. But only after I learned he'd killed another man and raped a sixteen-year-old girl. He's dead,

Agent DiMeglio. One of your many unsolved murders. You'll find what's left of him in the cellar."

She took another sip of tea. "At that point, I thought I'd be done with it. I'd killed the man that murdered my children and saw justice administered to his lawyer. *Dov'è l'offesa, lascia cadere la grande ascia.*"

"You'll need to translate that, Contessa."

"Let me, Chris," offered Lane, still listening to the conversation from outside the villa. "The Contessa said, *where the offense is, let the great axe fall.*"

"From *Hamlet*, Act IV, Agent DiMeglio," added the Contessa.

The Contessa reached across the table and pressed the button on the phone, ending the call. She was finished talking to Lane or anyone else except DiMeglio.

"I suspect you misquoted that, too, as you did the quote about killing all the lawyers."

She ignored his comment. "I tried to forget and go on with my life, raising my son as best I could. And now I attend to my grandchildren when they occasionally visit, but that's becoming increasingly rare as they grow older. So it's mostly just Luca and me now."

She leaned back in her chair, closing her eyes in thought. "But when I kept reading about killers in your country being set loose only to kill again, I could no longer stand by and do nothing. I kept thinking about those poor families. And the murders in other countries, too. Just like Johnson.

Every time I read about a case, my heart broke again."

"But why murder the lawyers and not the criminals?"

"There's a time for all things, Agent DiMeglio."

"There is never a time for murder, Contessa."

Ignoring his comment again, she continued, "You have a concept in your law, Agent DiMeglio. I believe they call it 'aiding and abetting.' If you aid and abet a crime, even if you're not actively involved, you are guilty of that crime. Correct?"

"That is a general rule in my country, yes. Accessories to a crime are guilty, as well as the person who actually commits the crime. If someone dies during a crime, everyone involved is guilty. It's called the felony-murder rule. Everyone taking part, whether or not they pulled the trigger, is guilty of murder."

"Do you now understand why I did what I did, Agent DiMeglio?"

He understood. "You killed the lawyers because they aided and abetted in the crimes their clients committed after they were set free? Is that about right?"

"Not any crimes, Agent DiMeglio. Murders. I only go after lawyers who help murderers murder again. I had the wealth and influence to do it, so I did."

She again leaned back in her chair, closing her eyes in thought. All DiMeglio could do was shake his head. He'd been asking her questions for months to get an accurate count on her murders, now realizing he may have only scratched the surface. He also wondered if some victims might have been saved if he and his team had connected Johnson to the crime spree. That would forever be another emotion haunting him. Such emotions burdened him each time he missed a connection.

"Contessa, I have listened to a lot of serial killers, but few who hired the guns rather than kill the victims themselves. But that makes no difference. If you help, you're as guilty as any accomplice to a crime."

"Yes, Agent DiMeglio, I guess I am. I aided and abetted. I was an accomplice. *Nocens sicut comminatus est.* Guilty as charged." DiMeglio found her calmness unnerving for someone about to spend the rest of her life in either an Italian or an American prison.

DiMeglio leaned forward in his chair, preparing to get up. He'd had enough for now. The questioning could continue later. "Contessa, it's time for you and me to go."

"Agent DiMeglio," she calmly replied, "I'm not going anywhere. Please sit down." He stood. Raising her voice, she added firmly, "I am the Contessa Sofia Bartolini! Sit down!"

DiMeglio sat back in his chair and calmly continued, "Quite to the contrary, Contessa, you are indeed leaving to face extradition to the United States, a trial, and imprisonment. Of course, that assumes the Italian government doesn't decide to put you away forever before American courts can get their hands on you. And while I doubt any lawyer can get you off, even if your trial is in the U.S., you will receive all the protections of our Constitution. Not that you deserve it. At least you'll probably avoid the gallows, something your wealthy ancestors apparently enjoyed watching for entertainment."

With her composure regained, she replied, "I'm eighty-two years old, Agent DiMeglio. If you think I intend to die in prison, you are indeed a fool."

DiMeglio looked at her closely, leaning forward, "What are you getting at, Contessa? Don't do anything foolish. You won't get away with it."

"I am not bound to please you with any more answers, Agent DiMeglio, but let's just say you made an excellent decision not to have any tea," she replied calmly as she finished her cup.

"You've poisoned yourself?!" DiMeglio asked incredulously.

"And it should complete its task shortly. I can already feel it working. Agent DiMeglio, only I shall choose the way and where I die. Not some judge or jury that you think knows how to mete out justice. I choose to die in the home where I have lived for over sixty years. Death rock me asleep. *King Henry*, Agent DiMeglio."

DiMeglio rose, rushing to the door to get Torchia. Perhaps they could take Bartolini to a hospital, and the poisoning reversed. He wanted her to face trial to bring closure to the families of those she killed. To give them a chance to confront the killer who stole their lives.

"Wait!" she yelled.

DiMeglio turned to look at her.

"I knew you didn't like tea and would decline to have any."

With that, she slumped over in her chair, dead.

They found Luca Romano's body in the kitchen, where he brewed and drank the tea that killed them both.

CHAPTER SEVENTY

Perhaps We Should Talk

Washington, D.C.

Two months back from Italy, Lane broke off her relationship with DiMeglio. She said the sex was great, and she was having fun, but needed to move on. She wrote a wonderful article about the search for the Shakespeare Killer and the brilliance of DiMeglio and his team tracking her down. Kinston could not have been happier. Frattarola resisted telling him she told him so. Lane won a Pulitzer Prize, locking her into a job with the *Gazette* and moving her persona into greater fame. An ongoing affair with an FBI agent wasn't in the cards.

DiMeglio was saddened she'd left him, but Sully was pleased. The evening sessions on the couch and long walks were once again pleasant.

The team went back to work and was well under way investigating a suspicious series of murders in Alabama and Mississippi. Stokes was tracking down some leads in Biloxi when he received a text on Signal.

"Perhaps we should talk."

In Wilmington, North Carolina, police found prominent criminal defense attorney Anthony Barlow and his wife, Charlotte, dead in the den at their home. Initial reports indicated that Barlow, in a murder/suicide, killed his wife and then shot himself in the head.

AUTHOR'S NOTE

The Shakespeare Killer is a sequel to my earlier book, *Blood on the Bayou*, chronicling the work of fictional FBI profiler Christopher DiMeglio. Foremost, I hope my readers find the book suspenseful and enjoyable. As I do with all my books, I endeavor to be as accurate as possible when I incorporate facts into a story, including serial killers, unsolved murders, and profiling. I do months of research on the underlying topics used to build the narrative before I write a single page. I interview professionals to confirm accuracy. While the book is a work of fiction and DiMeglio is a fictional character, readers may see the story as believable—something I like to call plausible fiction.

Readers will undoubtedly find some of the book unsettling. The premise of the book is frightening on several levels. Criminal defense lawyers are the backbone of our legal system. They stand on the front line, protecting our constitutionally protected rights. Our forefathers and ancestors fought a revolution to establish those rights. Defense attorneys now stand in their shoes.

But we also live in an increasingly dangerous society where the acts of the irrational often suspend adherence to the rule of law obeyed by reasonable men and women.

According to *Scientific American,* there are between twenty-five and fifty active serial killers in the United States at any given time. They account for about 150 murders in the U.S. per year. They are not loners or social misfits. They look completely normal and often hide in plain sight, blending in with their communities. They have families, homes, and jobs. They might be coaches, town council members, community organizers, or a neighbor. In short, they can be anyone, living anywhere. The FBI has, however, reported that there are traits common among some serial killers consistent with psychopathic personality disorders. They include a lack of remorse or guilt, impulsivity, the need for control, and predatory behavior. Their behavior is often a mixture of charm, manipulation, intimidation, and violence.

I hope readers enjoy reading the book and perhaps learn a little about serial killers and the threat they pose. Some readers may find the SMS texts' grammatical accuracy between characters too precise and not reflective of how most texts look in real life. That was intentional. I felt it would be easier for the story to flow and for readers to understand the dialog. I hope readers and critics allow me that indulgence. As readers will also see, the narrative includes quotes from Shakespeare. But can you identify passages from the Bard embedded throughout the text, some paraphrased? Enjoy the hunt.

ACKNOWLEDGMENTS

As always, there are many people to thank for their support and help in writing this novel. To Mitch Becker, my friend for nearly sixty years. Mitch has been a pre-reader of all my books and contributed essential thoughts and criticism that made them better, and he's an outstanding golfer who helped ensure my description of a skins game was correct. Special thanks to my friend and fellow lawyer Felix Hofer. Felix lives and practices law in Firenze, Italy. Without his help, I would have never written with the accuracy I try to include in my books in the many scenes in Italy or involving Italian dialog. I've had the pleasure of visiting him in the beautiful Tuscan region of Italy many times. His hospitality is amazing, and his friendship is invaluable. I'd also like to thank Michael Tiffany for his help in understanding the technology described in the book. Michael is a computer technology and communications expert and the founder of several cybersecurity firms. He has worked closely with the FBI on major investigations. Thanks go to my daughter, Meghan Wood, and to Brent Jostad, my son-in-law, both former Florida State Attorneys, for their insight about Signal. Thanks also to Nancy Schulein, my assistant for over twenty-five years. Her comments keep me focused and ensure I stay within my writing style and on schedule. Thanks also to my pre-readers from the Compass Pointe Stealth Book Club—Nancy Garland, Gayle Pfeiffer, and Cheryl Herland. Also to my neighbor, Roy Landreth, former Assistant Inspector General for Investigations, Office of Labor Racketeering, OIG, U.S. Labor Department (participant in the U.S. DOJ Organized Crime Strike Force) and a former Orlando Police Officer. Thank you to Brett Phillips, Management Assistant, Office of the Warden at the Idaho Maximum Security Institution, for his invaluable answers to my questions about the institution and its policies. And to my son, Joshua, and the support of his team at Ruckus Marketing in maintaining my website, www.douglasjwood.com. Of course, to Carol Ann, my wife of fifty years, for her support and many suggestions on the plot and characters. I could also never do this without the help of my publisher, Plum Bay Publishing, and its leader, Claire McKinney. Dee Dee Book Covers was terrific in designing the cover and jacket and Claire's staff, including Sonya Dalton, Jeremy Townsend, Stephen Orovich, Grace Remshifski, and Kate Petrella, did a fantastic job promoting, editing, and fact-checking. While the editing process can sometimes be emotionally painful for an author, it is essential to ensure a book is as good as it can be.

CAST OF CHARACTERS

Leading Roles

Name	Role	First Appearance (by Chapter)
Bartolini, Sofia	Contessa	Sixty-Seven
de' Conti, Giamani	Marchese	Fifty-Seven
DiMeglio, Christopher	FBI Agent; Chief of the Behavioral Analysis Unit	Two
Evans, Georgia	FBI Agent	Nine
Frattarola, Julie	FBI Assistant Director of Public Relations	Three
Kinston, George	FBI Director	Two
Lane, Carla nee Michelotti	Reporter	Eight
Mangold, Jeff	FBI Agent	Forty
Ricci, Antonio	Assassin	Thirty-Six
Sasha	Assassin	Five
Shakespeare, William	Playwright	Twenty-One
Stokes, Bradley	FBI Agent	Nine
Sully	Catahoula Leopard	Six
Torchia, Angelo	Carabinieri Inspector	Forty-One

Victims

Victim	Location	Cause of Death	Appearance (by Chapter)
Armand, Percy	New Orleans	Slit wrists	Twenty-Three
Barlow, Anthony	Wilmington, NC	Gunshot	Seventy
Bartlett, Joseph	Chicago	Hanged	Eleven
Clark, Geri	Unknown	Unknown	Sixty-Seven
Haynes, Justin	Miami	Overdose	Thirty-Four
Hunter, Nathan	Washington D.C.	Unknown	Sixty-Four

Victims, continued

Johnson, Michael	Unknown	Torture	Sixty-Nine
Létisse, Marie	Paris	Electrocution	Seventeen
Scarpa, Mario	Venice	Suffocation	Sixty-Nine
Schneider, Jacob	Key West	Drowning	One
Stafford, Paul	Los Angeles	Jump	Five
Williams, Charlotte	San Francisco	Bludgeoned	Fifty-Three

Extras

Name	Role	First Appearance (by Chapter)
Albertolli, Grato and Giocondo	Renaissance architects	Sixty
Allen, Steve	*Tonight Show* host	Seven
Baker, Ronald	Murderer	Forty
Berkowitz, David	Serial killer	Eleven
Bezos, Jeff	Book seller and space pioneer	Sixty
Broussard, Raleigh	Superintendent, New Orleans Police Department	Twenty-Four
Bundy, Ted	Serial killer	Eleven
Carpenter, Martina	Actor	Seven
Carson, Johnny	*Tonight Show* host	Seven
Christ, Jesus	Savior	Thirty-Three
Comey, James	FBI Director	Fifteen
de' Conti, Betsy	Wife of Giamani de' Conti	Sixty
De Niro, Robert	Actor	Fifty-Six
Dickerson, John	*60 Minutes* correspondent	Ten
Elena	Jeff Mangold's assistant	Forty-Eight
Fallon, Jimmy	*Tonight Show* host	Seven
Furini, Massimo	Server	Sixty-Five
Ford, Henry	Tycoon	Twenty-Eight

Gentile, Bartolo	Restaurateur	Sixty-Five
Gibson, Carter	George Kinston's Executive Assistant	Three
Hannity, Sean	Fox personality	Eighteen
Hitchcock, Richard	Murderer	Twenty-Eight
Hoover, J. Edgar	FBI Director	Fifteen
Kelley, David	Television writer, producer, and former attorney	Preamble
Kramer, Alan	Lawyer	Fifteen
Leno, Jay	*Tonight Show* host	Seven
Little, Chicken	Fairy tale character	Thirty-Three
Little, Samuel	Serial killer	Fourteen
Lombardo, Carlo	Chef	Sixty-Five
Manning, Wallis	Serial killer	Seven
Ness, Eliot	FBI Agent	Fifteen
Orwell, George	Author	Twenty-Eight
Paar, Jack	*Tonight Show* host	Seven
Pelley, Scott	*60 Minutes* correspondent	Ten
Pesci, Joe	Actor	Fifty-Six
Peters, Lenoir	Chris DiMeglio's Executive Assistant	Three
Polk, Rob	FBI techie	Forty-Nine
Pope	Pope	Thirty-Seven
Raphael	FBI driver	Forty-One
Reagan, Ronald	40th President of the United States	Twenty-Eight
Ridgway, Gary	Serial killer	Eleven
Roots	*Tonight Show* band	Seven
Simone, Rebecca	NOLA Police Detective	Three
Sister Agnes	Nun	Twenty-One
Smith, Perry	Murderer	Twenty-Eight
Stahl, Leslie	*60 Minutes* correspondent	Ten
Stimpson, Charles	Serial killer	Fifty-Three
Suggs, Horace	Congressman, Wyoming	Nine
Theron, Charlize	Actress	Fifty
Wallace, Mike	*60 Minutes* correspondent	Eleven

Extras, continued

Wilson, Philip	Congressman, New Jersey	Nine
Wuornos, Aileen	Serial killer	Fifty

Glossary

French	English
Une mort choquante (French)	A shocking death
Italian	**English**
la dolce vita	the sweet life
Ispettore	Inspector
Nessun problema, Signor Mangold. Non ho mai avuto un incidente. Record di guida perfetto!	No problem, Mr. Mangold. I've never had an accident. Perfect driving record!
Nessun problema, signorina. Record perfetto!	No problem, miss. Perfect record!
In piedi. Entrambi!	Stand up. Both of you!
Non ho niente da dire.	I do not have anything to say.
Come ho detto, non ho niente da dire.	As I said, I have nothing to say.
Vaffanculo	Fuck you
Ti capisco	You understand?
Comprendere	Comprehend
Comprendiamo	We understand
Voglio un avvocato	I want a lawyer
Mousse al Finocchietto, geletina di Lampone, Lampone giallo e granite di Bergamotto	Fennel mousse, raspberry gelatin, yellow raspberry, and Bergamot granita
Dietro ogni uomo intelligente, c'è una donna ancora più intelligente.	Behind every smart man, there is an even smarter woman.
Pici Cacio E Pepe	Thick spaghetti with cream and pepper sauce
Gran Selezione di salumi chiantigiani Platter	Great selection of Chianti cold-cut platter
Bistecca ala Florentina	Florentine steak

Salve, ha delle stanze?	Hi, do you have rooms?
Sì, quante persone?	Yes, how many people?
Due, per favore	Two, please.
C'è un problema, signora?	Is there a problem, ma'am?
Dov'è l'offesa, lascia cadere la grande ascia.	Where the offense is, let the great axe fall.
Nocens sicut comminatus est	Guilty as charged

CPSIA information can be obtained
at www.ICGtesting.com
Printed in the USA
BVHW041910010623
665240BV00003B/72